THE MILLION-DOLLAR TATTOO

THE MILLION-DOLLAR TATTOO

EARL EMERSON

BALLANTINE BOOKS
NEW YORK

http://www.randomhouse.com

Library of Congress Cataloging-in-Publication Data
Emerson, Earl W.
        The million-dollar tattoo / by Earl Emerson.
        p.   cm.
        ISBN 0-345-40066-6
        1. Black, Thomas (Fictitious character)—Fiction.   2. Private investigators—Washington (State)—Seattle—Fiction.   3. Seattle (Wash.)—Fiction.   I. Title.
PS3555.M39M55 1996
813'.54—dc20   96-2946

Manufactured in the United States of America
First Edition: October 1996
10 9 8 7 6 5 4 3 2 1

I never slept in the park but I came damn close to it. I went five days without anything to eat but soup once. . . . It didn't kill me, but neither did it increase my love of humanity. The best way to find out if you have any friends is to go broke. The ones that hang on longest are your friends. I don't mean the ones that hang on forever. There aren't any of those.

—*Raymond Chandler, in a letter to Carl Brandt*

THE MILLION-DOLLAR TATTOO

CHAPTER 1

I was working my way through a recurrent dream about a women's softball team when the phone woke me. The voice on the other end of the line was all too familiar and slurred, though not with sleep.

"What time is it, Thomas?" Kathy asked, pushing her pillow over her face.

"Four o'clock."

"Are we waking up from a nooner?"

"It's four in the morning, Sister," I said, peeved at being awakened from the softball dream.

"Good grief. Who is that on the phone? Snake Slezak?"

"Listen," I said into the receiver, "you're drunk. Get some sleep and I'll come over on my way to work."

"It *is* Snake." Kathy slammed her head into the pillow.

His voice sounding slightly metallic and raspy, Snake said, "There's a woman in my bed. What am I supposed to do, Thomas?"

"There's a woman in my bed too. If I have to tell you what to do, you've got a problem."

"But she's dead."

"What? Are you sure?"

"Her eyes are froze up and she stopped breathin'. She won't

leave. I *think* she's dead, Thomas. We gotta get her out of here before she stiffens up."

"How long has she been dead?"

Kathy sat up and knuckled the sleep out of her eyes, her dark hair huge from having slept on it.

"I don't know."

"A couple hours? A couple days? Give me a ballpark figure."

"A couple hours, I suppose."

If rigor mortis hadn't set in, she probably hadn't been dead more than two hours, for it generally took two to three hours for the process to begin. It took even longer for it to become complete, maybe eight to twelve hours. The clock across the room said three fifty-one A.M. If Snake was telling the truth, she'd died around one or two, perhaps earlier.

"Look, Snake. Hang up and call the medics."

"I ain't callin' no medics. They'll bring the police, and if the police come, I'm afraid I'll shoot one of 'em. Besides, she's long gone."

"Okay. Don't touch anything. Stay where you are and I'll come over."

"Right. But there's something else you should know."

"What's that?"

"She's an alien."

"What? Mexican?"

"I'm a little too drunk to explain now."

"Drunk might be the best way, Snake."

"Damn it, man. She's from another galaxy."

Kathy was watching me in the dark.

"Are you okay, Snake?" I said.

"You think I don't know it sounds crazy? Come over and look at her. She don't even look American. She's from outer space." The line was silent for almost thirty seconds.

Snake Slezak was in the habit of playing gags on his friends, at times elaborate gags, and I had to admit a dead woman from outer space was the sort of stunt he might pull, yet his voice was strained, his words halting and tremulous, and this didn't sound like a joke.

"Thomas? You there?"

"I'll be right over. Sit tight."

"Promise you won't tell Kathy."

"Kathy's right here. She already heard."

"And when you come, bring a jumbo freezer bag, okay?"

"Say again?"

"We'll stuff her in your freezer until we can make a deal with a museum. You got one of those big chest freezers, right? She'll fit in there perfect."

"You at your new apartment?"

He grunted.

"Ten minutes." I hung up. He'd been flush lately, rolling in dough, had a new apartment, a new Cadillac, lots of new girlfriends, as well as several new teeth.

"You're not going somewhere, are you?" Kathy's voice was soft and sleepy.

"You want to come?" I asked.

"Come where? What's going on?"

"Snake thinks he has a dead woman in his bed. He says she's from outer space."

Kathy sat up and dropped her legs over the edge of the bed. "Oh, boy."

"He's soused and he sounds confused."

"I wouldn't miss this for the world." Kathy gave a short sigh and walked across the hall to the bathroom. "You know, Snake should have a psychiatrist on call. Like those daredevil car-jumpers on motorcycles who have an ambulance standing by. Snake should have a psychiatrist and a bunch of guys in white coats and crew cuts following him around. This was bound to happen."

Kathy came back into the bedroom wearing a pair of jeans and nothing else, turned on the light, began bending over the opposite side of the unmade bed searching through the bedding for her nightshirt, an oversized football jersey. "Why aren't you getting dressed?" she asked.

"Wanted to make sure you found whatever you were looking for."

Kathy gave me a tiny smile and continued digging through the bedclothes. "Quit grinning. You look like a cat in a shrimp factory. And put your pants on."

I removed a pair of jeans from a chair back, sat on the edge of the bed, and began tugging them on. "How did Snake sound?" she asked.

"Quite reasonable, considering. A little swacked, but quite reasonable."

She found the football jersey and let it drift down over her outstretched arms. "Snake has always believed in little people from outer space, hasn't he?"

"I wouldn't get too revved up. This is probably a gag."

CHAPTER 2

Ten blocks west of the main entrance to the University of Washington and just south of Northeast Forty-fifth Street, one of the main drags in the U District, stood Elmer Slezak's small apartment house. I'd visited there twice, disheartened each time by the sound of the freeway through his flimsy back bedroom wall, though Snake claimed it lulled him to sleep on the nights he didn't have a woman.

He was reputed to be Tacoma's sleaziest private investigator, but if you knew him well, you knew the label was not entirely accurate. He *was* dirty-minded, opinionated, and cantankerous, but he had plenty of empathy for his clients. He'd once broken into tears over not locating a fifteen-year-old runaway, the daughter of a Boeing engineer, a girl he'd discovered had been sexually abused by a half brother and was now hooking somewhere along the coast. More than once he'd loaned cash to clients who hadn't been able to pay their bills.

Among his preferred hobbies were shooting rats in the county dump, homophobia, catching bullets in his teeth, and moral superiority, though his real passion was, as he put it, "chasing pussy."

With bricks in his pockets he weighed in at a hundred twenty-five pounds, and perhaps because of his Lilliputian stature, he was feistier than he needed to be. The hardest I ever laughed was in a bar in San Diego when he got the crap knocked out of him by a one-armed woman who'd retired from the Roller Derby. During the scrap he'd pulled off her prosthesis and was drunk enough to think he'd pulled off a real arm. He bawled about his own brutality even as she threw him across the floor with her good arm. The brawl lasted six or seven minutes, and Snake never got in a single lick.

Kathy maintained that I let him hang around out of guilt and gratitude because he'd saved my life years ago. She labored under the mistaken and, for her, necessary assumption that being private investigators was all Snake and I had in common.

Though she seldom disliked anyone, when she did, Kathy was unable to keep it a secret. She abhorred Snake, and Snake had known it for some years. Her antipathy stemmed, I believed, from their first meeting in a crowded room when he effected some unnamed minor physical assault on her—probably goosed her—then asked her to drive to Reno with him. Being groped wasn't high on Kathy's roster of preferred pastimes, ranking slightly above driving to Reno with lechers. In the years since, their relationship had smoothed out, but not by much. Kathy claimed Snake had equal regard for the philosophical precepts of Nietzsche, Kierkegaard, and Hugh Hefner.

Though he could now afford better, Elmer had recently moved into a somewhat shabby apartment in an area of mostly shared rental housing and student apartments, a neighborhood of slobs—more fastidious tenants and owners having been driven away by the exhaust and racket rising off of I-5.

It was a two-story brick apartment building with twelve units, open balconies, and steel railings that had once been aqua but were now mostly paint chips and rust. Three motorcycles, two padlocked mountain bikes without front wheels, as well as an illegally parked car were on the concrete patio on the wrong side of the sidewalk. The automobile was a forty-thousand-dollar Cadillac Snake had paid cash for sometime over the past year.

Beneath Snake's Cadillac the sidewalk was littered with empty beer cans, spilled french fries, and greasy Burger King wrappers waiting for a little wind to take them to a nicer neighborhood. A scruffy, bearded man wearing a watch cap who reminded me of Nick Nolte in *Down and Out in Beverly Hills* lay in a sleeping bag next to the green garbage container near the fence. As Kathy and I climbed out of my Ford and chunked our doors shut, he stirred slightly. Pretending we weren't there, a woman with bags under her eyes and Walkman headphones clamped to her ears jogged past in nylon shorts and a sports bra. It was a few minutes after four A.M.

Traffic on the nearby freeway was sparse enough to dupe a three-legged dog into crossing, and despite the pollution from the city lights, as well as the impending dawn, you could see six, maybe seven stars in the sky.

As we mounted the steps to the second-level apartments, Nick Nolte curled into a fetal position in his sleeping bag. Lately the U District had become a destination spot for the homeless. I wasn't sure why, but I thought it might have something to do with freshmen from small towns being easy marks. Then again, maybe it was the library. The U had a terrific library.

"You know what gives Snake these delusions?" Kathy asked as I knocked at the door, waited, then knocked again.

"Booze?"

"Watching cartoons."

"What?"

"When adults watch cartoons all day, their perception of the universe becomes warped."

Despite my glum mood, I laughed as I tried the knob and pushed the door with my fingertips. It was unlocked and swung open to reveal a heavily curtained apartment.

Elmer was twelve feet away in an armchair, his bony knees spraddled out in either direction. He wore boxer shorts and cowboy boots and had a large pistol nestled between his legs barely out of reach of his fingertips, and in the moment before I heard him snoring like an old dog, I thought he'd shot himself. He tended toward the morose, and if there really was a dead woman in his bed, suicide might have passed through his mind.

He had a mat of body hair that was mostly white. Though he still had all his toes and nine and a half fingers, his body was a mishmash of scars, some from traumas back in his rodeo days, others from a life of wild nights and no compromise. He had a couple of bullet holes in him and liked to show them to women he was trying to schmooze into bed. He told me once that if he could get a woman to look at his bullet wounds, his chance of scoring was automatically increased to fifty-fifty. Even when he wasn't trying to lure women, Snake had a fondness for flashing a patch of puckered skin and telling the story of how he'd acquired it. Embellishment having overwhelmed memory, only a few of his stories were true.

Even in his semiconscious and torpid state, or maybe especially in his semiconscious and torpid state, Snake was capable of lifting and firing the gun before I could spit. Guns were Snake's religion and he worshiped them zealously—not that he was much of a shot. I'd once seen him fritter away fifty rounds shooting at empty soda cans a snaggle-toothed girlfriend was tossing into the air, missing every time. But then, Kathy and I weren't soda cans and we weren't twenty feet in the air.

Motioning for Kathy to remain in the doorway, I took the revolver away from him and snapped open the cylinder, dropping six .44 Magnum rounds onto the carpet. The .44 Magnum was his favorite weapon, and Snake wasn't above carrying two of them in dual shoulder holsters.

The cool air from the doorway must have aroused him, because when I looked down, he had a nickel-plated .38 pointed at my chest, cocked and shaky. His bloodshot eyes were cocked and shaky too. It was hard to know how many guns he might have hidden in that chair.

"Snake. It's me. Thomas. Put the gun down."

Without lowering the revolver, Snake said, "Shouldn'a brought your woman, man."

Anybody who's ever been fired at on purpose doesn't want to be fired at by accident, and I am no exception. When I'd been a cop, I'd had a partner once who liked to calibrate various incidents by how many seconds away from death they put him—a maniac with a knife might be forty or fifty seconds, hiking along the freeway with your back to the traffic one second—but a cocked gun was maybe one one-hundredth of a second.

I stepped around the overstuffed chair, confiscated and

unloaded the .38, then dug down around the cushions. Up close his body emitted the stink of sex, beer, and dentures—a potent combination.

"How'd you two get in?" Elmer asked. "The door was locked."

"Not when I tried it."

Kathy stepped inside and said, "Elmer? You all right?"

"Sure." He turned back to me. "Shouldn'a brought your woman."

He looked as if he'd been melted into the chair like a slab of cheese. His bloodshot eyes were open now, though he hadn't moved except to point the gun at me. He slowly looked toward the dark bedroom and back at me, then at Kathy.

"I didn't want her to see this," he said.

"Elmer," Kathy said, "if you're in trouble, you're going to need an attorney. Maybe you don't want me working for you, but I can at least get things started."

"*You* would be willing to represent *me*?"

"If you're in trouble." She said it so matter-of-factly you'd have thought he'd been a lifelong friend of the family, so matter-of-factly it brought little squibs of water to his eyes. Some people would have called them tears. Elmer called them squibs.

"Really?"

"I said I would."

"You're hired, baby."

"Good. And you call me baby again, I double my fee."

"I didn't mean nuthin' by it."

"I know what you meant."

CHAPTER 3

It was an efficiency apartment, the kitchen opening out onto the living room, the bedroom buried at the end of an open passageway toward the rear. The only door inside the unit led to the john off the bedroom.

The place smelled of beer and perfume, a wonderful perfume, like some wildflower I'd encountered a long time ago when I was small, a scent I had forgotten until that moment. There was a combination of immediacy and nostalgia to it that made me long to remember where I'd come across it before.

Glancing past Snake into the darkness, I saw a form on the bed that became more distinct when Kathy moved away from the doorway and let the glow from the streetlights paint the unit in pastels instead of the blacks and grays it had been. Snake's breathing was audible, and I could hear the whisper of Kathy's jeans as she moved. No sound came from the bedroom.

Switching on the dim overhead light in the bedroom, I stepped around an empty brassiere, black high heels, and a splash of red we later discovered was a dress.

She lay on her back, a tiny, dark-complexioned woman with a waist a man could almost get his hands around and wrists as thin and reedy as cornstalks. You would be hard-pressed not to say she was pretty. She appeared to be half-black and half-Asian like some of the immigrating offspring from Vietnam, the product of Vietnamese women and African-American soldiers during the war, though she was probably from Tacoma, as was Snake.

She had long lustrous hair, pitch black, along with heavy eye shadow and bright lipstick. Elmer often posited that the primary advantage of being married would be you wouldn't have to kiss them anymore, and I wondered if he had bothered to kiss her tonight. A small bandage clung to the inside of her right breast, standing out because it was the color of Caucasian flesh.

When I gripped her wrist and pulled, she was relaxed and limp. Her flesh was cool. There were marks on her neck. Her eyes were closed. Rolling her lower eyelid down slightly with the pad of my thumb revealed a series of tiny red dots in the conjunctiva. She'd bitten her tongue too. A textbook case.

Her pocketbook was on the nightstand, and the credit card holder was open to her driver's license, as if she'd been asked to flash her ID before hopping into the sack with Snake—an unlikely occurrence at best, since Elmer had never been overly particular. In his time he'd slept with lady cabdrivers, cops, bartenders, lesbians who wanted to get pregnant, the wives of friends, the sisters of girlfriends, elderly widows, and once even with a gravedigger, a nice enough woman actually, who'd proposed marriage. I wasn't counting the two he-shes he'd been involved with by accident.

Kathy stepped into the room behind me and pressed up against my backside so that I could feel the heat from her body. "She dead?"

"Yes."

"Can't you cover her?"

"I could, but the cops would have a fit."

"Do you know how she died?"

"Yep."

"I wish we could cover her. She looks so . . ."

"Naked?"

"That too. I was going to say young. Do you think Elmer did it?"

"I heard that," said Snake from the other room.

After a moment Kathy read aloud the name off the driver's license on the nightstand. "Fleegle, Catherine Samantha."

Bound together with a simple beaded chain, two keys sat atop the driver's license. I moved one of the keys a fraction of an inch with my fingernail and said, "*Mc*Fleegle. It's *Mc*Fleegle." The Washington State license said she was born in July, was five feet tall, weighed ninety pounds, and lived in West Seattle. Her twenty-second birthday, only a couple of days away, could end up to be the date of her funeral.

"They're going to be madder than wet hornets." Somehow Snake had fallen to his hands and knees and was gawping at us from the living-room floor.

I helped him back into the chair. Kathy said, "Who's going to be madder than hornets?"

"The rest of them aliens."

"Elmer," Kathy said gently. "She's a woman. A human woman. She's got a driver's license and brown eyes and perfume that goes for a hundred ninety dollars an ounce. She's not an alien."

Rolling his eyes around in his head as if he'd lost control of them, Elmer said, "You think aliens don't know how to use mascara and eyeliner?"

"She's a *woman*."

"Wanna bet?"

"Anything you name," Kathy said, looking at me.

Snake stared at the wall. It was always awkward when somebody said something patently false, or worse, preposterous, and then waited for you to acknowledge the appropriateness of their position.

"Just 'cause somebody's not from this planet doesn't mean they wear tinfoil pajamas and look like insects. There's all kinds. Here in the States there's even some masquerading as doctors. You can tell 'em because they have a hard time naming body parts. There's all different species. That one in the other room's from stock been bred with earthlings. Maybe a couple of times."

"Is that what you were doing with her?" I asked. "Breeding?" Kathy gave me a censorious look. Elmer didn't reply. I said, "Let me find you some clothes. I don't want you going downtown like that."

"Downtown? You gonna call the police? Fuck the police. Get your freezer bag. We'll put her in with the frozen turkey and the blueberries. In a coupla weeks we'll thaw her out and sell her to the Japanese."

Kathy said, "We have to call the police."

"Dang," said Snake, slamming his head back against the chair. "Dang dang dang dang." The clothes he'd been wearing were scattered around the foot of the bed. We found fresh slacks and a shirt in his closet. The slightly cooler air coming in from outside was refreshing, but I closed the front door for privacy, then switched on a lamp in the living room.

"Look at her teeth," he said. "No cavities. Go look at her teeth if you don't believe me."

"It's the fluoride," Kathy said. "A lot of people don't have cavities these days."

"Yeah, well what about the marking?"

"What marking?" I said.

He placed a finger on the inside of his right pectoral muscle. "Right here you'll find a tattoo of a lopsided butterfly."

"Right there she's got a Band-Aid."

"Jesus," Snake said, vaulting from the chair and making a deceptively quick feint, diving under my outstretched arms. By the time I reached him, he had the Band-Aid in his hand. "Damn. See there? That's the scar you get when you have a tattoo removed. Look yourself."

"Lots of people have tattoos removed," I said. "Get dressed."

"I been screwed. This is a plot. It was a setup."

I went into the kitchen and phoned the police dispatcher. After I'd answered her questions, I returned to the living room to find Kathy eyeing Snake warily. "You want to tell us what happened while we're waiting?" I said.

"Not particularly."

"Why don't you try anyway? And you'd better get dressed."

Moving with agonizing slowness, Elmer dressed in front of us and then asked for a glass of water, which he bolted in one long, loud, gurgling swallow. I brought him a second glass. When he felt sufficiently lubricated, he leaned back in the chair and spoke in a dull monotone, as if narrating an old *Dragnet* episode. "Fact: I picked her up downtown at Fourth and Pike. Fact: It was prearranged. She called me. Fact: I didn't kill her. Fact: We went to bed. I boffed her. Fell asleep. Later I got up to piss and found her like *that*. Period."

"How much later?" I asked.

"Couple hours. I picked her up late. After eleven. Found her dead and called you."

"How was this date arranged?"

"It wasn't a date."

"What was it?"

"I can't say."

"Where do you know her from?"

"I never met her before tonight."

"She a hooker?"

"Hell, no. You know I don't pay for it."

"She called you? What? She get your name out of the phone book?"

"She phoned, gave me her number, and told me where to pick her up. I went and got her. It was that simple."

"She gave you her phone number? Do you have it?"

"It didn't have anything to do with her phone. It was her *number*."

"What was her number?" I asked.

"Seventy-three."

"Seventy-three what?"

"It was a number."

"Seventy-three have some special significance for you?"

"They all had numbers."

"There were others?"

"I don't want to say anything else. I gotta think about this."

"Snake. This is your lawyer standing here."

"I gotta think."

"If we don't find out here, we'll find out later." He didn't reply. "For the record, her name is Catherine Samantha

McFleegle. She lives in West Seattle. At least she did when she got her driver's license."

He only smiled. The room was quiet for a while. Kathy and I looked at each other, Kathy's eyes slightly wet.

I said, "Snake. There were only the two of you here tonight?"

"Right."

"What happened?"

"I told you."

"Snake," Kathy said. "Is it your belief that if you assault someone from another planet, you won't be held accountable?"

"Don't get cute with me. Why would I kill an alien? What would be the motive?"

"You never met McFleegle before tonight?" I asked. "Never even heard the name?"

"Never."

"But you'd met others like her?"

"They're all like her."

"They all have a tattoo?" Kathy asked.

"Every damn one of 'em."

CHAPTER 4

Looking at Kathy as she brushed some hair out of her face, I said, "Snake, why don't you explain what happened this evening the way you might explain it to the cops?"

"You mean about the tattoo and—"

"No hogwash. They're not going to believe she's an alien. Try the real stuff. Tell me how you would get out of this if you were explaining it to a couple of skeptical beat cops."

"No problemo. I picked her up at Fourth and Pike in my Caddy. I brought her here. We had a couple of drinks. She took her clothes off. I took mine off." He stared at us stupidly.

"There must be more."

"Sure, there's more. I got up to take a piss, came back, climbed aboard, and realized she was not with the program."

"And then you called me?"

"Not exactly."

"What'd you do before you called me?"

"Telephoned NASA."

"The National Aeronautics and Space Administration?"

"Right, Jacko. NASA." He stared up at us. "Only I couldn't get ahold of anybody with any rank." Perhaps mention of NASA made him realize how weird this sounded. He chewed the whiskers on his lower lip, ran both hands through his wiry hair, hawked up a gob of phlegm in his throat, swallowed it, and continued. "You think I fell asleep and smothered her?"

"No," I said. "And don't suggest that to the police."

"You didn't argue with her?" Kathy asked.

"These aren't like human women. None of 'em are the least bit argumentative."

"Was there a struggle?"

"No. She *wanted* to put out. You don't believe a woman would *want* to sleep with me, do you?"

"That's not it," said Kathy. "What I'm having trouble conceptualizing is a woman from another planet wanting to sleep with you."

"Neither one of you believes me."

"Snake," I said. "Something occurs to me. Did she speak English?"

"All of 'em did. They got a few phrases wrong—like they called Coca-Cola *cock-a-colla*. This one here said 'Ravenna Boulevard' but pronounced it 'Ra-veena.' And they didn't know any of the TV shows. Never heard of *The X Files*. I asked one of them about phasers and Mr. Spock, and she didn't know what I was talking about."

I said, "Did these women come right out and tell you they were from outer space?" Snake stared at us. "I mean, you're not going to believe a story like that without proof. What convinced you?"

"I can't tell ya."

"Why not?"

"I can't."

Kathy said, "How did she get the marks on her neck?"

"What are you talking about?"

"She's got marks on her neck," I said. "Probably from a pair of hands. And she's got what's known as petechial hemorrhaging in her eyes. She wet herself. You know what all that means."

"Strangulation. But I didn't do it." Snake looked pleadingly at Kathy. "Isn't it *possible* what I've been saying is true?"

"Well," said Kathy, "it's just . . ."

"Isn't it *possible* aliens are visiting our planet?"

"Just about anything's possible, but that doesn't mean it will play in a court of law," Kathy answered. "And we're talking about a court of law here, not what's possible. We start announcing she's from space and all the rest, we might as well drive you right on over to Walla Walla and request your cell assignment. Are you listening, Snake?" He nodded. "I want you to keep quiet about this. Not a peep."

Snake said, "We all have to keep quiet about it. You don't go around spouting off either. You're the only ones I ever told." He looked up at me. "That's why I didn't want your woman to come. You really don't get it, do you? They can come through the walls. Locks don't mean nothin'. Through them windows. Through the glass."

I said, "More likely somebody came in through your unlocked front door, a jealous boyfriend, a husband, an outraged brother, killed her, and left before you woke. Or you killed her."

"No, sir. I didn't. And I locked that door."

"It wasn't locked when we got here."

"And you say you didn't hear a thing," said Kathy. "Wouldn't you have heard something?"

When we'd walked in, we hadn't woken him from a chair, not at first, so I could see how, ensconced in his own bed, swaddled in his own blankets, drunk on booze and sex and that magnificent perfume, dreaming of women from distant planets, he could sleep through a murder. I said, "She was drinking half as much as he was, it wouldn't have been much of a struggle. Even if she weren't so small, a choke hold can render somebody unconscious in seven to ten seconds. Sometimes less. You start with a sleeping victim . . ."

"The doctors did it," Snake said.

"What doctors?" Kathy's voice had grown decidedly softer since concluding Snake was madder than a March hare.

"The ones who control the breeding program."

For the first time Kathy and I could see in each other's eyes that Snake wasn't going to snap out of this. He was going to spend some years sucking down Jell-O and little colored pills at Western State Hospital.

"Have you ever met anyone who claimed to be a doctor from space?" Kathy asked.

"No, but I heard about 'em."

"Where?"

"The breeders."

"I wonder where the cops are," I said.

"And I read about 'em too. I know this all sounds odd," said Snake. "But don't you think it's possible?"

"Look, Elmer," Kathy said. "From now on you say nothing. Anyone asks you a question, you refer them to me. I don't want you talking to the police or your cell mates or anybody. We'll prepare a written statement together. Understand? Everything you've been telling us is to remain between us."

"Of course. But I got about the most fantastic story anybody ever told, and when you and everybody else hears it, you'll be convinced. The police will be convinced. This shit I got would convince J. Edgar Hoover in his little dress and everything."

After I'd stepped outside to see if the police were anywhere close, I came back in and said, "You ever walk in your sleep, Elmer? Find yourself in another room and not know how you got there? Ever fall asleep at the wheel of your car?"

"Years ago in the hospital on morphine I had some curious dreams."

Kathy, who was on her knees beside the armchair Elmer had collapsed into, touched his hand and said, "Have you been under the care of a mental health professional?"

"No!"

The first homicide detective came half an hour after the uniforms. By then Snake had been frisked and cuffed and stashed in the backseat of a squad car, his whiskers flat against the cruiser window, eyes closed, spit trickling down the glass. Kathy and I leaned against the fender of my new Ford sedan.

Short, bald, round, and tight, Arnold Haldeman, the homicide dick, was chubby enough to make you think he could fall off a ladder and bounce, a man without wrinkles on his nuts. An in-your-face cop with a chip on his shoulder, Haldeman was a man who feigned camaraderie with everyone, but in fact experienced it with no one. I'd seen him around and knew he wasn't much liked by the troops. I had the feeling he'd never been one of the gang, not in the SPD, not in college, and not in the Boy Scouts. I had never been one of the gang either, but I hadn't dedicated my life to getting even.

When he'd gone upstairs, Kathy, who had never met Haldeman, said, "I sure wouldn't buy a used car from that man."

"I love it when your ESP kicks in."

"Why did he give me that creepy look?"

"Could be he doesn't like being dragged from bed at five in the morning. Could be he hates cross-eyed private eyes and gorgeous brunettes."

"He didn't even look at you. Besides, your eyes aren't crossed—not since the operation."

"Very funny. Okay. He hates brunettes."

"Gorgeous brunettes, you said."

"I did, didn't I."

Ten minutes later Haldeman came down the stairs and walked over to Kathy, pushing out his thick sausage-fingered hand. As they shook, he said, "Counselor. I understand you're representing the man in custody."

"Yes. I'm Kathy Birchfield, and Elmer Slezak is my client. I've given Mr. Slezak instructions not to say anything until we can prepare a statement. I should have that for you sometime this morning."

Haldeman smiled as if she'd said something not entirely amusing. "Oh, surely you can let him talk. We're not going to ask him who killed Nicole Simpson. Nothing tricky. You want, you can sit on his lap and hold his hand. How would that be?"

"Don't patronize me." Kathy returned his smile.

"Sorry. I didn't mean to suggest I didn't think you were effective counsel, counselor. I hope you didn't come away with that idea."

"As a matter of fact I did."

He laughed, and then his tone changed, but only by a notch, the implication being that now we were going to get the real Haldeman. Despite the early hour the Windsor knot in his tie was crisp, his starched shirt immaculate. "I understand you disturbed the crime scene."

"My client called early this morning and said there was a woman in his apartment he thought had died. We got dressed, drove over, and saw for ourselves. We touched nothing."

"Who's we?" Haldeman asked.

"Myself and my associate, Thomas Black."

Arnold Haldeman regarded me for the first time. "You a lawyer too?"

"He's a private investigator working for me," Kathy said.

"Black? Don't I know you? You were linked to that death over near First Avenue South. About a year ago?"

"Not linked exactly. I knew him."

"Yeah. You sure did." His eyes were gray and carried condescension, confidence, as well as the arrogance of power. It was funny because if you'd seen Haldeman on the street, you wouldn't have looked at him twice. But here he was with a badge making me nervous. Then, too, I had a history to be nervous about. There was no statute of limitations on a killing, and "linked" was a nice way of putting my involvement.

"Surely you can tell me something before you make your *official* statement? Like who's that girl up there? How about a couple of clues. His wife? Sister? Mother? Somebody he found in *The Stranger*?"

"I need to talk to my client before we say anything," Kathy said.

"What time did you get the call?"

"The call came through at three fifty-one," Kathy said.

Haldeman made a play of looking at his wristwatch. "Let's see. You didn't call our dispatcher until four-forty. You live a mile from here. That's forty-nine minutes from the time of Slezak's call until you dialed 911. Why so long?"

"How do you know where I live?" Kathy asked.

"Come, come, come, dear. That's my job. Why so long?"

"It's hard to tell what happened to the time. We must have taken a while to get dressed."

"Did you, now?" He was staring at her jersey.

"Yes."

"Well, let's figure this out, why don't we? Three fifty-one you get the call. Let's say you get out of your house by four. That's nine minutes to use the Water Pik and find the car keys. More than generous, don't you think? So unless you stopped for breakfast at Denny's in Ballard, you're here around, what, four-oh-five? Thirty seconds to park—I see you didn't waste any time looking for a spot—which tells me you might have been in a little bit of a hurry—and what, a minute to get inside? That puts us at, let's see, four-oh-seven? That means you were inside without calling for thirty-three minutes."

Kathy said nothing. I folded my arms and looked at the rapidly bluing sky. The apartment door was open and we could see evidence technicians and police department personnel wandering around inside.

"I'm wondering what took you so long. And hoping it wasn't because you were waiting for your client to sober up or maybe until you could dispose of some evidence."

"We didn't touch a thing," I said.

To anyone watching from across the street, Arnold Haldeman no doubt seemed friendly enough, riding up on the balls of his feet, smiling, chewing gum, offering us the pack. "Suppose you tell me what you found when you got here."

"Same as you did. Except Mr. Slezak was in the living room," Kathy said.

"And what was he doing in the living room?"

"Waiting for us."

"Did he seem agitated?"

"Not exactly."

"Not exactly? What does that mean? When somebody says not exactly, I have two ways to look at that. It could mean he was agitated but not as much as they would've expected, or it could mean he wasn't agitated at all. Which?"

"Somewhere in between," Kathy said.

"Somewhere in between. Hmmm." Haldeman looked at me. "How well do you both know Mr. Slezak?"

"I've known him ten years," I said.

"Maybe three years," Kathy said.

"Does he have a lot of women friends?"

"Couldn't tell you," I said.

"Has he ever assaulted one before?"

"You can find that out easier than we can," Kathy said.

"What I don't understand is why, when he murders one, the first thing he does is call you two over. Now, why is that?"

I was tempted to say something smart, but it wouldn't have helped Elmer, and Kathy would have been furious. Kathy said, "We don't know that she was murdered."

"Yeah, well I can see you two are going to be about as useful as an extra pecker on my poodle. Listen. I'm going to help you both out. I'm going to tell you what I'm planning. How about first-degree murder? How does that sound?"

"It's interesting to hear the prosecutor's office is letting the police decide the charges now," said Kathy sweetly.

Haldeman smiled below his wire-rimmed glasses, exposing a mouthful of ground-down nubs that looked like baby teeth. "We can work together on this. I want to know who the woman upstairs is and what went on."

"I always work with the city," Kathy said.

"Me too," I chimed in, only because I could see how peeved he was.

"Here's what I think," Haldeman said. "I think he brought this woman up here for some kinky sex and she wouldn't go for it. I think if we ask around, we'll find Slezak engaged in kinky sex most of the time. I think we'll find he got rough with his girlfriends when they didn't go along with his games. I think he was probably playing around with sexual asphyxia. Went overboard."

"That wouldn't be murder in the first," Kathy said.

"Why don't you let me worry about the charges, okay, honey? You can just keep your pretty little self reserved for your client. I don't know the story yet, but this is a stinker. A real stinker."

After we were in the car, Kathy said, "That little son of a bitch."

"He watches too many movies. Don't let him get to you."

I backed across the curb onto the street, then drove past two police cruisers. It was almost five-thirty and my eyeballs felt as if they'd been rolled in sand and dropped into a wool pocket. Kathy slid close and slipped a hand between my thighs, cradling my leg with her warm palm. "Thomas, we both know it's a sign of guilt when a person can fall asleep after being arrested."

"It can be."

"Elmer was sleeping in the squad car like a drunk in the back of a bus."

"I saw."

"You know what I think? I think he hallucinated while he was having sex with her, strangled her, then dozed off. He woke up and honestly didn't know what he'd done. I don't suppose there will be any doubt that strangulation was the cause of death?"

"Nope."

"First degree," Kathy said. "He'll never get first degree. But we've got to have Elmer's mental state evaluated."

"You have somebody in mind?"

"Ellen would be perfect." Ellen Burgess and Kathy had gone to school together. Ellen had a Ph.D. in psychology and had worked for Kathy before, as well as having her own practice. She could probably give us a report after one or two visits, depending upon how cooperative Elmer was. "I'll ask her to see him today or tomorrow."

As we pulled onto our street off Roosevelt, I laughed. "Alien women. Doctors who don't know the names of body parts. Breeders from outer space. Phone calls in the middle of the night. It would be funny if she wasn't dead."

"It's so like Snake."

"They can go through walls, you know."

"It is possible. Don't you think it's *possible*?"

We looked at each other. Kathy lowered her voice and said, "You have just entered . . . *The Twilight Zone*. Do-do do-do, do-do do-do . . ."

CHAPTER 5

When we got married, Kathy and I made two decisions: the first, that she would keep her surname, Birchfield; the second, that we would live in my three-bedroom bungalow. The house was old, somewhat battered, but held fond memories for us. Situated in one of the less trafficked neighborhoods in the U District, we had only one bad neighbor that we were aware of—Horace, right next door.

The basement contained a tiny apartment that Kathy had once rented. Presently it housed a six-foot Swedish foreign student with hair so pale her eyebrows were nearly invisible. We called her The Mole because it was rare to actually catch sight of her. Ironically, before renting it out, I'd joked about finding a giant Swedish goddess to live in the basement. A masseuse was what I'd actually hoped for, but so far we hadn't seen enough of her to ascertain if she knew the art of massage. Ingrid wasn't a goddess exactly, but halfway across a dark nightclub floor she might pass for one. I liked having her around because Kathy, who normally didn't lack self-confidence, was just a tad uneasy around all that Nordic altitude.

In my spare time I grew roses and, along the south wall of the house where it was hot, tomatoes. I also maintained a vegetable garden in back where we had a mixture of sun and shade. A grand old crab apple tree grew in the yard, equipping us with ammunition each fall for apple wars with Kathy's nephews, the boys wearing thick ski hats, two pairs of pants, fencing masks, and bulky winter clothing, Kathy and I in wraparound shatterproof sunglasses and parkas. So, okay, it was pretty juvenile, but so much fun we didn't care.

Half asleep in a corner of the back porch, L.C. greeted us when we finally got home that morning with a lazy slap of his tail, cautious not to move any other part of his body and spoil us with too much affection.

We went inside and dropped onto the bed on our backs. The room was dark. "I can't believe he accused us of tampering with evidence," Kathy said.

"Look at it from his point of view. He's at square one. We wouldn't give him a statement. He doesn't know if there were fifty people in the apartment when she died or two. He doesn't know if she's an ex-wife or the Federal Express driver. Maybe she's a mail-order bride from the Philippines. Or a business associate. A prostitute. Maybe our story is going to be that Elmer got up in the middle of the night and went out for a pack of cigarettes, came back, and found her that way. You think about it, until they get some physical evidence, they don't have jack."

"Whatever he thinks, they're not going to charge Elmer with murder one. There's an interesting court case, *Bingham versus the State of Washington*, that says you can't presume because it was strangulation that there was premeditation. I'm sure Haldeman doesn't know about it."

"Tell you the truth, I'm not entirely sure Snake did it," I said.

"Because the door was open?"

"Elmer's a man who routinely carries five guns. Somebody that nervous doesn't make love without a locked door protecting his backside. So I'm thinking somebody had a key. Or maybe the woman unlocked it from the inside. It could have been a scam. She flirts with Snake, goes home with him, then the out-raged husband or boyfriend breaks in and demands money.

Except he came in and for reasons unknown killed her. It'll be interesting to see what the forensics people come up with. That and McFleegle's history." I kissed her. "Breeders from distant galaxies. That gets me sooooo hot."

"You think I'll let you have your way with me while you're thinking about aliens?"

"I *always* think about aliens when I'm having my way with you." I kissed her ear. "The way I figure it, we could go one of two ways here. We could grab an hour of superficial sleep, or we could earn a glow that would surely give us many minutes of quality sleep. Which would you prefer? The illusive? Or the genuine?"

"You should have been an attorney." She wrapped her arms around my neck.

"I sleep with an attorney."

"You sure do."

We woke up a little after seven, at least I did. Because of our relative arrangement, it was impossible to get out of bed without disturbing her. I walked into the bathroom and turned on the shower, but before I could step under it, Kathy was in the room. She tucked her hair into a shower cap. "Thomas. Has Elmer ever done anything like this before? That you know of?"

"Kill a woman? Not that I know of." She stepped in, took the shampoo away from me, squirted a gob into her palm, and began kneading my hair. I groped for the bar of soap and began reciprocating. Kathy was short and fit with just the hint of a little rounded underbelly even slim women seem to carry. It was my favorite part, but she didn't know it. "You know this never works," I said. "One of us is always soapy and one of us is always cold."

"I'll be Soapy," she said, turning me around and forcing me out from under the spray. "You be Cold. And don't keep washing the same part."

"Parts."

"All of me needs to be clean."

"I have it," I said, turning her around again so that I was under the spray. "I'll be Sleepy. You be Dopey."

"Dopey? Thomas, you should be Dopey. It fits you better. Now, see how much fun this is?"

"I didn't say it wasn't fun. I said one of us was always cold. And *you* be Dopey. I'm *always* Dopey."

"If you say so."

"Whoa. Maybe I'd better be . . . Bashful."

"No, this is Bashful right here. Well . . . *whoa* is right. This *was* Bashful. How did that happen?"

I grinned through the soap. "You know how it happened."

CHAPTER 6

Tuesday was spent in court chaperoning a nervous, elderly witness to a hit-and-run involving a woman on horseback on the Burke-Gilman Trail near Marymoor Park who'd collided with a young man on in-line skates.

It was half past noon when I got back to Pioneer Square and the Mutual Life Building. We had a large office on the fourth floor, Kathy and another attorney, a couple of paralegals, and myself.

On First Avenue near the corner of First and Yesler Way, the Mutual Life Building had housed the city's earliest jail. It was a stone-faced, flat-roofed, narrow building four stories tall, lacking spatial separations from the buildings on either side. A set of worn steps led up to the front doors. Below on the corner was a toy shop filled with colorful kites and gewgaws. Across the street was a small park haunted by winos, jumpy tourists, and the homeless. One of my favorite cookie stands was catty-corner from the building.

Stepping off the elevator on the top floor, the first obstacle one saw was a set of glass doors with a reception island behind them. The office arrangement formed an L, with the corner of the L pointing at the elevators. Kathy's office was on the right at the end of the long leg. Along that same leg was a combination corridor/waiting room with couches and chairs for clients. At the end of the other leg of the L, the short leg, stood a coffee machine and beyond that, my space, a pebbled-glass door leading into what was virtually a converted closet. Should a crazed gunman or a Jehovah's Witness break into the office spraying bullets or pamphlets, I would surely be overlooked, a fact I regularly relayed to those wallowing in more luxurious quarters.

The two paralegals and Kathy were out to lunch, Kathy to visit Elmer in jail directly afterward. The other lawyer was behind a closed door with a client. I could hear the client's voice, but not what she was saying. Our receptionist, Beulah, greeted me with a wink and a twinkle. Beulah was robust, or thunderously fat, depending on how you looked at it, and as was the case with a lot of people in her situation, you never saw her eating.

She told me Arnold Haldeman had called twice, probably because Kathy had rescheduled Elmer Slezak's statement twice, promising it later in the afternoon. Elmer didn't have to give one at all, but I reckoned Kathy had been postponing it both to keep Haldeman hooked and to piss him off.

Cocooning myself in my office, I reviewed my phone messages. An outfit called IGP Systems had called and left an incredibly long message basically asking me to come over and apply for a job. On the personal side, an ex-girlfriend called sounding tentative but also interested. We hadn't been all that involved when she had dumped me for a rowing jock in the spring of our sophomore year in college, so I wondered why she was calling now so many years later.

While I was in the office, I decided to do some preliminary research on Elmer's victim: Catherine Samantha McFleegle.

A little roaming on the computer produced a mild shock. McFleegle didn't live in West Seattle, at least not at the address on her driver's license. That didn't bother me. People moved. What bothered me was that there was no dwelling at the address, never had been.

A couple of phone calls revealed additional peculiarities. Her Washington State driver's license was a fake. DMV had never issued a license to a Catherine McFleegle. Nor to a *Mac*Fleegle. A search on the CD-ROM phone directories in the office didn't produce any McFleegles in the Northwest.

Stumped, I called an information broker in Oregon who was tapped into about every database there was, some legally, a few otherwise. Without leaving her castle, Hilda could procure an amazing amount of information on almost anybody.

She called back forty-five minutes later and told me Catherine McFleegle didn't have a driver's license in any of the thirty-nine compact states, at least under that name, wasn't listed on any voter registration she could find, and apparently had no credit history. She didn't turn the name up in any of her phone directories, and a check with her confidential sources at the banks in the area didn't yield any accounts or activity. "This woman hid herself real good," said Hilda.

"Either that or she never existed."

"Listen. I can go through arrest records, adoption records, a bunch more."

"Don't waste your time. I'm almost sure now the name's an alias. Besides, the cops will do all this if I wait."

"Call me if you need me. I'll put it on the tab."

I drove home in midafternoon and found time for a thirty-mile bike ride through the University of Washington Arboretum and down along Lake Washington Boulevard, into Renton along Renton Avenue near the airport. I came back over the hill in Skyway, climbing hard in the heat. The digital readout on a bank claimed the air temperature was eighty-two degrees Fahrenheit. We'd been having an unusual summer for the Northwest. In fact it had been ideal weather since early May— blue skies, light breezes, and daytime temperatures hovering at or topping eighty. Kathy griped that truckloads of tourists were flying straight home to pack up and move here permanently.

After stretching and showering, I met Kathy at Rosita's, a Mexican restaurant near Green Lake, where you were served all the hot tortillas you could eat while you waited. "You're looking good," I said, kissing her cheek.

"You *always* look good," she returned.

It had been a long day and I was tired and hungry from my

ride, but she seemed as fresh as a kitten. Over fajitas and gua-camole she told me of her visit to the King County Jail that after-noon. "The only aspect of this I feel good about," Kathy said, "is that Elmer seems to be keeping mum about the aliens."

"What about Ellen?"

"She's going to see him tomorrow."

"Does Elmer know she's coming?"

"Not really."

"Not really? Hmmm. What does that mean?"

"I'm hoping he'll be more receptive tomorrow. They took his fingerprints, then they took saliva samples, blood, hair. They scraped under his fingernails. He was furious. Then he wanted to know what they'd taken from his apartment."

"Did you tell him?"

"I had the list with me. I didn't see why not. It seemed to appease him a little, as if he'd been expecting them to find some-thing they didn't."

"How was he?"

"Sober. He still swears he never met her before last night. He kept asking about the autopsy. Thomas, I think he really believes the autopsy is going to turn up something fantastic, like two hearts or a bunch of livers. He thinks the newspeople are going to be interviewing him. That he'll be a national celebrity."

"They should be through with the autopsy by now. They usu-ally do them the next morning."

"Every time it came up, he'd get this little smirk on his face."

"There has been one odd circumstance." I told Kathy about my search for Catherine Samantha McFleegle.

"So what do you make of it?"

"I don't know. What else did he tell you?"

"He claims he's been meeting with different alien women for two weeks. He claims they call him up and make arrangements and he impregnates them."

"So he was serious when he called them breeders?"

"He's been chosen, he thinks, to put his seed into a par-ticular strain or species or whatever you wish to call it. He said he's impregnated about twenty-five already and they had him lined up to do two hundred more."

"Good grief."

"That's what I said."

"And why, I wonder, did they pick Elmer to populate the galaxies? They wanted a crowd with hair growing out of their ears?"

"By the way. He said men in black cars would be following you. I swear. Black cars, he said. Usually Buicks. They all wear black suits. They'll be traveling in pairs or foursomes."

"This is a joke, right?"

"He said he thought the ones following him were dwarfs."

CHAPTER 7

By Wednesday afternoon the case against Elmer Slezak looked even more grim. After charging him with second-degree murder, the prosecutors asked for and received a bail of seventy-five thousand dollars, a figure that made it unlikely Elmer would be released anytime soon, since he had only the Cadillac and sixty-five hundred bucks in a savings account, no house or property to sign over to the bail bondsman, and no wealthy relatives; in fact only a few of his relatives spoke to him. Friend or not, I certainly wasn't going to empty my savings account or put my house on the line, for they wanted ten percent in cash as well as securities for the rest.

Kathy and the psychologist, Ellen Burgess, visited Elmer in the King County Jail after the bail hearing, but Elmer, while conceding he was in a pickle, refused to talk with Ellen, expressing a fatuous and clearly false confidence that the truth would come out and he would be released.

After Ellen left, Kathy said, "Why on earth didn't you tell her what you told me? The breeders? The men in black?"

"You told me not to talk about it with anybody."

"But she's on our side."

"Some stuff is private."

"But you told *me*."

"You're my lawyer."

"And she's a *psychologist* I hired. What you say will be held in confidence."

"Believe me, it's for her own good." When Kathy stared at him, he continued. "People who know about this . . . strange things happen. Events are unfolding. You'll see. You read the *PI* this morning?"

"I saw the article."

Slezak had smiled knowingly.

Page three of that morning's *Seattle Post-Intelligencer* had contained a sketchy article about the murder, accompanied by the driver's-license photo of the dead woman, not a bad likeness, and beneath the photo a plea to the public: *Anybody with information please contact the Seattle Police Department. This woman may have been using the name Catherine Samantha McFleegle.*

I'd lunched that Wednesday at Palomino's with a couple of clients who'd hired me to check out their respective boyfriends: bad news for one—her prospective mate had gotten cold feet and broken off four previous engagements; worse news for the other, whose boyfriend was gay and was looking for a wife to satisfy his deeply religious and wealthy parents. Unknown to her, he'd had two earlier marriages that had gone sour, the last on the eve of the wedding.

Lunch turned out to be twenty minutes of food, twenty minutes of dispensing information, and two hours of counseling. One client spent the meal dripping tears into her blue cheese dressing. The other talked openly about becoming a lesbian. "I mean, let's face it. At our age men are either taken, ruined by some other woman, socially disabled, or out-and-out pigs. You want somebody as sensitive and caring as a woman, you need a woman."

"But I *like* men," said her companion.

"I know," she said. "Me too."

It was almost three o'clock when I walked the twelve blocks to the office and found another message from the IGP Systems woman, an oleaginous young lady with perfect diction and a studied and seductive voice that might have been generated by computer. They'd heard good words about my investigative skills and needed another operative in the region. Beginning tomorrow they had a job that was "tailored" for me. The money was nearly four times my going rate. I knew local PIs who worked for IGP and who considered them a first-class employer, but I had a bugaboo about big corporations. Besides, I had a feeling Snake's case was going to take up a lot of time.

I was still pondering the call when Kathy came into my office in a summery white shift that buttoned up the front and extended almost to her ankles. She dropped a heavy manila envelope onto the desk. "Thomas? You want to take a look at this package from the prosecutors and tell me what you think?"

"You read it?"

"Some. Elmer was legally drunk on the morning of the murder. And you were right. She *was* definitely strangled."

"What planet was she from?"

Kathy smiled grimly. "*This* one, apparently. I don't know if I can make jokes about it anymore. I wish for once I'd get a client who was innocent."

"Or sane?"

"That might help too. I suppose somebody has to make certain all the losers in the world get a fair shake. I'm only tired of it being me. By the way. They said that *was* a tattoo-removal scar, done in the last few days."

"Interesting. I'll be on the roof, okay?"

"Trying to get skin cancer? You're already brown as a nut."

"All for you, Sister."

My excuse was that cyclists tended to get farmers' tans, a small half moon on the back of the hand where the gloves opened, brown from the biceps down the arm, white everywhere else, strap marks from the helmet crisscrossing your face. It looked particularly funny on me, since I tanned instantly, making the corresponding white marks all the more distinct. An outing in the sun a couple of times a week helped flatten the effect.

Hedged in by a chest-high parapet, the flat, tarred roof of our building allowed a view of the roofs of nearby lower buildings, penthouse apartments, greenhouses, the tops of the maple trees across the street in the park, the Alaskan Way Viaduct to the west, Elliott Bay, and a sweep of the snow-capped Olympic Mountains beyond on the horizon. If you were snoopy and went to the back over the alley, you could look into the windows of a couple of seedy hotels on Yesler Way and watch the unfortunate carrying on with their lives.

The building tenants had donated an assortment of mismatched lawn furniture along with a small glass-topped table and a strip of AstroTurf. A cardboard box filled with sand served as that summer's ashtray and pigeon roost. The only thing missing was a wading pool.

Stripping down to a pair of running shorts, I leaned back in a lawn chair and thumbed through the prosecutor's discovery papers.

According to the autopsy report, there had been extensive trauma and bruising to her throat and larynx consistent with manual strangulation. They'd taken sperm from her vagina and belly and it was being tested at the state lab. There would be no surprises there. Elmer admitted having sex with her. Her teeth were cavity free and there was no evidence of orthodontic work. She'd been wearing contact lenses of the type one leaves in for a week before disposal. There had been no signs of a struggle, no torn hair, no extraneous bruising, and no evidence under her nails.

Her blood alcohol content had been .05, and there had been a strong sedative in her bloodstream. They had also sent the dregs from several drinking glasses found in the apartment to the state lab, hoping to detect a drugged drink. Alcohol and tranquilizers together were always dangerous, and the medical examiner had written a note to the effect that she probably would have remained unconscious for many hours. I wondered how much strength or awareness she would have had to fight off an assailant.

Kathy had been hoping to plea-bargain the charges down to manslaughter, but the presence of drugs in her system hinted strongly of premeditation. If we could prove she'd taken the alcohol and drugs on her own, perhaps in a downtown bar prior to their meeting, or if we could show she was in the habit of mixing alcohol and drugs, Snake would benefit.

Haldeman had interviewed every neighbor with a view of Elmer's door, which was on an open balcony facing the street, and had produced almost two dozen witness statements from twelve students, two cabdrivers, two nurses, a hospital orderly, a convention decorator, a teaching assistant in the philosophy department at the university, a meat cutter in the middle of a divorce, and two women who were co-writing a book about butterflies in city environments.

All of Haldeman's witness statements were overlong, many were immaterial, and unless he owned a brand-new word processor he needed to dick around with, I couldn't think of any reason for him to have gone overboard this way.

Piecing together the accounts, it became clear, in contradiction to what Elmer had told us, that the victim had been frequenting his apartment for a couple of weeks, sometimes visiting two or three times in an evening. Despite all these visits Haldeman had failed to locate a single witness who had spoken to the victim.

"He's had trashy women up there from the start," said his apartment manager, a woman named Magdanz. "If he hadn't been driving that Caddy, we never would have let him in, not with his rent history." Haldeman was apparently recording minutia such as this in order to portray Elmer as a scumbag. Or perhaps he wanted to give the appearance of having been so thorough that there would be no point in our traversing the same ground.

Snake had clearly lied to us about not having met the victim prior to the night of her death, but the questions confronting us were more complex than Snake's lies. Was he being evasive, or did he believe the tales he was spinning? If evasion was his game, why such ridiculous evasions? Surely he didn't think he was going to get off the hook with an insanity plea. The other possibility, and the one that shook me up, was that Elmer Slezak *was* losing his marbles.

It was difficult enough to have a friend move away or die, but to watch a personality unravel before your eyes was to visit a small place very few of us had been and fewer would care to return to.

According to the witness statements, Elmer was a lousy neighbor, surly when encountered on the breezeways, sometimes inebriated, often confrontational, rarely helpful. He parked on the wrong side of the sidewalk, kept late hours, listened to noisy honky-tonk or country western music, snarled at people, and from time to time entertained transients, unbathed men carrying knapsacks, bedrolls, and in one instance a large knife.

Haldeman had used his expertise to paint a vivid and thoroughly one-dimensional portrait.

Elmer *did* drink. He *did* listen to country music. He *did* like women. Whether they were "trashy" was a matter of perspective. And he *was* a soft touch. I'd seen him give ten bucks to a man on the street who'd asked for a quarter. Hopelessly swayed by hard-luck stories, he let the homeless sleep on his couch, in his car, and had once driven two destitute women to Spokane, where they had been promised jobs, and then back to Seattle again when the jobs didn't pan out. No hitchhiker was ever left on a road Snake was driving on. If Snake had been a whore, people would have said he had a heart of gold. And of course it was a given that if Snake had been a woman, he would have been a whore.

All in all, the police and prosecutors were beginning to paint Elmer into a corner. He'd been meeting with the deceased for weeks. She'd had sex the night of her death, with him by his own admission. She'd been drugged the night of her death, probably by him. All that was missing were witnesses to document discord between them.

The last sheet in the packet the prosecutors had sent over was a list of items the police had seized. From Elmer's apartment they had confiscated the sheets and bedding, the dead woman's clothing, Snake's clothing off the floor, his pistols from the kitchen, six more revolvers from other areas of the apartment, an address book, drinking glasses from the kitchen sink, an assortment of prescription medications from his medicine cabinet in the bathroom, and an album of photographs. The list from his office was smaller: an appointment book, a Rolodex, a desk calender, and several bottles of medications.

"So," Kathy said, her heels making a hollow sound on the tar roof as she walked toward me from the doorway. She sat on the edge of a folding beach chair three feet away. When the breeze swirled around on the roof, a hint of her perfume wafted past me. "So? What do you think?"

"I'll go back to his apartment and see if the police missed anything. And I need to visit his office. He's got a garage in Tacoma where he stores stuff, so maybe if I get desperate, I'll head down south. I'm pretty sure the police don't know about it."

"You told me the garage was filled floor-to-ceiling with pornographic magazines and videos."

"That's what it seemed like when I was there a couple of years ago, but he's also got a grand piano his mother used to own. And there's a ton of other stuff."

"Do you think he drugged her?"

"She might have a history. She might have done it herself."

"But do you think he did it?"

"Yes."

Kathy watched the breeze ruffle the papers in my hands while I watched it play with a few loose strands of her hair. A ferry skated out from the dock toward Bremerton. "What are you thinking?"

"I'm thinking you have entirely too many buttons on that dress. Here, let me help you."

"If this were the tallest building in sight, I might be tempted to consider such a gallant proposal." She stood, the sunlight exposing the outline of her legs through the thin, white material. Opening the metal door that led downstairs, she said, "By the way. Whose turn to cook tonight?"

"Yours."

"I thought Wednesday was your night."

"No, yours."

"Liar."

"I'll make it up to you. Leave that dress on and I'll make it up to you."

"You can make it up to me by doing the dishes."

Downstairs, Haldeman was unexpectedly cooperative when I phoned Homicide and asked him to fax me the blown-up photo from the dead woman's driver's license. While I had him on the line, I said, "You get any tips from the paper?"

"Not yet. We're running it again tomorrow and in tonight's *Times*. You don't have any ideas, do you?" Asking for help was a major concession from an anal-retentive control freak such as Haldeman. Yet, when I thought about it, this new wrinkle ran true to form. Feigning false candor and pretending to be pleasant were part of his act.

"I was as surprised as you to find out the license was fake," I said.

"You don't see many phony driver's licenses these days. You folks aren't foolin' with Uncle Arnold are you? Sure you don't have any idea who she is?"

For a moment I considered telling him she was a breeder from another planet, but I said, "If I knew, I'd tell you."

CHAPTER 8

After running off twenty copies of the photo Haldeman had faxed, I took Elmer's keys and drove the ten or so blocks to his office on Jackson Street in the International District.

The office was on the second floor over a small Chinese grocery and herb shop in a block of three-story buildings. The nameplate had been done up in bronze (ELMER SLEZAK INVESTIGA-TIONS—CONFIDENTIAL) and bolted to the brick face of the building, as if he expected to be around in twenty years. On the same block was an Asian dentist, an optometrist, an Asian newspaper, a Chinatown tour-guide business, and several music stores specializing in Chinese and Japanese CDs.

Snake's key ring had maybe forty keys on it, so it took a while to find the one for the street door, longer for the one to his office at the top of a long flight of creaky wooden steps.

The office overlooked the street and was bright despite the lack of direct sunlight. As I entered, a pair of trolley poles sparked and skittered along wires over an electric bus outside the window.

On the walls were old lobby posters of Humphrey Bogart in *The Maltese Falcon*, Robert Mitchum in *The Big Sleep*, and Robert Montgomery in *Lady in the Lake*. All three were encased in glass and signed by the actors, though the dipsy-doodle penmanship on each looked suspiciously similar to Snake's.

In one corner stood my stuffed yellow dog, Alfred, an item Snake had "burrowed" several months ago. Alfred had an eye patch, purple jockey shorts, and he had recently acquired a wooden leg from an old coffee table to replace one of his that had snapped off. I carried the stuffed dog over to the door so that I wouldn't forget him on the way out. He'd been a gift from a group of clients, but Elmer liked to take him to bars and order drinks for two, the best gimmick for picking up women ever, he claimed. "If I'd known about this damned dog when I was eighteen, I wouldn'a got myself shot so many times."

The drawers and tabletops produced little that might pertain to the dead woman, or any woman who might have passed for an alien in Elmer's fried circuitry.

On his desk were a couple of magazines devoted to ufology and a fat tome called *A History of the World*, not the type of book you would expect in the library of Tacoma's sleaziest private gumshoe.

In the top drawer of the desk were two uncashed checks from an outfit called Green International; one for $16,050 and the second for $6,590. I took them with me. They probably weren't enough to get him out on bail, but Kathy would want to deposit them before they got lost. Or forgotten.

In a corner near a sofa stood a stack of videotapes about aliens, space travel, the Bermuda Triangle, theories on ancient mysteries, and stories of alien abduction. There were thirty or forty books on spacemen, government conspiracies to cover up spacemen, mysterious sightings, aliens who came from inside the earth, from other life zones, etcetera. I'd spoken to Elmer two weeks ago and he hadn't mentioned any of this.

The padlocks on two huge steel cabinets at the west end of the office had been sheared off, probably with police bolt cutters. Elmer had always been a sucker for gadgets, listening devices, and exotic weapons, but his current collection was breathtaking. The second cabinet was loaded with electronic equipment: expensive bug-detector systems still in the boxes; wiretap detectors; voice scramblers; miniature tape recorders; voice-activated bugging devices; a pen microphone; a product called Thief Detection Powder, to be sprayed on bundles of currency or jewelry or whatever was apt to be stolen, the thieves later to be identified with the use of ultraviolet light; fingerprint kits; invisible ink; a spray to allow one to read through sealed envelopes.

A parabolic microphone looked as if it had seen some wear and tear, but many of the items hadn't even been removed from their original packages, as if he'd gone on a recent spending spree.

In the weapons cabinet were two .44 Magnum handguns identical to the ones the police had confiscated from his apartment, a variety of other guns, handcuffs, thumb cuffs, boxes of ammunition, a case of Riot Buster Smoke Grenades and several models of electrical stun guns. He had Mace and pepper spray. In a corner a small leather satchel contained Elmer's lock-picking set.

I picked up a unit called the Powermax Double Shocker and turned it on, triggering a loud crackling sound. Seven inches long, it looked almost like a walkie-talkie, except for a pair of metal prods at one end. It was from between these prods that, according to the wording on the package, 150,000 volts spewed forth. I triggered it again. It was a menacing sound indeed.

The computer was on a table beside the desk. I was surprised the police hadn't carted it off with their other loot, but maybe the astounding array of computer games and game magazines had persuaded them he used it only as a toy.

I sat down and switched it on.

After it booted up, a screen came on asking for a password. I knew if I called Snake at the jail and asked for the password, he'd tell me to go piss up a rope. Nobody was as secretive as Snake, and even the prospect of going to prison wouldn't have deterred him from keeping me out of his files. In fact his passion for keeping secrets was probably the real reason he'd refused to talk to Ellen Burgess.

After trying every four-letter word I could think of, I began experimenting with more scholarly references, jotting each on a sheet of paper after it failed. Thirty-five minutes later I opened the computer with a rather nasty Spanish slang term for a small but intimate part of a woman's anatomy.

In the computer was a list of Snake's cases for the past two years, as well as copies of what appeared to be every report he'd written during that time. It took a while to get used to his word processor, but eventually I figured out the search function and began scanning the files for McFleegle's name. When that came up empty, I ran a search for the word *alien*.

Nothing.

I did find out that in the past six weeks Elmer had worked on forty projects, most of them small. Twenty-seven of those projects had been at the behest of IGP Systems, the outfit that had been courting me.

Glancing through the reports one by one, the only case that stood out, not an IGP case, was one in which a young man's girlfriend turned up in an alley, half dressed and dead from an overdose of heroin. The boyfriend, Snake's client, swore his girlfriend had never taken drugs but had been pursued by a Mexican who did. The Mexican had spent five years in a California prison for drug-related offenses and had been accused but never convicted of rape. Snake found another ex-boyfriend of the deceased who said she'd occasionally smoked marijuana or snorted cocaine at parties, smoked crack once or twice, and had been taking amphetamines for years to keep off weight. Clearly she'd put on a new face for Snake's client.

Locking the front door, I drove to Welch's Hardware on the corner of Twenty-third and Jackson, bought two large padlocks, returned to the office, and secured the cabinets.

I took a couple of blank computer disks from my car and downloaded all of Snake's recent files onto them, then loaded my car with Alfred, a couple of the more interesting UFO videotapes, and some items from the weapons cabinet I felt needed further examination.

On my final trip out the door I spotted an object under the

sofa on the far side of the room, a book swiped from the Tacoma Public Library, typical of Snake, who was addicted to committing minor infractions. It was titled *Diagnostic and Statistical Manual of Mental Disorders*. Several sections had been dog-eared and windowed with yellow and green highlighter pens. I took it and locked up the office.

CHAPTER 9

Kathy was cooking dinner in shorts, sandals, and a sleeveless blouse. I was on my back on the couch. Life was as it should be.

Powered by two tiny nine-volt batteries, which produced 150,000 volts at the press of a switch, the Double Shocker turned out to be an amazing piece of machinery that begged me to discharge it as quickly as it would recharge. "It's too bad you shucked that dress," I said.

"Why?"

"I wanted to take it off."

"I'll tell you what. You can wear it with your brown loafers. Then you can take it off as many times as you want."

"Thanks. I need an outfit for the private investigators' convention in Duluth. By the way, I got Alfred back."

"I'm so glad. Alfred. Gee. Be careful where you put him, would you? He's been with Snake and I'm afraid he might give L.C. fleas."

"I *was* careful. I put him in your closet. And I like having Alfred around. It keeps L.C. on his toes. He thinks we're going to stuff him too."

"That's mean, Thomas."

"I know." I triggered the Double Shocker and watched the sparks.

"Are you going to keep playing with that all night?"

"I think I am."

The phone rang. Answering it in the kitchen, Kathy spoke quietly for a minute, then carried it across the living room to me. Our fingertips lingered as she handed it to me. "It's Elmer," she whispered.

"Snake, old boy."

"Thomas. Did you get my message?"

"Which message was that?"

"About the boys in the Buick. You seen 'em?"

"Not yet."

"Keep your eyes peeled. They're around. And I don't want you to eat. Stay away from food."

"That's going to be a little tough, Snake. I get pretty hungry after a couple of days."

"Eat out of cans. Sealed packages. Open them yourself and don't take your eyes off 'em. Shop at a different store each meal."

"I'll think about it. How are they treating you?"

"They don't know nuthin' here. But forget about that. Why wasn't the photo of my alien on page one?"

"Gee, Snake. I guess the president and the governor had some items they wanted to let us know about."

"Don't make sport of me, Thomas."

"I don't have any idea why it wasn't on page one. Why didn't you talk to the psychologist?"

"Why the hell should I?"

"Because she might be able to give us a handle on what's going on."

"I didn't like her."

"Any particular reason?"

"For one, she had big boobs."

"That's two reasons. But I would have thought that would make your day."

"You think I'm an imbecile? Of course it makes my day. But when you get down to it, you gotta realize a woman with big tits hasn't got any brains. God only gives so much to any one person. You know that."

"If I promised you Ellen's breasts were implants, then would you talk to her?" Kathy gave me a strange look from the kitchen.

"No way. I can't have them making a record on me. Besides, them weren't implants."

"Who would make a record?"

"You know who."

"A record? You've *got* a record. Where do you think you are now? When they send you up, you'll really have a record."

"It won't be a *psychiatric* record."

"You'd rather be in prison?"

"I can't have *them* getting ahold of a psychiatric record."

I thought about it for a few seconds. I'd known more than one screwball who didn't want a psychiatric record, usually somebody who'd fallen off his medication and already had files thicker than Bill Gates's tax return. "Okay. Let's move on. The witness statements the police gathered indicate you had been seeing the dead woman for two weeks."

"Buuuullshiiiiit! I never saw her before Monday."

"The neighbors claim she's been in and out of your place for weeks."

"The neighbors are lying."

"Why would your neighbors all tell the same lie?"

"For all we know the aliens have some sort of poison makes everyone tell the same story. Tell me that's not possible."

"It's not possible." The line went quiet. "None of this is possible, Snake. Look, I've about reached my limit. You were seeing her for two weeks. Own up to it and we'll move on to something meaningful."

"I'm not coppin' to it 'cause it's not true. Don't you get it, Thomas? In the past two weeks I've had a whole passel of girls, each one different. But they're all from the same gene pool. And because they all *look* the same, the neighbors think they're the same girl."

"Everybody's confused but you?"

"Now you got it."

"The neighbors said you had street people in and out of that place. Lots of them."

"It's all being reversed from the actuality here. They're

saying it was *one* woman and a *bunch* of street people. But it was a whole passel of women and one street person, a dude named Barber. Think about it. I banged two women a night for two weeks, three women on the nights I'd had a nap and a tonic. That's more than twenty-eight *different* babes. Not *one* babe twenty-eight times. What woman would stand for getting rattled twenty-eight times in two weeks? I never met her. Just shows you how twitterpated your ordinary witness can be. Especially when they've been poisoned. Anyways I'm glad I'm in jail. At least I don't have to put ice on my *cojones* every evening."

"Tell me about this street person. Barber."

"I felt sorry for the sumbitch. I ran into him on a case a couple years ago and then recently saw him downtown in a soup line. I mean, two years ago he was driving a Lexus and sitting around in handmade Italian suits. Now he's got holes in his shoes and has his hair clipped at the beauty college twice a year."

"Where can I reach him?"

"I couldn't tell ya. Haven't seen him in a couple of weeks myself."

"And he's the only street person you've been seeing?"

"He's got a friend or two, but I don't even know their names."

"Snake. You think it's possible the dead woman is linked to a case you worked on?"

The line was silent for a few beats. "I *did* think that. I remember now. I *did* think that."

"I went to your office. I couldn't help noticing most of your recent work has been for IGP Systems."

"They pay good. Damn good."

"You think something you did for them was connected to all this?"

"I don't see how. We had a blowout anyways."

"What kind of blowout?"

"Never did know. They just started bein' unhappy with me." He hadn't yet caught on to the fact that if I knew about his recent cases, I'd broken into his computer. It was easy enough to figure out why they'd stopped giving him work. Delusions as spirited as the ones Snake was entertaining had to affect every aspect of his life, including his job. "Listen. I gotta go now. Remember, Thomas, the phones are tapped. And not just this jail phone. Every phone you got."

"I'll remember."

"And don't drink anything. It's poison."

"I'll bear that in mind."

When I hung up, Kathy came into the living room, standing out of reach of the Double Shocker. "Why were you two talking about Ellen Burgess's breasts?"

"Just guy talk." She gave me a suspicious look. I made the stunner pop. "Why do you think they came up with such a dumb name? Double Shocker? This should be called the Zapper. No. The Zinger. Or maybe—" I lowered my voice. "The Eliminator. I wonder what it would do to a dog."

"I want to know why you were talking about Ellen's breasts."

"And I want to know what this would do to a dog."

"Don't you dare use that on L.C."

"I'm not talking about *my* dog."

"Don't try it on Horace's dog either. What would the rest of the neighbors think? You're like a little boy with a new toy."

"I know I am. I'm ashamed."

"Whose dog are you going to try it on?"

"Horace's dog is too small. It'd fry him."

"You want to see what it does, give it to me. I'll show you."

I turned it off and stuffed it behind the cushions on the couch. Kathy sat beside me, leaned down, and kissed me. "What did our client have to say when he wasn't talking about Ellen's boobs?"

"That's all we talked about. Wasn't time for much else."

"You're not going to tell me, are you?"

"Nope."

"Guy talk?"

"Right."

During dinner Kathy filled me in on a case she'd been handling. Three months ago her client, Wilkerson, a tall, thin youngster, had gotten into a shoving match with an older man in a Ballard nightclub, had gone outside, retrieved a gun from his car, waited, then ambushed the older man in front of the club, killing him and wounding two bystanders, expending thirteen rounds in all. Almost a hundred people saw it. He was arrested at the scene with the gun in his possession, and the prosecutors charged him with second-degree murder. Eventually they offered a plea bargain: manslaughter if he would plead guilty.

Wilkerson, who was only twenty, let his mother convince him to "stand his ground and fight with his last breath," good tactics in a jungle battle, not so hot in an open-and-shut criminal case. Her reasoning? The other man was larger and older and had been pushing Wilkerson, had been impugning his manhood. Why cop a plea when the other fellow started it?

Kathy told them to take the plea—any lawyer in town would have advised the same action, and several had—but ensnared in their own self-righteous indignation, mother and client refused. The guilty verdict had been a fait accompli, but Kathy'd had her fingers crossed for the sentencing, which had taken place that morning. Fifteen years. Even after predicting it, Kathy was devastated.

After I'd washed the dishes and policed the kitchen, I settled myself on the couch and triggered the Double Shocker while Kathy finished the evening paper in an easy chair, her legs tucked under her. "You know, Thomas, ever since you got that shocker, L.C.'s been cowering in the backyard."

"He likes it back there. It's shady."

"He's cowering." Kathy put the paper down, came over, and knelt beside the couch, leaning her elbows on the cushion, her nose touching my face. "I've had such a rotten week. First Elmer. And then this Wilkerson kid. People commit his kind of crime and do five years. Three with good time. So he figures out a way to do ten, maybe the whole fifteen. And that damn Haldeman. He's taken Elmer's case personally. I know he has. He's got a vendetta against Snake."

"You know the trouble with Haldeman? He doesn't have a wonderful wife to keep him contented."

"Do I keep you contented?"

"Oh. Did you think I was talking about us?"

She kissed my cheek. "Of course you were, darling. Do I keep you contented?"

"Haven't you noticed how tranquil I've been since we got married? My legs don't jerk around by themselves. That tic in my eye is gone. Hardly any more hiccups."

"Yes. And I've noticed you don't slobber quite so much when you sleep."

I pulled her on top of me. "Right now I'd like to be *reeeeally* tranquil."

"I suppose you think I'm going to do this every time you need to relax."

I kissed her ear. Then her other ear. "You have so far."

CHAPTER 10

Mrs. Magdanz, Snake's apartment house manager, lived four doors down from Snake's second-floor unit and looked enough like a cadaver made up by a student mortician that I took a step backward when she opened the door.

I'd knocked earlier, received no answer, and then had gone around the neighborhood retracing Haldeman's route as closely as possible, although almost half of his respondents weren't home. I would have questioned these people in any case, but in addition to that, Haldeman's witness statements had seemed a little staged, and maybe even edited.

"I'm a private investigator," I said. "I'm working for Elmer Slezak's attorney."

"Is he still in jail?"

"As far as I know."

"Good. I'd like a little more shut-eye before he comes back." I didn't bother to mention he might not be back for ten years. We exchanged names, trounced the subject of the weather, and looked each other over.

Magdanz appeared to be in her mid-sixties and had colorless skin and limp hair, as if she'd been created in black and white. Her emaciated physique was clad in ethnic-looking baggy pants and a too-large blouse in a salmon color, a huge black plastic belt holding it all together. She wore sandals that revealed a map of blue veins on the tops of her feet. Her eyebrows were plucked and penciled in, too high and rather witchlike. She had thick lips that formed a natural pucker and had daubed them with bright red lipstick, slashes of which adhered to her teeth.

Her reddish-brown hair was short, the bangs chopped straight across, and her voice, probably behind forty years of cigarettes, sounded like a Louisiana frog, a sound she accentuated by speaking on the croak the way you might clap on the beat.

"You mind if I ask a few questions?"

"I suppose. Come on in. Excuse the mess." She led me into a fastidious apartment that appeared to be identical to Elmer's unit. I assumed the cardboard boxes along one wall were the mess. A small sofa and love seat were pushed against another wall. A spotless coffee table sat in front of them. A pink bed was visible down the open corridor in the bedroom. One corner of the living room seemed to be a shrine of some sort, with red lights and lit candles. The room reeked of cinnamon, incense, and smoke.

"My sister's storing some of her books here," Magdanz said. "I don't know when I'll get rid of them. Why don't you sit down here?" She pointed to a chair with a twenty-pound cat in it. The cat gave me an evil look, but when I reached down and petted him, he closed his eyes, leaned into my hand.

"I'll stand. Thanks." I tried to stop petting the cat, but as soon as his motor stopped, he bit me.

"A police detective named Arnold Haldeman was here too. Do you know him?"

"Yes."

"Sweet man, isn't he? He told me he has six cats." A lie, no doubt. According to other witnesses I'd already spoken to on the block Haldeman was restoring an antique car, had a brother who was a lepidopterist, took care of five adopted Korean children, and had an ex-stepfather who'd written a study of gay and lesbian job discrimination in public service. Interviewers used various techniques to get next to their prey, and Haldeman's technique seemed to be in aligning his own hobbies and interests with those of his subjects. Backtracking his handiwork, I was surprised he hadn't done better with Kathy the other morning, but then, Kathy had seen through him almost instantly. "You know, too, there were some men here yesterday. They went into Mr. Slezak's apartment. Last night it was. Around . . . let me see. Must have been eightish. They were government men. Would you care for some tea?"

Tea wasn't my drink, and despite myself I couldn't help thinking about Elmer's admonition not to eat or drink. It had been bothering me because it gave me the idea that maybe Elmer *had* been poisoned. But then, there were a lot of ways to turn paranoid, and I didn't need to indulge any of them myself. "Tea would be great."

Magdanz disappeared into the kitchen. The corner of the room was set up like a Buddhist shrine, except there weren't any Buddhist artifacts. An inset photograph on the wall had a felt cover draped over it. I lifted the felt and found a glossy black-and-white photo of Marilyn Monroe. After a moment I realized the photo was autographed. The cover was probably to keep the ink from fading, which it was doing anyway. Other objects in the corner began to make sense. A *Life* magazine with Marilyn on the cover. A single shoe in a glass case. Sixty or eighty books on Marilyn on two shelves.

The drapes across the only window in the front of the unit plainly hadn't been opened in years, for the draw cord in the corner had been tied in a knot. Magdanz lived in a cave the way The Mole in our basement lived in a cave. "How do you know they were government men?"

"Listen," she shouted from the kitchen. "I worked in Olympia thirty-five years. I know government men."

I espied two more enormous cats perched around the apartment, one asleep, a second watching me and wiggling his haunches as if to attack. I kept my eye on the second one.

Making her shaky way back into the room, Magdanz balanced two china saucers and cups, handed me one, and then backed up and slowly lowered herself onto the cat in the chair until he squeezed free and dropped heavily to the floor. I pretended to sip, but even that scorched my lips.

Magdanz's apartment faced the same open-air hallway Elmer's apartment did, and from the grease spot at the curtains by her door, she would be able to see anyone who came or left Slezak's unit.

"I've got ten cats," I lied.

She looked me over and said, "Ten's too many."

"Yeah, I thought so too. Actually Haldeman gave me a couple of his extras. I'm going to try to get it down to six, maybe seven. Through attrition of course. So how do you get yours so big?"

"It's a tough neighborhood. The little ones don't come back."

"I see. How long were the government men in Slezak's apartment?"

"Oh, I don't know. Ten minutes. Maybe an hour."

"They take anything?"

"Not that I could see. One of them did have a small case."

"What'd it look like?"

"It was black and square."

"Did he take it in with him, or just out?"

"I *think* he took it in. I *know* he took it out."

"You sure they weren't police?"

"I don't see how they could have been. The police didn't have a key."

"And the government men did?"

"Of course."

"You see their car?"

"I looked, but it was down the street. Parking's always so bad around here. That's why people thought Mr. Slezak was gauche, driving up over the sidewalk the way he did every night. I take the bus since my eyesight's gone haywire." I'd have to remember the remark if she ever got to court.

"What can you tell me about Slezak?"

"The eight months he's been here we all thought he was a pimp." Letting remarks sink in was a big part of Magdanz's conversational repertoire, as well as letting certain words crack open on her froggy voice the way eggs crack on the edge of a skillet. I wondered if a vitamin supplement might take some of the gray out of her skin. "And then the last little bit, he had this one gal coming and going day and night. Colored or Chinese. I liked to call the Sex Crimes Unit a couple of times, but I never did. I had, I might have saved that poor girl Sunday night." Magdanz looked at me and pursed her heavy lips as if she'd barely missed being important.

"I believe it was *Monday* night."

"It was Sunday. I was watching an old Tyrone Power movie, so I know."

I let it pass. Her cats were malicious, her tea was scalding, her eyesight had gone haywire, and her calendar was cockeyed by a day, but I let it pass. "You said you thought about calling the Sex Crimes Unit. Did you know of any sex crimes over there?"

"They certainly weren't playing Parcheesi. I used to walk by his door on my way to the laundry room. You could hear them inside."

"What did you hear?"

Magdanz gulped some of the scalding tea without wincing, and her face took on a simpering look. It took me a moment to realize she was flirting. "What do you think I heard? He was yelling. Giving her orders. Do this. Do that. Put it here. Like the Gestapo. I shoulda called Sex Crimes. I have their number right here."

"Aside from that, did Elmer do anything that might have made you think he wasn't right in the head?"

She blew air between her protuberant lips, disdainful of my question. The teacup was jittery in her hands, but that could have been the excitement of having a guest, clearly a rare event here. "One day I saw him swatting at his leg. I watched for a while, but it didn't make any kind of sense, so I went out to see. You realize I'm normally not a busybody."

"I *do* realize that. And I like your cats."

"Thank you." I realized she wasn't a busybody, despite the grease smear on the curtain where she spied on people and the opera glasses within easy reach.

"When I got out there, he was all in a panic. He said for me to help him swat the spiders off his leg. At first I thought he was playing with me, but then he ran downstairs, and you could tell he really thought there were spiders. When I saw him a couple of hours later, I would have asked about it, but he had that little gal with him. Know what I think?"

"No, Mrs. Magdanz. What do you think?"

"I think he was running some sort of immigration racket."

"Really?"

"And furthermore I think he was taking advantage of that poor young girl." Maybe Magdanz was crazy, but on the other hand, an immigration racket would explain the false ID on the dead woman. Was it possible that in Elmer's mental illness he'd fixated on the word *alien* and built some sort of sci-fi fantasy around it?

"Did you see anything the night of the death?"

"I seen everything."

"Did you see them come in?"

"Around seven-thirty. The two of them."

Seven-thirty didn't jibe with Elmer's description of picking the woman up at eleven, but then, Elmer said she was from another planet too. None of the other witness statements nor the statement the police had taken from Magdanz described anyone arriving at seven-thirty. "Are you sure, Mrs. Magdanz?"

"Call me Annie. Of course I'm sure. I may be retired—I'm not confused."

"Then what?"

"She left around eight-thirty, and he went out at about ten-thirty. When he came back, she was with him again."

"Did you tell the police this?"

"Golly sakes. I don't remember what all I told the police."

I set the saucer and cup on the coffee table.

"You think it might have been two different women?"

"Oh, no, honey. It was the same one."

"Did Mr. Slezak have any trouble paying his rent?"

"Never. He paid three or four months in advance. In cash. He'd haul out his wallet and count it out for me. All in hundreds."

"Thank you for your time." On the way to the door I said, "I couldn't help noticing your Marilyn Monroe memorabilia."

"I keep a few items here in the apartment. The rest are in security storage. I rotate them. But you came at a good time. Of course I always keep the picture. Did you see it?"

"Yes."

She slopped some tea onto the saucer when she put it down, pushed herself up from her spot on the chair, and moved quickly to the draped photo, lifting the flap. When she moved, she looked like a skeleton in clothes. Together we studied a woman neither of us had known, a woman who'd been dead almost thirty-five years. "This of course was taken when she was doing calendar modeling. It was never published, which makes it even more valuable. The signature is in ballpoint pen, which fades. Someday it will be gone.

"I also have a ring she wore before she was famous." She held her bony, veined hand up for inspection. There were three rings, two sporting clusters of diamonds, so I assumed Marilyn's was the one with the small blue stone. "I'll probably die with a piece of Marilyn's clothing against my skin." She turned back to the photograph admiringly. "It's worth eight or ten thousand on the open market. The shoe was worn in *Some Like It Hot*. Remember the movie?"

"One of my favorites."

Magdanz gazed fondly at the photograph for a long while, long enough that I thought she might be asleep on her feet. "Wasn't she lovely? Even when she got older, she was so lovely."

"Indeed she was."

Magdanz followed me onto the breezeway, closing the door behind her. "That's where she did it."

"Did what?"

"One of Slezak's girlfriends. The giant. They were out here quarreling about two months ago. I was trying to watch a *Rockford* episode, so I rapped on the window. She looked in at me and spit. Right there on the window."

"Nervy. Just out of curiosity, Mrs. Magdanz, who owns the building?"

"I do. My late husband owned this and two apartment buildings on the next block. My son inherited one of them, but he's in Denver, so I manage all three." Magdanz glanced around to see what her tenants were doing, but nobody was in sight. "And then she brings her motorcycle down and guns the motor. That's how Mr. Johnson downstairs got on the wrong end of a fat lip. Went out one evening and told her to pipe down. I never saw it, but those who did said she threw him around like a rag-doll baby."

The story about Elmer coming in at seven-thirty with the woman, leaving, and then coming back again after ten-thirty was probably bogus. Elmer had said he'd come in at eleven, and the two neighbors writing the butterfly book had confirmed that for the police, and then for me. No one else had mentioned any movement at seven-thirty. To cast more doubt on it, the statement she'd given Haldeman hadn't mentioned two trips. But then, perhaps Haldeman hadn't asked. Or for some reason hadn't wanted to know. Mistakes by witnesses and falsehoods by the police always worried me, but not as much as government men.

CHAPTER 11

Searching for a breeze, I left the front door open and cracked a window in the bathroom of Elmer's apartment, which smelled musty after two days without an occupant. The SPD had done a thorough job, leaving a bare mattress in the bedroom, fingerprint dust on doorknobs and counters, and a strip of carpet razored out of the bedroom floor. If there had been other visitors, they hadn't left calling cards.

The tape in Snake's answering machine had been on the list of confiscated items Haldeman had removed with the warrant Monday morning, but what Haldeman hadn't mentioned in his report was that he'd replaced the tape with a blank, undoubtedly planning to come back and pick up messages, or call for them.

Already there were seven fresh messages. Two were hang-ups. One was Mrs. Magdanz asking Snake to get in touch with her when he got back. One was a woman with a rough, husky voice who didn't identify herself but asked Snake to call her. The last three were also from a woman. The first two times she called, she said, "Hellooooo. Hellooooo. Pick up if you're there." It was her third message that bothered me. "One of our numbers is missing. We're calling you about one of our numbers. Hellooooo. Pick up." Snake had told us the alien women each had a number, and I hoped she wasn't alluding to that, because if she was, Snake had put her up to it, and as far as I was concerned, that would be one machination too many.

In the kitchen an Endless Light Mission brochure was mixed in with a stack of take-out restaurant menus. Three blocks from our office in Pioneer Square, the Endless Light had been established forty years ago based on soup, soap, and salvation, and fed a queue of men each evening at six o'clock, supplying forty-five of them with beds. As far as I knew, they hadn't had a vacant bunk in five years, not even on warm summer nights like these when the waterfront offered a hundred cubbyholes for itinerant campers.

The menus under the brochure surprised me: Thai, Vietnamese, Japanese. Snake typically ate meat-and-potatoes TV dinners or at Mexican restaurants.

The phone rang. "Hello," I said.

"Snake? Is that . . . who is this?"

"My name is Thomas Black. I'm working for Elmer's attorney and I—" She hung up.

Two more women called, one who might have been the first caller trying again, and another whose voice I thought I recognized from elsewhere, sort of a worn-down southern-belle act. None identified themselves, and Elmer did not have caller ID on his phone, which seemed odd to me, considering his paranoia.

I went back out to my car and brought in a small tape recorder, discovering yet another message on the machine upon my return, this from a man named George, who said he was a nephew of Elmer's and wanted to know if Elmer needed legal counsel. After recording all the messages onto my tape, I reset the answering machine, closed the front door, opened the drapes, sat at the kitchen table, and began writing up my notes from my interviews that morning.

Magdanz's assessment of Elmer hadn't been dissimilar to the other neighbors'. The two ladies writing the butterfly book lived directly next door and were terrified of him, had seen him walking around the breezeway carrying my stuffed dog, Alfred, and barking in two voices, one for Alfred and one for himself. Several times they'd seen him step out to get his mail with a pistol in his hand. Once he'd been naked except for his boots, a jockstrap, and the pistol. They'd seen him with electronic instruments they couldn't even guess the uses of.

He'd been in the apartment eight months, and they said they'd never before witnessed such a procession of floozies. They had believed the African-Asian woman he'd been seeing lately was more than a floozy, different from his other "dates," though they couldn't put their finger on why.

We'd secured Elmer's last three months of phone records from the phone company yesterday, and I sat and sorted them, knowing I might be forced to put a name on every number. I'd already identified the lion's share using a phone register Snake had left in his computer. He'd called the Smithsonian in Washington, D.C., eight times during the past month, one of the calls lasting forty minutes. On the day of the murder he'd phoned the science department at the University of Colorado and was on the line twenty-two minutes.

As I studied the phone bills, a man carrying a bedroll and a small pack shuffled past the picture window, looking directly at me for a moment. I opened the door and called out. "Hey?"

He was almost as thin as the cadaver, Magdanz, and if he'd been a woman, you would have said he was anorexic. "Me?" he squeaked. Even in stocking feet I intimidated him. He was almost six feet but weighed maybe forty or forty-five pounds less than I did.

"You come to see Elmer?" I said.

"Snake? I mean Mr. Slezak? Yes. That's who I came to see. But I don't want to bother anybody. I'll come back some other time."

"You Barber?"

Where most people would have taken a step forward, he took a tentative step backward. "Yes."

"Come on in." I turned my back on him to help ease his anxiety, went into the kitchen, rummaged through the cupboards, and came up with a package of spaghetti, a jar of sauce, some canned mushrooms and black olives, and an onion, stacking the booty on the countertop. I passed up the greenish-looking sausages I found in the refrigerator. It took a few seconds before he darkened the doorway, looking like a kid on his first trip to the doctor.

"I was . . . I was wondering if Elmer was around."

"Come on in. You hungry?"

"Not much."

"It's almost lunchtime, so I'm going to cook up a mess of spaghetti. I need somebody to help me eat it. You got time?"

"Well, sure, yeah, I guess."

He moved and spoke like a man who'd been pushed around and had subsequently learned to make himself look harmless and invisible. He had fair skin, winsome, cornflower-blue eyes, and white hair swept back in a cut worthy of a corporate executive. His diction and manners were impeccable and, as did most street people, he wore too many clothes for the weather: a winter coat, a sport coat under that, a rumpled dress shirt, two T-shirts that I could see. His body was a human clothes rack.

"Go ahead and wash up. The bathroom's back there."

"You sure it's all right?"

"No problemo, pal. I can't eat this much," I said, puncturing the spaghetti package with a knife. He looked educated, reminded me of John Updike, his face a tad pink where the sun had gotten to it. By the time he came back, the water was boiling and I was dropping a handful of dry spaghetti into it. The sauce was simmering. I looked around for vegetables or bread, but found none.

"I'm uh, uh, really here . . . to see Snake," he said. "Meade Barber." He stuck his hand out. I took it and tried not to break any bones. He had that look.

"Thomas Black. I'm working for Snake's attorney. Maybe you haven't heard. Snake's in jail."

The news knocked him into the chair I'd been using at the table. "He is?"

"Here. Let me clear this stuff off." I picked up the phone records and my notes and put them on one of the other chairs. "A woman was killed here Monday night. The police think Elmer did it."

"Here?"

"Not here at the table. In the other room."

"Holy shit." Barber fell into a thousand-yard stare as if he was a man who fell into it often.

"You okay?"

"Yeah. Sure. But he seemed like such an honest guy. He's been very good to me. I don't . . . believe he could have done that. The police think . . ."

"They've charged him with second-degree murder." I stepped back into the kitchen and stirred the sauce. "I hope you like olives."

"Yeah. Oh, yeah."

"How long have you known Snake?"

"I don't know. Maybe a couple of months. He's been good to me."

"Yeah, he's like that."

"You think it would do any good if some of his friends talked to the police. I mean, I'd be willing to—"

"We're going to have to save the character-witness stuff for the sentencing, if it comes to that. Snake said you hadn't been around for a while."

"You talked about me?"

"We talked about everyone."

"I've been busy lately."

"Maybe you could help me out."

"With lunch?"

"Defending Snake." Even though his slightly wrinkled, silky skin made him look around fifty, his little-boy act didn't seem a bit faked. "Tell me what you know about Snake's life. Any friends of his you've met. Anybody he talked about. Tell me how you two came to know each other."

"Jesus. We met on the street. He came up with some money and decided we should eat in the Westlake Mall. Snake is one of those rarities, he's got ten dollars, five of it's yours."

"Yes, he is." Snake was another person entirely around the wealthy, the arrogant, or the powerful, but I didn't see any point in mentioning it. "So you met on the street?"

"Actually we were in the chow line at the Millionair Club. We just started hanging around together."

"Snake drives a pretty nice car for a man eating at the Millionair Club."

"He said he was a private investigator."

"He tell you much about his job?"

"I guess not."

"So what'd you talk about?"

"He was helping me. I've had problems, but I'm starting to see a turnaround. Snake was a big part of that."

"What kind of problems?"

"Trying to get a job. Get back on my feet. When you're on the street, you know, it's hard to keep your self-respect. He let me shower here a couple of times when I had job interviews. But mostly he listened and gave advice. Elmer's a fantastic counselor. I think he's pretty much got my life straightened around."

"You ever stay here?"

"The first night we met. He wanted to know all about me. Every little particular. He's a real sympathetic listener. We stayed up till four talking, then he let me crash on the couch." Meade kept talking while I found plates and dished up the spaghetti. We ate; he talked. He turned out to be ravenous, touching his mouth with his napkin each time he spoke through his food until I thought he was going to drive me nuts. "Snake is the nicest man I've ever met. And I don't believe he killed anyone. He couldn't. Say, did you know he got hit by lightning once?"

"What?"

"We were down by the waterfront. He bought me some ice cream while we were figuring out how to get my life back together. Out on the pier. It was storming, so we probably shouldn't have been out. Then this lightning bolt hit him. Knocked him about five feet onto his butt. I was right next to him. It could have been me. I could have been killed. I know that sounds selfish, but I always think of him as indestructible. He's just so . . . I don't know. Macho."

"What happened after the lightning hit him?"

"Well, he got up and started looking for his shoes. They were smoking. Some lady in a boat not far off the pier must have seen it, because she called 911 and then they came in to see if he was all right. The aid car took him up to the hospital."

"When was all this?"

"May. A month ago."

I wondered if a lightning bolt might not have been the cause of Snake's fried circuitry. The struck-by-lightning defense. Kathy would make legal history. "Tell me about his girlfriends."

"When I saw him, it was mostly just me and Snake."

"You never met any of them?"

"A couple, I did."

"Did you meet her?" I asked, pulling a copy of the newspaper photo of McFleegle out from my papers and laying it on the table between us.

He studied it. "I believe so. No. I'm not sure. Uh, the only one I remember for sure was . . . *there* she is."

Staring at us from the window was Desiree Nash. Obviously she was the woman Magdanz called "the giant."

"Desiree," I whispered.

"You know her?" Barber asked.

"Desiree and I go way back."

CHAPTER 12

Before I could respond to Desiree's loud knocking, she was in the apartment. "Black, you bastard. What the hell are you doing here?"

"I could ask the same question."

"Came to talk to my old man."

"Elmer?"

"Where the fuck is he?"

"You and Elmer? Are you kidding me?"

"What is this? *Oprah?* I called him up one day. We went out for beer a few times. Now we're making history together."

She looked at me out of eyes that were a deceptively gentle blue, almost the same blue as her ex-husband's before the state hanged him. She hadn't changed much, except she wasn't wearing the biker regalia or the Jolly Rogers' colors. She was my height but weighed more; had a thick torso; long, pipe-stem legs; and breasts that somebody like Elmer would idolize. Elmer was five-five, or thereabouts, depending on how badly he was lying that day, and she was six-one or two, so they would be a sight together. She had a large, flat face, four earrings in one ear. Blackish lipstick. Her hair was dyed black and fell in wet-looking ringlets around her neck. She wore tight jeans and a tighter T-shirt with writing on it that I didn't have the guts to

read. Hers had been the worn-down southern-belle accent that
had hung up on me earlier.

"Elmer's away," I said.

"With some whore?" Stepping toward the bedroom, Desiree
surveyed the apartment. "Where'd he go?"

"The King County Jail."

"You putting me on, sweetheart?"

"I wish I were. Don't you read the papers?"

"No time. I work. What'd he do? Get rough with a meter
maid? Welsh on a bet with his accountant?"

"Second-degree murder."

If she was surprised, she concealed it well. I wanted to ask
her how she was doing, where she was living, wanted to deter-
mine how she might be involved, because she could throw the
case into another dimension. "Stupid butthole. Second-degree
murder? Who'd he off?"

"I'll tell you all about it, but you and I need to sit down and
talk."

"Sure. Sure, Black. But I got my car idlin' out here in the
street." She glanced at Meade Barber, who'd stood meekly when
she'd come in and who hadn't said a word; then she stared at
our lunch, at the picture of the dead woman on the table. "I
gotta move it before some gangbanger decides to see if it's got
light speed on the gearshift. Where do you want to meet?"

"You got time now?"

"Sure."

"How about here? We're about finished."

"Snake'd be pissed. Know where the Monkey is?"

"On Roosevelt?"

"See you in twenty minutes."

It was only a few blocks from my house, and I wondered
if she'd chosen it for that reason. Desiree had expressed a
romantic—if that's the word—interest in me a couple of times,
and I had little reason to believe she'd abandoned that bent.
Being Snake's woman would make little difference to her. Sex
for Desiree had always been like cigarettes, gum, or more likely,
in her case, chewing tobacco. Open up the package and pass
it around. It had to do with her life history, her mother's

infidelities, her own early seduction and subsequent abuse by male relatives, and numerous other footprints on her psyche, which she'd revealed to me one night while she was surrounding ? beer in a motel restaurant in Walla Walla.

After she left, Meade Barber sat back down and began eating as fast as he could. "Take your time. It's only a two-minute drive," I said.

"I don't want to be in your way." He patted his lips tidily with his still-folded paper napkin.

"Where can I find you if I need to talk to you again?"

Meade looked up, furrows of worry creasing his brow. "Me? I get my mail at the Endless Light. Maybe you could leave a note there."

"Okeydoke."

Still eating, Meade said, "I'm not so sure Snake and that woman were getting along."

"I wouldn't be surprised. Neither one of them's what you'd call easygoing. By the way, Snake ever talk about Martians or spacemen or anything like that?"

"We mostly talked about my life. Getting it straightened out. I can't tell you how bad I feel about him being in jail."

"Don't worry about it. We'll get him out."

I cleaned up the kitchen, hastily washed our dishes in the sink, and gathered up the materials I'd been studying. Barber had put his packsack strap over one shoulder. "Thank you for the meal."

I tucked a twenty-dollar bill into his coat pocket. "For the information you gave me. I'd offer to drop you somewhere but . . ."

"You have to meet that woman."

"Right. Take care."

Five minutes later, I described Desiree to the bartender at the Monkey, but he thought I was joking. He'd never seen or heard of her. Holding on to the unlikely possibility that she might show up still, I frittered away half an hour in the car.

I called a source at the phone company, who gave me Desiree's address and unlisted number, confirming that she was still using the surname of Nash. Curiously I'd bicycled to within a mile of her house yesterday.

John Coulter Nash, her ex, had been the instrument of our initial meeting, back when I'd been a young, unseasoned police officer working Seattle's north end. I'd apprehended Nash running a stop sign, run his name through the computer, and discovered an outstanding warrant for robbery. When I'd searched him for weapons, he'd dropped a length of pipe out of a sleeve, swung it around, and clipped my shoulder, hard. He'd been aiming for my temple. He outweighed me and had a certain flair for street fighting, and as we tussled, I began to think I was going to lose, and that when I did lose, he would kill me. It was one of three incidents in my short police career that I'd thought might get me killed. Though the scuffle occurred on Northeast Eightieth, a busy enough thoroughfare, and traffic slowed to watch, nobody stopped. Eventually I broke one of his eardrums and three of his fingers in a maneuver he'd not encountered before. On the way to the precinct he kept asking where I'd learned it. It had been a lucky move, but I didn't tell him that.

Years later, long after I'd left the SPD, and long after he'd gone to prison for the last time for a trio of brutal murders, he begged me to drive to eastern Washington to witness his execution. Aside from his wife, Desiree, I was the only person he requested. It was easy to conjecture that he blamed some, if not all, of his problems on me and knew intuitively how upsetting it would be for me to watch him hang; had invited me to witness his end as an act of retaliation.

Desiree and I stayed at the same hotel, ostensibly so that I could look after her as I had promised Nash I would, but deep inside somewhere, I'd had a nasty feeling he'd told her to seduce me and murder me in my sleep, though not much in the real world ever confirmed my paranoia. In the years since, I'd run across her several times, and I now had the uneasy notion she'd discovered Elmer through something I had inadvertently told her, had the feeling she might have looked him up because he was my friend.

When I got home that evening, Kathy handed me a registered letter from IGP Systems. There was also a message on my answering machine from them. The money offer had gone up. For the first time, an officer of the corporation was mentioned, a man named Rakubian, his title: Vice President in Charge of Domestic Affairs—whatever that meant. Interestingly enough, the letterhead on the paper indicated approximately fifty companies under IGP's flag, some of which I recognized and some of which I did not.

While I prepared supper, Kathy sat at the table in the dining room casually leafing through the evening paper. I told her about Snake's neighbors, about Meade Barber, Desiree, and Magdanz, the apartment owner. "Desiree? Isn't she that Amazon biker babe who knocked you senseless with an alarm clock?"

"It wasn't senseless exactly. And she didn't—"

"Her and that other motorcycle mama. Both of them had body odor too. Didn't they want to have an orgy with you?"

"I'm not sure."

"By the way, I talked to Elmer again today. He tried his best to fill me in on what *really* happened."

"What *really* happened?"

"He's part of an interplanetary breeding program. He's been selected to impregnate hundreds of alien females in some huge genetic experiment devised to find the right population base for a planet they're colonizing about twenty light-years from here. He swears he was having sex with virgins from this interplanetary breeding program, dozens of them."

"That's pathetic."

"Isn't it? It's even worse than your fantasy about a women's softball team."

"I never should have mentioned that. So what's his explanation for the dead woman?"

"He still doesn't have one."

"The neighbors say that for the last few weeks he's had only the one woman up there at his place. The dead one."

"That's the beauty of this particular delusion. Snake says he's serviced twenty or thirty of them. Says they're clones. They all look alike. Exactly alike."

"Bullshit."

"That's what I said."

CHAPTER 13

Desiree lived on Avon Street in a section of South Seattle called Skyway. Her house sat halfway down the dead-end street and was small enough that a runaway pickup truck could erase it. Ten or fifteen years ago some hapless painter had begun spreading blue over the tea-brown and then abandoned the project, and now it looked like a hideout for a gang of motor-cycle outlaws, which coincidentally was what Desiree had hung around with when I knew her, a flock of no-goods known as the Jolly Rogers, most of whom were in prison now for running drugs.

Lying in the brown grass and tall thistles in front of the house like rusty alligators waiting for quarry were three junked cars. In front of the dead cars stood a bright orange Camaro with a black air scoop on the hood, wide slicks in the rear and enough pin-striping and chrome and tailpipes to make any grade-school boy turn his head. Desiree's car. A tarp that looked as if it hadn't been moved in a year was lumped over an object alongside the house, the Harley. Ex-bikers never got rid of the hog.

I snapped my cleats out of the pedals and walked my twenty-pound Eddy Merckx through the spiky grass to the front door, leaned it against an engine block on a tilting stand, and knocked.

When she finally answered the door, it was plain to see she'd only recently climbed out of bed, even though it was after ten o'clock on a Friday morning and the temperature was already bumping eighty.

"Black. You bastard."

"That's what you said yesterday."

"How'd you find me?"

"I called your pastor."

"Come on in. You want some decaf?"

"No thanks." Under a tatty white robe, she wore a pink chiffon affair that looked like a leftover costume from the circus, all of it ending at mid thigh. Her legs were bare, and without her customary caked-on makeup, her face looked like a deforested hillside. The house was tiny and messier than the yard. She knocked a pyramid of magazines and feminine hair-care products off a straight-backed chair onto the floor and bid me to sit while she went into the kitchen and rattled utensils.

"Dale," she said. "This is Thomas Black. He's a private peeper." A young man who didn't look too bright and who couldn't have been older than eighteen, maybe even sixteen, poked his head around the kitchen corner and, without a word, crept past me to the front door, barefoot, carrying shoes, socks, and a shirt, skulking out like a cat caught in the neighbor's garage.

She entered the room, set a cup of steaming liquid on the hull of a disassembled motorcycle gas tank, and flopped across a sofa, dangling her legs over the end, arranging herself so she could watch me. If she thought her legs were alluring, she had the wrong audience. She picked up her cup and sipped. "So tell me, pretty boy. How'd Snake come to have a woman in his room?"

"You mean a dead woman?"

"A *woman*."

"You'll have to ask Snake. Did you ever meet her?" I unfolded the circular the cops were printing in the papers and held it up.

She looked at it for a few seconds. "That the bitch he offed?"

"It's the woman who died in his apartment."

"I never saw her."

"How long have you known Elmer?"

"Listen to me, Black. I'm tired, okay? I wait tables until two and then it takes me a while to unwind, so you got me up in like the middle of the night for you. And then there was Dale."

"Babysitting for the neighbors, were you?"

"Now, don't go off on Dale. He's only a kid."

"That was my point."

"He lives up the street. He's got a sniffle brain from glue and gasoline. It's funny because I used to inhale gasoline my own self."

"That *is* funny."

"You're just the same old tight-ass you always were, aren't you?"

"I suppose so. What can you tell me about Snake? Was he acting oddly?"

"It's kind of hard for me to tell because he's been odd ever since I've known him." She sipped again and carefully placed the cup back on the gas tank.

"And how long has that been?"

"Six months. He disappeared a couple of times in there. Maybe two weeks at a pop. I don't know if he always does that or what." She looked at me questioningly.

"I wouldn't think so."

"I didn't either. He never would tell me where he went or what he was doing. It was too bad, because he had a hell of a job and he blew it. Bringing in damn good money."

"IGP Systems?"

She snapped her fingers. "Yeah. That was it. IGP. He used to call it I-Get-Pissed. He got seven hundred dollars once for delivering an envelope."

"Was he seeing a shrink?"

"Somebody down the hill here in Renton. Claimed it had something to do with one of his clients, but he'd been having all sorts of problems his own self."

"Tell me about them."

"For one thing he was runnin' around on me."

"Running around on a girlfriend is not exactly abnormal behavior for Elmer."

"He was afraid to be close. His mom ran out on them. Did you know that?"

"Yes."

"He never would explain why he got canned. But the odd part was, he stayed busy, maybe busier than he had been."

"Doing what?"

"Working with winos. Walking the streets. I couldn't figure out what the hell it was about, and he wouldn't tell me."

"You ever see him with another woman?"

"Just once. I followed him to some gal's house over in West Seattle. I was tempted to go in and let them both have it." She slammed a balled-up fist into her open palm. "But then I saw some kids' junk laying around in her yard and decided to talk to him later. I don't like messing around when there's kids."

"Except for Dale."

"Don't be pickin' on Dale. He's got almost no brain left."

"Sounds like the perfect man for you. Did you talk to Elmer later? About this woman?"

"Fuck you. I talked to him. This was maybe . . . three weeks ago. Her name was Margery Billingham. First he denied going over there. Then he denied having sex with her. Christ. I waited three hours. Snake's not capable of spending three hours with a woman and *not* having sex with her. So we had this big blowout. I was just looking him up when I met you yesterday."

"That's the first time you'd been over there in weeks?"

"Yeah. What'd you think? I went over and killed his bitch?"

"Something like that."

"You know me better than that."

"I hardly know you at all, Desiree."

"Know this. I wouldn't have left him running around. I woulda killed them both."

"The house in West Seattle. You remember the address?"

"Up on Twenty-first Southwest, up behind the community college." She gave me the address from memory, and I wrote it down. "He probably had women all over town. I just happened to catch him with *this* particular tramp. You know, now that I think about it, he did act really weird one time. He came over smelling of it. Like I wasn't going to know he'd been with a woman. I would have belted him, but he was crying and saying all kinds of stuff didn't make sense. He said his face was falling off. Wanted me to hold his ears so they wouldn't fly away and then I had to count his fingers. Said *they* were going to give him an extra finger. He cried for a coupla hours. I thought he was on shit, but he swore he wasn't."

"You sure he wasn't?"

"I never saw Snake take any shit."

"You ever talk to this Margery Billingham?"

"Like I said, I considered going over and busting her up, but she had those kids. I did give her a jingle. Every time I called, one of the rugrats answered and told me she was at work. After I heard those little voices enough times, I gave it up. I always been a sucker for kids, Black. Besides, by that time Snake and I were on the skids."

"And you're not now?"

"We are, but I'm going to patch it up."

"You sure you never saw this woman in the flier?"

"Never."

"Did Snake ever talk to you about beings from UFOs?"

"He and I used to watch these movies. *ET. Plan Nine from Outer Space.* His favorite was *Invasion of the Body Snatchers.* He even had old TV episodes from *The Invaders.*"

"He ever talk about any of it being real?"

"No more than anybody else. Why?"

"If he wasn't on drugs, and he was seeing a mental health professional, and he was having delusions, maybe he thought some of this stuff was real."

"Martians?"

"Sounds crazy, right?"

"Not Snake."

I stood up to leave. Desiree rolled off the couch and gave a long, slow look at my getup, a Banesto team jersey, Lycra shorts, cycling shoes, and gloves. I was carrying a Giro helmet and sunglasses. "Why didn't you show up at the Monkey?"

"Hey, the whole world doesn't revolve around you. I have a life, you know."

"You were never going to talk to me, were you?"

"I told you. I had to get to work yesterday. I was going to call this afternoon." She looked me over. "Come on, Black. You can't keep me hanging on about Snake and spacemen. What's going on?"

"You ask him. When you find out, tell me, because I don't have a clue. By the way, whatever happened to Queenie?"

"Moved back to Georgia. Had a kid a year since you saw her. Squirtin' em out like a goat. You still with that malnourished brunette wears the painted contact lenses?"

"She doesn't wear contacts. And yes. I'm still with her. We're married."

"Well, hey, congratulations. Married? Geez Louise. I never figured you for the marryin' kind. Come on over to mama and I'll give you a great big hug." She held out her arms. I stepped toward the door. "John always did like you."

"That's what he said. I never really believed him."

"He did. He liked you."

John was her ex, the man whose execution we'd witnessed together. He'd been a monster.

CHAPTER 14

It was late Friday by the time I got to West Seattle.

Distanced from Seattle proper by the bay and the Duwamish River, West Seattle had the feel of a small town, was mostly housing, schools, restaurants, small shops, with a steel mill at the base of the hill off Delridge Way.

A good portion of my afternoon had been spent sorting the materials I'd taken from Elmer's office and apartment, working on his phone bills, poring over the *Diagnostic and Statistical Manual of Mental Disorders* to see what he had highlighted, and then speaking to Ellen Burgess, the psychologist, who ultimately refused to speculate. The book was thoroughly marked up, probably not all of it by Elmer, since he'd stolen it from the Tacoma Public Library.

As of three-thirty that afternoon the police still hadn't identified the dead woman.

Elmer's cellular-phone bill had come in the mail that morning, and it included numerous calls to a West Seattle number that might have coincided with the address Desiree had given me. When I cross-checked in our CD-ROM phone directory, the name that went with the number wasn't Margery Billingham, though, it was JoAnne Barber—at the same address Desiree had given me. It was typical that she'd argued with

Snake about the woman but Snake had not corrected her on the name. It took me a minute to connect the name Barber to the homeless man I'd met at Elmer's apartment house: Meade Barber.

Twenty-first Southwest ran north and south along the ridge of a small, woodsy hill over Delridge Way. It was a high, two-lane road with a gravel shoulder, dozens of cars parked helter-skelter, and modestly priced houses crowded along either side.

The address Desiree had followed Elmer to was a two-bedroom rambler with an overgrown laurel hedge on one side, a rickety wooden fence on the other. The relatively barren yard was typical of someone who didn't have time to do more than police the litter and mow the grass. There were ten or twelve weedy perennials, none that had been put in recently. A new portable basketball hoop sat in the grass alongside the driveway. Judging by the height, the player in the family wasn't much older than twelve or thirteen.

A faded name—Margery Billingham—on the mailbox across the street was what had spawned Desiree's blunder. An open carport attached to the house contained three sad-looking bicycles, a lawn mower, a barbecue, stored snow tires, and enough empty space for a car.

A gust of stale summer heat pushed out of the house when the boy opened the door. He told me his name was Cormick and confirmed his mother's name was JoAnne Barber, said she wasn't home from work yet.

"When do you think she'll be in?" I asked.

"Maybe after seven." It was already six-thirty.

He was a good-looking boy—short, blond, around thirteen, with blue eyes and short-cropped hair that showed off a serious cowlick in front. He wore basketball shoes, nylon shorts, and a large, black Saint Louis Rams T-shirt. Half collie and half mongrel, a mutt came to the door behind him and eyed me. Beyond Cormick in the doorway a younger boy was on his knees in front of a television set.

"Maybe I should come back and talk to your mother tomorrow."

"She works at Kmart on weekends."

I would have left then if not for the newspaper clipping and photo of Elmer's dead alien affixed to their refrigerator with magnets.

I went out to the car and thought about it.

From the look of the kitchen they'd been home alone all day; mom at work, keeping tabs on them by phone, if they were lucky. In some ways it reminded me of my own childhood.

When I checked the office for incoming messages, I learned IGP Systems had called again. Persistent little buggers. Because of Elmer's involvement I had decided to learn more about them, but I knew they weren't going to get chatty if I asked the wrong questions. Inquiries concerning Elmer would be related back to the cases he'd worked, and their assumption, perhaps true, would be that I was running down one of those cases. They would not want that.

The sexy computer-sounding voice answered my call. "Mr. Black. I'm so happy we finally made contact. We've had so many favorable comments about you. When can we see you?"

"I was thinking about Monday."

"Monday's a little late for what we had in mind. Arthur will be out of town all weekend. Could you hold for a moment?" I listened to a string ensemble for almost two minutes before she came back on the line. "Can you come in this evening? Arthur will be here until seven-thirty, but then he has a plane to catch."

"Sorry. I can't make it."

"This involves a fair sum of money, Mr. Black." She named a truly obscene sum and let the germ of greed sprout for a while. "The job is for this weekend and two days thereafter."

"Can't make it tonight. Sorry." There was a long, pregnant pause. Her voice was chilly when she said, "I guess it will have to be Monday." Even chillier when she added, "Nine o'clock at our office in the Meany Tower?"

"Sounds fine."

"See you then."

If they'd had a job that weekend, they would have hired somebody for it long before Friday afternoon.

When Cormick came out of the house and began shooting hoops, I asked him if he wanted to play H-O-R-S-E. He wasn't a bad little shooter and beat me three out of five. The smaller boy, Powell, glanced out the window from time to time as we dribbled the ball and made our shots. "I noticed you got a couple of flat tires on your bikes. You know how to fix them?"

"Not really," Cormick said, bouncing the basketball slowly.

"You got a pump? I have a patch kit in the car."

"Sure."

It took only a few minutes a bike; three bikes, one for each of the boys and the last for Mom. All of them had flats. Powell came out to watch, but said little except that the bikes had been out of commission since last summer. I had the feeling Powell rarely said much. He had red hair and freckles that had been bronzed into patches on his face and arms. He told me he was going into fifth grade next year. Cormick was going into seventh. After we got the wheels back on and secured, the tires pumped to pressure, we oiled the chains, then discussed chain tension, seat-height adjustment, and related topics.

When the conversation dried up, I held out my dirty hands and said, "There someplace I can wash up?"

The boys looked at each other, and I could see the household dictum against letting strangers inside beginning to topple even before Cormick made the decision. "We have some Lava soap in the kitchen. The only thing it doesn't work too good on is pitch."

"It works on bird crap but not on Super Glue," volunteered Powell bravely.

"It's good to know that," I said, smiling.

Smelling thoroughly of dog and boy, it was a small house with pathways worn into the carpets. There were two birdcages with canaries in the corner. Powell had turned off the TV when he came out, so there was only the noise from the panting mongrel at my heels. The door had been open for a few minutes now, so the house was cooler. The cold-water tap had a washer that needed replacing.

"You know that lady?" I asked Cormick, pointing at the newspaper clipping stuck to the refrigerator with a happy-face magnet. Powell had turned the television back on.

"Not really. Mom just put that up."

"You know why?"

"No. Do you?"

I smiled. "No, I don't."

Also on the refrigerator were two open report cards and a couple of receipts for children's clothing. The older boy had gotten straight As and good notices in the comments section. Powell had gotten an A in art, but apart from that, mostly Cs and one D. The clothing had all been bought at bargain stores.

A handmade Father's Day card with glued-on photos of Powell and his older brother alongside a man in a business suit had crept, probably over a period of weeks, to a spot near the bottom of the refrigerator door. The man in the suit was the man I'd lunched with yesterday, Meade Barber.

"That your dad?" I asked, looking at Cormick.

He nodded. "We used to be rich. We had a house with a swimming pool. I had my own ATV. We could see Mount Rainier *and* Mount Baker. We had jet skis. We used to snowboard in Colorado."

"Do you miss it?"

"Not really."

I went outside and sat on the step near the front door. Cormick and the dog came out and sat beside me. It was almost seven-thirty. "See your dad much?"

"He was supposed to come over on Father's Day, but he couldn't make it. He has to take the bus and then walk up the stairs from Delridge, and his leg hurts."

"What happened to his leg?"

"Some man who used to be a cop beat him up. Dad's not a fighter. He tried to use reason."

"I guess sometimes reason doesn't work."

"That's what Dad said."

"Your mom and him are divorced?"

"Last year. He used to visit everyday. Then somebody took his car and he had to use the bus. When he gets his job back, he's going to buy a condo down on Alki and have us over on weekends."

"That'll be nice."

A gray Chevrolet station wagon came up the street and swung into the drive, coasting down the slight slope into the carport, the muffler hanging low off a wire. The engine dieseled twice before it died.

Her shoulder-length blond hair was full and, according to the older photographs in the house, dyed. She wore a skirt and blouse and open-toed shoes with a wedge heel. As she climbed out of the car, the dog showed up and licked her hand. She looked at me with gray eyes and raised eyebrows, as sour a look as I'd received all day. Cormick said, "Mom, this is Mr. Black. He's a real private eye."

She looked me over wearily. "You a friend of Mr. Slezak's?"

"I'm working for his attorney."

"I read about him in the paper. I don't know what you want from me."

Cormick had opened the tailgate and was hauling groceries into the house. When he was out of earshot, I said, "He's a good kid."

"You think so?"

"He is. So's Powell."

She looked at me curiously. "How long have you been here?"

"An hour. I hope you don't mind."

"I *do* mind." She grabbed a sack of groceries. "I guess you have to do what you have to do." With her free hand she picked up a flat, greasy box that had a pizza-company name on it and carried it into the house, leaving the aroma of hot cheese and pepperoni in her wake. Cormick and Powell came out and carried three more bags of groceries and a carton of milk inside. I closed the hatch on the station wagon and waited. Five minutes later JoAnne Barber came out in denim shorts, an old blouse, and thongs that revealed meticulously painted toenails.

CHAPTER 15

"**W**hat do you want, Mr. Black?"

She crossed her arms and remained on the step, so that her eyes were nearly level with mine. She was a trifle plump and had pale skin, the type of pulchritudinous figure men would have raved about two hundred years ago when starvation was a frequent enough cause of death in the Western world. She wasn't pretty, but she was cute, and her complexion was flawless. She'd scrubbed her face, and damp tendrils of hair clung to the fringes of her face. She looked cooler but no more relaxed than before.

"I don't want to keep you from dinner," I said.

"But you are, aren't you?"

"I guess so. Elmer Slezak came to visit you a few weeks ago."

"I read where he's in jail."

"Is that why you cut the article out?"

"What article?"

"The one on the refrigerator."

"Oh, that." She seemed chagrined, her cheeks flushing. "The boys aren't supposed to be letting anybody in the house."

"Cormick let me wash up."

"He said you fixed their bikes. Thank you. So you want to know about Slezak? What?"

"What did he want from you?"

She crossed her arms over her chest again. "Mr. Slezak came several times starting about two months ago. He said he was investigating something concerning my ex. He never was clear on what. I assumed Meade was in another jam. I'm afraid I was in a talkative frame of mind that first evening. I probably told him more about our divorce than I should have."

"Did he phone you later?"

"He came back twice, but he never phoned."

"Could you check with the boys? Maybe he spoke to them on the phone." She stepped inside the house and asked her sons, who were at the dinner table dismantling the pizza wedge by wedge. They shook their heads, strings of cheese webbed off their chins. Elmer's cellular-phone bill had been laced with calls to her number.

"You mind telling me what you told Slezak?"

"If you're working for Mr. Slezak's attorney, why don't you ask Slezak?"

"That's a long story."

She thought about that for a few moments. "Is Meade, my ex, in some sort of trouble? Because Elmer asked about him."

"I don't know yet."

"Because if he's in trouble again, I can readily believe that."

"How long have you been divorced?"

"A little over a year. We'd been separated off and on another year before that. In fact, now that you ask, that was the time period Mr. Slezak seemed most interested in. The period around the time we separated."

I nodded.

"We were married twelve years. My father . . . Meade worked for my father, but that didn't work out, so he ended up working for various building-maintenance companies. He was a vice president at the last one, doing quite well. Before that, when he was still working for my father, somebody called one evening and asked if I knew where my husband was. They said he was at a motel with some woman. I drove there and was across the lot when they came out. They never saw me. A half hour later at home when I confronted him about it, he denied it. I was beginning to think maybe I was going crazy, that I hadn't actually seen them. But then he broke down and told the truth.

"Meade was always such a sap. When I first met him, I thought he was just a super nice guy. But he's a sap. The bimbo he was running around with talked him into investing our life savings in a pyramid scheme. A Ponzi scheme they called it. Some other people got caught up in it. It was in all the papers. Everything we had in the world, including the house, which he'd taken a second mortgage on.

"I could have lived with losing it all. I'd lost my mother's trust fund earlier. He kept telling me he loved me and the children and wanted to make it up to us. Then he lost another job under cloudy circumstances."

"Can I ask what those circumstances entailed?"

"They claimed he was sexually harassing his secretary, as well as another woman in the company. He said he wasn't, and I believed him. I don't know why. Then after only a month another outfit in town hired him at a much higher salary. The chief executive over there accused him of harassing his secretary, who, according to Meade, the chief executive had been sleeping with. I told Meade to get out."

"And?"

"He denied it all, the way he'd denied it all when I caught him at the motel, said he was going to find another job and make it up to me, pay it all back. You can see how much he's paid back. Even child support only lasted two months. We lost the house, the cabin, our vehicles, land investments, all of it. I had to declare bankruptcy. Standing in front of that judge was the most humiliating afternoon of my life. And still, I wanted the boys to have a father. Now he doesn't even visit." She chewed off her words and folded her arms, the flesh bulging like pale balloons.

"You know where he's been staying?" I asked.

"I don't want to know. If he dropped off the face of the earth, it wouldn't bother me one little bit."

"How do you reach him?"

"I don't."

She gave me the names of the companies her husband had worked for. When I'd spoken to Meade, he hadn't struck me as either a playboy or a wheeler-dealer, and I said as much.

"You met my husband?"

"Yesterday."

She took a deep breath. "I know. He wasn't a playboy. Not for eleven and a half years, anyway. His trouble was he was so easy to lead around by the nose. *Anybody* could talk him into *anything*. He never had a distrustful thought in his life. Tonight you could walk up to him and take every cent he's got with some trumped-up story."

"It's probably not much."

"It's probably not *anything*."

JoAnne stared across the street at a yellow house, where a woman with white hair stood in the window watching us. JoAnne waved. The woman waved back. "I don't know what happened to him. He started off as such an idealist. When we were first married, his dream was to write science fiction novels. He wrote every night after work. Spent most of his weekends writing. I thought it was great. When Cormick started to get older, Meade realized he was going to have to focus on earning a living. On the family."

"So what did Slezak say when he came around the second time?"

"The same questions, basically."

"You never had a personal relationship with him?"

Her eyes tightened down into blue screw heads. She looked at me hard. "Even if I had, I wouldn't tell you. And what makes you think I'd be interested in an old bag of bones like him? What makes you think I even have time for a man in my life? I barely see my kids."

"I wasn't trying to insult you."

"You did a pretty fair job of it."

"As long as we're not friends anymore, maybe you'll tell me the real reason you cut that photo out of the paper?"

"I cut it out because it was her."

"Who?"

"The woman Meade was at the motel with."

"Are you sure?"

"Yes."

"It had to be about, what, two years ago?"

"Don't try to tell me I can't remember that far back. I'll remember that woman's face two years after I'm dead."

"You realize she's the same woman Slezak has been accused of murdering, don't you?"

"Sure."

"Have you called the authorities?"

"Why should I? I don't have the faintest idea who she is."

"Meade does."

"I guess it's possible he asked for her name when he was screwing her."

"Don't you think it extraordinary your husband and Slezak were involved with the same woman?"

"Yes, I do. I don't know what to make of it. Except maybe it had something to do with all the questions Mr. Slezak was asking. I never did quite understand Slezak's precise relationship to Meade."

"My impression was that he was trying to help."

"Meade? Everybody tries to help Meade. Sooner or later they realize it's hopeless and give up. What? Why are you looking at me like that? You didn't give him money, did you? His so-called friends'll have it off him before he can spend a red cent. Did you give him money?"

"Not much," I lied.

CHAPTER 16

On our backs on a blanket under the crab apple tree, we waited for the first star to wink through the penumbra radiating off the city lights. It was nine-thirty, and already Horace's house next door was dark and buttoned up. A gentle breeze played across our bodies and held the summer insects at bay. A few doors north of our yard a cadre of small children were gleefully playing hide-and-seek. It was Friday night. It was summer. What could go wrong?

"Thomas, I had a bizarre experience today. I knew you were going to be late, so I walked down to the Safeway on Brooklyn. To get taco shells and more salsa."

"Always a good move."

"Thank you. On the way home at the corner of Fiftieth and Brooklyn a man and a woman were fighting. I shouldn't say *fighting* actually, because it was more like he was yelling at her and shaking her by the shoulders and she was simply absorbing it. You could actually hear him inside the store, but I didn't know what the noise was until I got outside. A crowd had bunched up in the parking lot to watch, but nobody moved to help. There was this inertia that seemed to take over everyone. For just a second I became part of it and it scared me."

"It's a self-protective mechanism," I said. "You have to make a decision *now*, but your natural instincts are working against a decision that could get you hurt. So you freeze. I remember when I was a cop once coming up on some little ruckus when I was off-duty and realizing that I was shaking. A little pissant hassle I normally handled two or three times a shift without blinking. It's funny, but just being mentally prepared to handle a situation like that makes all the difference in how you react."

"I think that's true. Because of the way he was manhandling her and the way she was standing next to the street, I was afraid he would shove her into traffic. You know how fast they drive on Fiftieth. So he's yelling at her and then he slugs her in the belly."

"How big was this guy?"

"Not so big. He was in his late forties, all wrinkled up like he'd been left out in the sun since he was two. His clothes were dirty, and he looked as mean as a bull in the blackberries. From the way *she* was reacting, she had to be his wife or his woman or whatever. So I crossed the street and said, 'Hey, you ignorant sonofabitch. Why don't you pick on somebody your own size?' Wasn't that mature of me? I just couldn't stand by and watch, though."

"You should be careful. You're not exactly a giant. Most people could level you with a good backhand."

"I don't know that *he* had a good backhand. He'd already hit her two or three times and she was still standing."

"I'm sure she's had more practice taking punches than you. What happened?"

"He hardly paid any attention to me. Fortunately a police car happened to be going up Brooklyn and he hit her again while they were watching. It turned out these two people were married and had driven here from Tennessee and somehow she'd lost their car. Don't ask me how. She told the cops to let him go, said she deserved 'a good paste-up.' "

"What were you planning if the police hadn't shown up?"

"I don't know. On the way home I realized he could have turned away from her and punched me."

"Or shot you. People who slap women around on crowded street corners generally don't take derogatory comments too kindly."

"So, what would you have done in my place? What if he'd been as large in comparison to you as most men are in comparison to me? Then what?"

"You mean about three hundred pounds?"

"And you knew if you stepped in, he would not only put you in the hospital but humiliate you doing it? Would you watch some poor woman take a beating? Or step in and take the beating yourself?"

"Something like that's only happened to me once, and my reaction still bothers me. It was ten years ago."

"What was it?"

"I waited, like the bystanders in that parking lot. Nobody got hurt, but they could have."

"And it still bothers you?"

"Sometimes."

The tale of my day took somewhat longer than her story. When I'd finished, she said, "So you're going to interview for IGP Systems? You going to tell them what you're really after?"

"I might if I knew what it was. You realize they weren't interested in me until we took on Elmer?"

"Don't get paranoid on me, Thomas."

"I've always been paranoid. It's just that now people are following me."

"Men in black? Dwarfs?"

"A coupla ex-girlfriends is all."

"So what else is new? How curious that this JoAnne Barber says Elmer's dead alien was the woman who broke up her marriage."

"You know how fickle the human memory is. What are the odds she would remember a woman from two years before, even if it *was* the woman who broke up her marriage, and remember her well enough to recognize her driver's-license photo after it's been reproduced in black and white in a newspaper?"

"Sorry, buster, I'd say about a million to one. No woman's going to forget that. The image would be indelibly burned into her memory. I wonder why she denied getting phone calls from Snake, though. You have the phone records, right? Tell you what I think. I think Snake made a pass at her. I think he was calling her trying to get into her pants, that or they were having an affair and she saw Snake with McFleegle. She Snake's type?"

"Every woman is Snake's type."

"I guess I should have asked is Snake her type? If they were having an affair, she's a suspect. She might have become jealous and sneaked into the apartment and killed McFleegle. Snake may have given her a key, which would explain the unlocked door. She had a powerful incentive if McFleegle actually did ruin her marriage with one man and then her affair with another. Desiree's a suspect too. And all the other women Snake knows. Or had you considered that?"

"I've been considering it all day. But that puts the suspect list into the dozens."

"Where is it without all those women?"

"One."

"Elmer?"

"Right. But you know? Desiree could strangle a woman the size of McFleegle one-handed. Hell, she could strangle *me* one-handed."

"I have a feeling she has other business in mind for you."

CHAPTER 17

Saturday morning I received a telephone call from a woman who wanted to talk about the heat. After about a minute of listening to her, I recognized her voice. "Mrs. Magdanz. How nice to hear from you."

"According to this morning's paper, they still haven't confirmed who the dead woman is."

"Yes, I saw that. What can I do for you?" I was half dressed for a bike ride, companions due in minutes. The tires on my bike needed air and my water bottles were empty. It would be in the upper eighties before we got back, and I would need water.

"I've been thinking about it, and I've decided *Gentlemen Prefer Blondes* is the one you ought to see. Marilyn was perfectly lovely in that. I believe her comic timing was at its height."

"Actually I'm on my way out, Mrs. Magdanz."

"You watch it, then come over here sometime next week and I'll show you Marilyn's earrings from the scene where she was wedged in the porthole. If you're interested, I also have the script Marilyn worked from. Oh, and I have Tommy Noonan's glasses."

"I'd love to see those items, Mrs. Magdanz, but I'm not sure I can clear my calendar for next week. To tell you the truth, I thought you called to tell me something more about Elmer Slezak."

Bare feet propped up on a chair, Kathy watched me from across the kitchen, tasting cherries from a bowl on the table as the morning sunlight tasted her.

"Oh, yes. The man in the beard. I called about the man in the beard. There was a hobo or a tramp of some sort. I saw him knocking at Mr. Slezak's door earlier on the evening of the murder, and when Slezak didn't answer, he hung around so long, I was tempted to call the police. Even Mr. Haldeman said it would have been appropriate."

"You told Haldeman about a bearded man?"

"I certainly did."

"Did you know this man?"

"I believe he was a friend of Slezak's. That's why I didn't call the police. He'd visited other times. That's also one of the fundamental reasons I wanted Mr. Slezak out of this apartment complex. Filthy hobos running around our breezeways scaring our tenants."

When I'd spoken to Magdanz the first time, she claimed to be confused about what she had told Haldeman. That was easy enough to believe, because she was confused about a lot of things. Now she swore Haldeman had been told of a man loitering around the apartment complex the night of the murder. If he had, he'd larded his witness statements with trivialities while neglecting to mention an item of possible momentous import.

"Can you describe this man, Mrs. Magdanz?"

"He was large and dirty and had a beard."

"What else?"

"His coat was filthy."

"Was he white? Black? Asian?"

"You mean Chinese? That's funny. I've never seen a Chinese bum. Have you?"

"So he was white?"

"Yes. A hulking man who walked like an ape."

"Do you recall the color of his hair?"

"Goodness, no."

"Wearing what else besides a coat?"

"I don't know. Trousers. A couple of coats."

"Overdressed for the weather?"

"I don't recall the weather."

"It was warm. A lot like today."

"I guess he was, then."

"What time did he show up?"

"I'm not sure. Sometime that Sunday evening."

"The evening of the murder?"

"Yes."

The murder had been Monday, but there was little point in correcting her again. "Did you see him make contact with Slezak?"

"Not that night. But like I said, I'd seen him with Slezak on other occasions."

The ubiquitous mysterious bearded stranger. Every murder case had one. On Monday night Kathy and I had seen a homeless man in a grimy sleeping bag near the Dempsey Dumpster. It occurred to me after we discovered the dead woman in Elmer's bed that the man in the sleeping bag might be a witness, that perhaps he'd seen someone entering or exiting Elmer's apartment, but by the time we called the police and stepped outside, he'd gone.

Of course the bearded-stranger defense was an old and well-known strategy, a sorry cliché, pursued after all other defenses had collapsed on the swords of their own logic or for lack of evidence. In our case there actually had been a bearded stranger, and the police probably knew about him, but that wouldn't make it any less laughable in court. If it came to a jury trial, the police definitely did not want this testimony coming from one of their people, hence Haldeman's convenient memory lapse.

The man near the Dumpster had looked innocuous enough, as did a lot of homeless people, a man who spent his days and nights trying to keep from being booted out of doorways, heated libraries, warm buses; trying not to get pounded, swindled, raped, robbed, burned, mutilated, or tattooed.

"Mrs. Magdanz. About a half hour after I visited you, a gentleman came to Slezak's apartment. I mention this only on the one-in-a-million chance that you happened to catch a glimpse of him."

"Oh, I caught a glimpse, all right. And I saw that fifty-foot woman Slezak calls a girlfriend too. I was glad to see you threw her out right away."

"Did you recognize the man?"

"I don't think so."

"You don't think he might have been the gentleman from the other night? With his beard shaved?"

"Why would he shave his beard?"

"He didn't look like the same man? Was he the same size? Weight? The same approximate height?"

"He wasn't any of those. The man last Sunday night had a scruffy beard. Reddish in color. He was dirty. And mean-looking. This man you spoke to wasn't dirty. And he was smaller. The man with the beard was a much larger man. And he didn't have all that silver hair." I didn't recall any silver hair on the man by the Dumpster either, but then, he'd been wearing a watch cap when I saw him.

"What time did he show up?"

"Oh, it was probably close to eleven. Slezak was still out."

"And you say he hung around?"

"For a long time. He had a jug of milk in his hand. He was drinking from it."

"Did he have a pack with him?"

"I believe so. I turned in, so I don't know how long he was there."

"You've been helpful, Mrs. Magdanz. If you think of anything else or see this man again, would you give me a call?"

"*Gentlemen Prefer Blondes*. Not all of her movies hold up, but that one does."

"We'll rent it."

I was deep in thought when Kathy said, "Mrs. Magdanz? What's she like?"

"Like Jane Russell in her prime. Gorgeous. Buxom. Whoo.

She invited me over next week, but I told her I had a hangnail operation scheduled."

"Oh, you did, did you?"

"Yes."

"Why didn't you just tell her you were married?"

"I have to keep a few irons in the fire. What if you decide to leave me for one of those fancy-pants attorneys down at the courthouse?"

"I would never leave you for an attorney. A judge, maybe. A cabdriver. A mailman. A coffee vendor. A . . ."

"I wouldn't leave you either. Not unless a real cute Dumpster diver showed up."

While I finished dressing, I told her what Magdanz had said. "So Mrs. Magdanz told Arnold Haldeman about a stranger hanging around Elmer's apartment the night of the murder, and he didn't think it important enough to include in the witness statement?"

"You challenge him on it, he'll say he didn't recall it. You put her on the stand, they'll eat her alive. She's already got the day wrong."

"Too bad."

"It is. But you saw him yourself. Nick Nolte by the Dumpster."

"Haldeman wrote such meticulous reports so that we would believe he was putting down every little tidbit, when in fact he only wrote what supported his own theories."

"Looks that way."

My two riding companions picked me up a few minutes later, the three of us coasting down Ravenna and pedaling to the Burke-Gilman Trail. We took the trail to Redmond and then got onto Highway 202 and rode as far as North Bend, where we stopped and snacked at the bakery, then rode back. It was almost four o'clock before I'd showered and eaten and driven to Elmer's apartment complex.

I managed both to elude Mrs. Magdanz and to find four individuals I hadn't spoken to earlier, only one of whom, Felix Trosper, a compulsive talker with a bobbing Adam's apple, had any useful information. I quickly found out that he'd dropped out of college and was working in a record store, that his parents were sending him money under the mistaken notion that he was still a student, that a girlfriend had jilted him recently, and that he was thinking of starting a band and making a movie about it. He said he would appreciate it if I tried to keep his name out of the papers. I said I would try.

"I see bums over there all the time." We were looking across the street at Elmer's apartment from Felix's small second-story room, the walls of which were plastered with rock posters.

"The same individual, or different people?"

"I couldn't say for sure. Bums sort of all look the same, know what I mean?"

"And the night of the murder? Monday night? Did you see anybody?"

"Some dude. I've seen him around before with the man who drives the Cadillac."

"Would you recognize him if you saw him again?"

"The dude with the Cadillac?"

"The other one."

"Probably. He hasn't been around, though. Not since the murder. Not that I've seen."

"What'd he look like?"

His description was similar to Magdanz's, though more detailed. A tall man wearing lots of clothes and carrying a knapsack. With a beard. Reddish in color.

"See anybody else hanging around?"

"I did. About a week ago. A woman came a couple of times. The reason I noticed, she parked right in front, and the first time she did it, I was expecting somebody, so I kept looking out. She was there about two hours. I know she was waiting for the dude with the Cadillac because when the Cadillac showed up, she got out and started across the street. But then I guess she noticed he had a woman with him, 'cause she just turned around and went straight back to her car. Like a dog somebody'd hosed down."

"Then what'd she do?"

"She was still out there staring at the apartment across the street when I left. I don't know how long she stayed. But it was a bad look she was giving that place. It was really bad. Just the evil eye."

"What'd this woman look like?"

"Nice. Blonde. About your age, maybe. A pretty good build on her. A little heavy in the legs."

"And she wasn't there when you came home?"

"No. But she showed up the next night. The Cadillac was there when she got here, but she didn't go in. She sat out in her car for a couple of hours staring at the place across the street."

"You only saw her from up here that second time?"

"Yeah. So I don't know if she was still pissed."

"See her any other times?"

"That was it."

"You didn't happen to get the license number of the car, did you?"

"No. But it was a brown Chevy wagon with a bad muffler. And there was a little crease running along the passenger side of the car. Not deep, but real long."

I didn't remember a crease along the side of JoAnne Barber's car, but it would be easy enough to check out. Before I left, he explained in detail about the band he wanted to start.

Expecting to be disappointed, we sat in front of *Gentlemen Prefer Blondes* that evening, downing strawberry shortcake built with the last berries of the season. The movie was funny and camp, filled with clever performances and witty writing. Magdanz had been right. It was Monroe at her best.

Sunday morning we slept in, then baked biscuits and smothered them in jam while they were still hot. I took a long, easy bike ride with the same two friends from yesterday. The afternoon was spent around the house, Kathy altering a 1950s dress she'd picked up in a thrift shop and reading while I deadheaded roses, weeded the vegetable beds, and scanned *The New York Times*.

Our domestic tranquillity was interrupted during dinner by the front bell. Before I had the door all the way open, Elmer Slezak blew past me and headed for Kathy in the kitchen. "Can we talk?" he said, taking my place at the table. He reached into my salad with two fingers and snatched out a slice of cucumber, tossing it into his maw.

I said, "Well, hello, Snake. Long time no see. It's good to see you, too, Thomas."

"Oh. Sorry," Elmer said, holding his head in his hands. His shirt was rumpled, his hair tousled, and his eyebrows, always wild, looked like a pair of hedgehogs squaring off for a spat. He wore the same silver-toed cowboy boots, slacks, and shirt he'd worn to jail early Tuesday morning.

"How'd you get sprung, Elmer?" Kathy said.

"Forget how I got sprung. Look outside. They're following me." When I went to the front window, I saw only the rear of a black car as it disappeared up the street. I waited, but it didn't come back.

"Was that somebody?" I asked.

"Them dwarfs."

CHAPTER 18

"**T**hey been following me for two days."

"I didn't get a good look," I said, turning from the window.

"Why would dwarfs follow you?" Kathy said. "You want something to eat?"

Elmer shook his head. I sat at the table and dragged my soup and salad over to a new spot. Elmer's breath was beery and his eyes looked like olives floating in tomato juice. "I don't know why. They were just after me. Government men, I believe."

"You sure?"

"No, I'm not sure! I'm not even sure they were dwarfs. They looked short enough. But maybe they weren't even following me. I've been pretty confused."

"Did you know your landlady claims government men broke into your apartment the other day?" I said.

"They were probably checking the electronic bugs."

"Hell, Snake. You've got a shitload of debugging toys in your office. And you're telling me your apartment is bugged?"

"I just figured that part out in jail." Distracted, he got up and walked to the back door, peered out, then bobbed his head at the kitchen window, then the windows in the living room. He walked bowlegged back to the kitchen table like a disappointed bronc rider who'd been thrown and disqualified. "I don't know. Maybe nobody's following me. Maybe I'm nuts."

"When were you released?" Kathy asked.

"Friday. The paperwork said it was a place on Second Avenue sprung me, so I went down and asked about it, but they were full of shit up to their eyebrows. Said a man came in, gave them the bail money and a fee in cash, and left. No questions asked."

"Was he a dwarf?" I asked.

"I forgot to ask."

"Friday?" said Kathy, giving me a nasty look for teasing Snake. "Where have you been for the last two days?"

"Checking out the titty palaces."

Kathy looked puzzled.

"Topless dance joints," I said.

"They've all got these tattoos. If I can find another one, she can lead me to the hive. Don't look at me like that. That's what one of them called it. The hive. Told me despite the way they look, they think and behave more like insects than people. That's why they want to breed with us. To become more human. Right now they all work together the way bees work together. One brain. Don't you see? They admire our independence. They want it."

Kathy and I looked at each other while Snake stared anxiously at the front windows. Kathy said, "You couldn't have spent two whole days checking out topless bars. What else did you do?"

"I mighta picked up a woman."

"You might have? Did you or didn't you?"

"I guess I did."

"You remember her name?" Kathy asked.

"Don't worry. She was double-u oh tee."

"What?" I said.

"Not *what*. Wot. *W-O-T*. Without Tattoos."

"Somebody walked in off the street and paid your bail?" Kathy said. "Seventy-five thousand dollars cash. Who would do that?"

"Maybe them aliens want me out so they can ice me 'cause they think I killed one of theirs."

"I thought you said they could go through walls," I said. "Through locks. Windows. If they wanted to kill you, why didn't they do it in jail?"

"Or one of my ex-girlfriends? I haven't had time to think about all the ramifications. I been looking for clones. You been lookin', too, haven't you, Tommy?"

"Don't call me Tommy. And no, I haven't been looking. I don't believe there are any clones."

He gave me an incredulous look, then turned to Kathy questioningly. "I'm sorry, Elmer," she said. "I don't believe in clones either."

"Well sheeeit!" he said.

I said, "I did learn that about half the apartment complex where you live says you'd been dating the dead woman for two weeks."

"I explained that. Okay. Shit. Damn it. Now I *am* hungry. How about some grub?"

"What would you like?"

"Steak. Rare. Sirloin or T-bone's okay. A baked potato about yea big. Lobster. Spinach salad. Maybe some steamed asparagus tips. And two fried eggs on the side. Sunny-side up and soft in the center. Then vanilla ice cream with colored sprinkles on it. Or jelly beans. Whichever you got."

Kathy looked at me. "We were thinking more along the lines of what we were having, soup and salad," I said. "And rolls. We don't have any steak. We can nuke some enchiladas from last night. Maybe rustle up the eggs."

"Whatever."

"Elmer," I said, sliding the pan of enchiladas out of the refrigerator. "How did you meet Desiree Nash?"

He gave me a startled look, and then, without a word, stood up and went into the bathroom, where he remained for nearly fifteen minutes. Kathy whispered across the kitchen, "Who would have let him out?"

"I'll check tomorrow."

"And what is all this about dwarfs following him?"

"I'm taking anything he says with a grain of salt until I confirm it elsewhere. He's been seeing a lot of stuff."

"What about the government men, the ones the landlady saw?"

"I don't know."

When Elmer finally emerged from the bathroom, the cuffs of his shirt were rolled up and a pistol was sticking out of his belt. I said, "Where'd you get the gun? Your office?"

"Haven't been to the office."

"Hand it over." Like a child caught with candy he'd snitched out of the bowl on Halloween morning, Elmer gave it to me. I unloaded it and put it into a drawer.

"Desiree called me up one day out of the blue, started talkin' dirty on the phone," he said. "That's where I met her."

"On the phone?"

"You gotta love a woman who talks like that."

"Called you out of the blue?"

"We agreed to meet at a dim sum place in Chinatown. We ate ourselves sick and went back to her place. She can drink more and cuss worse than just about any woman I ever knowed."

"That's because you haven't seen Kathy on a toot," I said, earning a theatrically sour look from Kathy. "You think Desiree could have sneaked in and killed McFleegle?"

"She gets mighty jealous," Elmer said. "I don't recall she knew any of the clones, though."

"Quit the clone crap, Elmer!" I said. "I've had enough of this! We need information, and sitting around talking about intergalactic breeding programs isn't doing anything but puffing up your ego."

"My ego? Why, I don't have any personal stake in this, boy. You think this is all because of my ego? Why, you're blind. It's not my fault they like the look of my DNA. They needed DNA and stamina, and I gave it to 'em."

"Give me a break. Hundreds of virgins throwing themselves into your bed? It's all a script made up in your own head. It's pure horseshit."

He was quiet for a full minute. Kathy said nothing. In the other room the regulator clock ticked away. "When was the last time you saw Desiree?" Kathy asked.

"Two weeks?"

"Right about the time you say the clone business began," I said. "Right about the time the neighbors say you started dating the dead woman. Does Desiree have a key to your place?"

"Not that I'm aware of. But she might."

"She ever threaten you over other women?"

"A few times. She followed me a few times, but an amateur is easy to ditch. You know that."

"You ditch her driving over to JoAnne Barber's house, did you?"

"How did you know that?"

"Because she gave me Barber's street number. She said she would have followed you right into the house if it hadn't been for the kids. Tell us about Meade Barber."

Snake scooped up a forkful of hot enchilada off the plate I'd taken out of the microwave, stared at the coppery-orange roses in the center of the table, Troikas, and considered the new information. "You know, I thought he was the cause of this fandango. In the beginning I thought he was. Before it got out of hand."

"Barber?"

"Yep. But it doesn't make sense."

"Is he the only homeless person you know?"

"He has a couple friends show up once in a blue moon."

"Is one of them a big, hulking man with a reddish beard?"

"Maybe. Yes. He's got a buddy who fits that description."

"You know the buddy's name?"

"Arliss somebody or other."

"On the night of the murder, did you see Barber or Arliss or anybody?"

"No."

"Why did you think Barber was the cause of this?"

"The seed, really. Not of this breeding program but of something. This was all back months ago. It's ancient history."

"I'm a student of ancient history."

"Okay. Sure. Christ. I saw him in a food line. I recognized him from a job I did maybe two years ago. I'd followed him for Green International. That's the security outfit inside of IGP Systems. The head honcho, Rakubian, wanted information on his day-to-day activities. They have a regular form you fill out.

Strengths. Weaknesses. Hobbies. Time per week spent with the kiddies. The wife. Does he look at babes on the street? Drugs? Alcohol? Does he exceed the speed limit? Don't ask me why they were interested. I've done a hundred of those surveillance gigs for Green International, and I never hardly knew what any of them was about."

"You never told me any of this," I said.

"You sign a pledge of confidentiality. Besides, it wasn't stuff to brag over. Some of my assignments included sabotaging Joe Blow's car three nights running. Air out of the tires one night. Bad gas in the tank the next. Fuck up his windshield wipers with a razor the next."

"Who's Joe Blow?"

"Anybody the company wants to unbalance. Sometimes there's no discernible reason. Maybe somebody in the office has a grudge. I mean, they were *that* cavalier about it. I did a surveillance once on the lead negotiator for a union that was giving one of their printing plants a rough time. I followed men and I followed women. I spied on homosexuals. Everything you can imagine."

"Printing plants?" Kathy asked.

"They got a foods division. A trucking division. A plant that makes airplane parts. Two or three dozen companies maybe. Worldwide they claim close to half a million employees. And with Rakubian, you never knew which company you were doing a job for, or why. Questions weren't tolerated. You did the job. You took the money. You kept quiet."

"And Barber?"

"An executive I wrote a report on a couple of years ago. I spent maybe two, three weeks on it. Pictures, videos, maps. I even bugged his car and listened to conversations he had on his cell phone."

"What'd you find?"

"He worked for a trucking outfit IGP owned. Left for work at eight. Skipped lunches to run the track at the Washington Athletic Club. Got home at six or seven. Sometimes later if they were busy. The only vice I could put my finger on was Lotto tickets."

"What's the rest?"

"There *is* no rest. I made my report. That was it. About a year, year and a half later I see him in a soup line. This is a guy who had his house almost paid off. Owned a brand-new motor home free and clear. Had property and a cabin over on Lake Roosevelt. A healthy stock portfolio. A nice wife. Two great kids. Now I see him in a soup line with everything he owns wrapped up in a newspaper."

"What happened?"

"From what I could piece together, he went nuts over some woman. His wife caught him, and then while they were patching it up, he lost his concentration and started getting sloppy at his job and they canned him. Also he got into some sort of Ponzi scheme. Meade is such a wuss, so anxious to get suckered. Even his kids push him around. Just before he got fired, he failed to finish a report he needed for a big new account 'cause he couldn't get his kids off the home computer so's he could work on it. Then he was caught with a secretary or somebody, and his ass was grass."

"You didn't call his wife and tell her she could find him at a certain motel with a woman?"

"It wasn't me. That happened after."

"Did JoAnne Barber tell you the woman she saw at the motel was the same one who died in your bed?"

Snake looked at me and then at Kathy. "You shittin' your old friend, Thomas?"

"That's what she said."

"Meade Barber was part of the fertility program?"

Kathy and I exchanged looks. Snake was so delusional, it was hard to know which part of his story was worthwhile and which was batty.

"Kathy, dear," said Snake after he'd finished his meal. "You think if a woman tells you she loves you but you've only known her six hours, it's legit?"

"Six hours?" Kathy said, sighing. She'd been through this before. "Was she drunk?"

"Seven beers was all. She could walk."

"It's not legit, Elmer."

"What if I'm with one lady, except I keep thinking about another lady? Does that mean I'm in love with the other lady?"

Whenever his love life took a bruising, Elmer showed up at our house asking to see Kathy. They would sit up for hours, she patiently listening and counseling, he sniveling and whining. Even though there had never been any love lost between the two, this had become a sorry ritual.

I wandered into the other room and tried to read a book, abandoned that to watch an old movie on video, *Hobson's Choice*. From time to time Kathy shushed my laughter from the other room.

CHAPTER 19

The next morning I called Arnold Haldeman at the Seattle Police Department, dispensed with the pleasantries, and asked about Catherine Samantha McFleegle.

"Don't worry yourself over her. We'll let you know when we find out anything. You're on our list to call."

"Thanks."

It was either the nonchalance in Haldeman's tone or the arrogance, or maybe it was the mention of being on a list that prompted me to make another call, this to an old friend in the SPD who had formerly worked in Homicide/Assault. "Ralph? This is Black. Listen, I'm calling—"

"I think I know why. The dead woman's name is Roberta Capshaw Sams. That's with one M. Nobody knows why she was using the McFleegle alias."

"You heard about this already?"

"A little." He gave me an address on South Ferdinand Street. "One of her neighbors just got back from vacation, was going through her newspapers, and saw the photo. Haldeman's going to open up the house as soon as he gets a court order."

"When I called him a minute ago, he said he didn't know who she was."

"I couldn't tell you about that."

I dialed my information broker in Oregon and gave her the name and address Ralph had given me. "Everything you can dig up, Hilda."

"Is this the woman you were hunting before?"

"That's her."

It was a short walk to the Meany Hotel. Entering through the north door, I went down a hallway past meeting rooms and into the foyer, where a young man and woman at the desk were checking in a group of business travelers. The reader board near the elevators around the corner gave the only clue that IGP Systems had any offices in the building. On twelve there was a *G.I.* listed. Green International? IGP Systems, as I recalled, stood for International Green-Turtle Products, though the full name was rarely used. On twelve I walked down a carpeted hallway and found suite 1201.

A young woman in a navy-blue suit answered the door. "Yes?"

"My name is Thomas Black. I'm—"

"Come in."

She walked in front of me. Trim, of medium height, she was young and well groomed with a wide rear and full calves working navy pumps. She stepped around a desk and sat, her short dark hair bisected by a wireless headphone. Her brown eyes were dark, slightly liquid, and heavily made up. If she was the sexy computer voice on the phone, I couldn't tell it. The name plaque on the corner of her desk read, CYNTHIA WEBBER.

She handed me a sheaf of papers on a clipboard and said, "Please fill these out." She entered my name and the time on a check-in sheet at her desk, and then when a light on her phone console lit up, she answered, "Green Division."

They wanted to know every place I'd ever worked, the street address of every house I'd lived in since birth, any trouble with the law including traffic tickets, my service record, schooling, formal classes since college, and the full names and addresses of all close relatives. There was even a section on hobbies.

Had it not been for Elmer's involvement here, I would have walked out, for I found the questionnaire intrusive, as if I were being checked out for a national security clearance—or quizzed by a first date who was already making plans for the rest of my life.

Fifty-two minutes later I passed the forms back to Ms. Webber, who asked me to sit and relax.

The suite consisted of the large main room, a rest room, and two back rooms, their doors closed. The large room contained Webber's desk, a second desk with very little on it, two sofas and three chairs in front of a set of windows sporting a panoramic view to the west. I could see Green Lake. The zoo. The freeway. Elmer's neighborhood. A chunk of brown-red air roosting on the city. I stood in the corner and tried to spot my neighborhood, but the angle was wrong. It was a strange waiting room, not a magazine or tropical fish in sight, nothing to keep the customers amused but the view and a prim Cynthia Webber with her back turned.

"Mr. Black?"

He'd sneaked up on me, a genial-looking man in his fifties; early or late, it was hard to tell. He looked weathered and fit and gripped my hand like a terrorist sizing up a captive. "Mr. Rakubian?"

He smiled. "No, no. I'm afraid I'm only here as a consultant. Art does the hiring and firing. I work downstairs." He had my paperwork in his hands, but I'd not heard him come into the room and wasn't sure how long he'd been there. "We have hiring autonomy in each of our departments, but the bigwigs like us to bring another manager into the room when we interview. A matter of policy."

"So you're on the same level as Rakubian, only in a different section of the company?"

"Rakubian's above me actually. And he works in Green Division. I work in Diesel Works Matters."

"The toy company?"

"Ordinarily Rakubian wouldn't choose me to sit in on a hiring interview, but I'm afraid with all the summer vacations and the out-of-state conferences there aren't many of us to choose from. Anybody else would have to fly up from our headquarters in San Francisco."

"I can't believe IGP owns a toy company. You make those little colored doggie-clown puzzles?"

"There's a long story behind those, but I won't bore you with it. They own BrelCo too. By the way. My name's Fitt. Ernest Fitt. It says here you ride bicycles. You ever race?"

"My friends do. Did you say they owned BrelCo?" Fitt smiled and nodded. His round head gave the impression of chubbiness, though his face was etched with character lines and his suit hung loosely, his neck lean and muscled. He had half-moon tan marks on the backs of his hands similar to the ones imprinted by my cycling gloves.

"The great advantage of working for this company isn't the pay. It's the perks. You can scratch up the airfare, the company'll put you up in Majorca in January and you can rub shoulders with the BrelCo cycling team while they're putting in winter mileage. You get tested by team trainers, run a VO-two max test on an ergometer. Hell, they'll even analyze your turds." He gave me a little-boy grin.

"Where do I sign up?"

"There were twelve of us last year. Dykstra from the film division. Me. Some others from the plants in California. We had a blast."

"So you ride too?"

"Before the Majorca trips my fastest twenty-five was a one-oh-three. In the last three years I've gotten it down to a long fifty-seven." Comparable to the mile for runners, a twenty-five-mile time trial was a universal yardstick for cyclists. Doing twenty-five miles in under an hour was the rough equivalent to a four-minute mile, and Fitt claimed to have beat an hour by more than two minutes. At his age, even on a tricked-out bike, it was not likely.

The door behind us opened and a saturnine man in a vest and a bow tie dabbed his tongue to his lips and looked us over. Looked me over.

Rakubian was a small, thin man with the ruddy complexion and webs of exploded veins in his face like those of a heavy drinker. His white hair was brushed straight back and groomed close to his skull. He had an erect military bearing. It wasn't until he spoke and the British accent materialized that I recalled Elmer telling me Rakubian had spent twenty years in MI6, the British intelligence agency.

"Mr. Black. Won't you please step inside?"

It was a small office with three chairs, one behind the desk, one alongside it, and one six or eight feet out into the room, a power arrangement, carefully laid out in advance and probably used on all guests. Along one wall stood a bookcase filled with thick tomes relating to U.S. and international tax codes, suggesting that the office was used by someone else, though I had the feeling it was not. The desk was old and scarred and had a lamp, an ashtray, and one pencil on it. The ashtray was half full.

After we were seated, Arthur Rakubian leaned back in his swivel chair and perused the stack of forms I'd filled out. From time to time he would make small sounds in his throat, but he did not look up. Ernest Fitt sat staring at the carpet with a smile on his face befitting a manager in the toy division.

Admiring their interview strategy, I waited. First it was the good-cop, bad-cop routine, Fitt taking on the role of good cop, Rakubian putting the screws to me with his silence. They'd probably had a professional come in and advise them on exactly where to place the chairs, how long to read the paperwork, whether or not to fart. A small stereo against the wall played Mahler, or something that sounded as if it could have been Mahler.

"So," Rakubian said when he'd finished eight minutes later. "Nothing surprising here. Of course there wouldn't be. We've been keen on you for some time, Mr. Black. Did you know that?"

"No, I didn't."

"More than one of our operatives in the area has recommended you. Tenacious but honest is what we've heard. And that interests us. You seem to have a code of ethics. Not many do these days."

"Thank you."

"Do you have any idea what we do here at Green, Mr. Black?"

"I have an idea."

"And what is it you think we do?"

"Industrial security."

"Close. What we require of you, if you decide to work with us, is absolute loyalty. You will not discuss your work with anybody, not even your wife. Understood?"

"Certainly."

"Your assignments will come through this office. I will give them, or Ms. Webber will. Should it be discovered you've spoken out of turn, however obliquely, you will be dismissed forthwith. Understood?"

"Yes."

"Should the police question you about any job you're performing or have performed for us, you're to contact this office immediately. A lawyer will be assigned."

"I'm not in the habit of breaking the law or going to jail."

"No. Of course not. These are extreme-action clauses and are rarely, if ever, invoked."

"By the way. Did Elmer Slezak recommend me?"

Rakubian looked hard at me, folded his hands together, and propped them under his chin. He had a small mouth, a narrow nose, and ears that stuck out like wind cups on a weather station. He appeared to be an emotionless man, and I could readily believe he'd once worked for MI6.

"I cannot discuss Slezak with you in the same way that I cannot discuss you with him. From top to bottom this is a quiet shop."

Rakubian sat back and put his thumbs into his vest. Fitt shuffled his feet. Twice now Rakubian had fumbled for a pack of cigarettes and thought better of it, refraining on Fitt's behalf no doubt. I had the feeling that if it had been just the two of us, his lungs would be filled.

Rakubian watched me for a few seconds. "We've prepared an offer for you." He pulled open a drawer and took out a single sheet of paper. "An attorney in Spokane named Gary Parsons. Follow him. We have standard forms for you to fill out. It might help to read through them before you begin so you know what we're looking for. Day-and-night surveillance from now until Wednesday morning. Fill out the paperwork. Return it to me or Ms. Webber by Thursday morning. It's a relatively simple job."

"I should have explained. I'm not available the first part of this week."

The room grew quiet. Even the Mahler on the stereo seemed softer. Rakubian slowly traced his lips with his tongue. "We haven't discussed the fee. For two days it will be very close to five thousand dollars."

"I'm working on a case this week. I'll have to pass."

"If the money's not sufficient . . ."

"The money's great. I have—"

"Ten thousand," Rakubian said. "That's five a day."

"I have the other case."

"You have obligations and you must honor them. We respect that. We'll call." He said it in a way that insinuated he never would. I had been dismissed.

"I look forward to it," I said, in a manner that hinted I knew he never would call. I wasn't sure exactly what was going on, but I didn't want to seem like a rube.

Ernest Fitt walked me to the door while Rakubian lit a cigarette and read some papers in his lap. I had been turned over to an underling, shooed out the door on a wave of smoke and ennui. It was hard to tell what had taken place. Had I applied for a job or had I performed a subtle interrogation of Snake's former employers? Had they offered me a job, or had they only conned me into writing down every fact and reference they needed to check out my life? The surveillance offer a few minutes earlier had seemed genuine enough, but Rakubian's dismissal had been swift and self-consciously boorish.

In the anteroom near the front door Fitt shook my hand again, not as vigorously as the first time. His smile was warm. "Look," he said. "Why were you asking about your friend?"

"No reason."

"Compartmentalization is what Rakubian's section is about. I suppose another word for it is secrecy. What was your friend's name again?"

"Elmer Slezak."

"Whatever you've got going, you'd better get rid of it. What you got here is a nickel holding up a dollar, son. Too bad. Your being busy. I was hoping you might have time to go riding.

Since I got into town, I haven't had that many people to ride with."

"What time did you have in mind?"

"This afternoon? This evening? I'll be here until about eight, but I'd like to get out for a couple of hours somewhere in the middle. My bike's here in the office."

"I'll give you a call. If you don't hear from me by four, go without me."

"I don't hear from you, I'll probably work straight on through."

I'd seen his kind before. A fifty-seven-minute twenty-five-mile time trial? Not likely. He was the type who bought a four-thousand-dollar bike and wore a brand-new team jersey from BrelCo and the first time we came to a hill he'd get out of the saddle and attack, pedaling as hard as he could, thrusting his bike back and forth between his legs. It wouldn't do him a bit of good. His kind thought forty miles a week was a regimen.

"By the way," Fitt said, lowering his voice as we stepped into the hall. "Art runs this whole schmear like some sort of spy operation. Don't let that fool you. It's mostly industrial-information gathering. 'Know thine enemy.' Harmless stuff."

"I figured as much."

After I'd walked home, I drove downtown to Second Avenue, where I dropped in at the bail bond company that had posted the bond for Elmer. Their description of the man who'd brought seventy-five thousand dollars cash into their office was vague, deliberately vague I thought. A white male in a suit, they said. Might have been an attorney. A small mustache. Medium height. Medium weight. Medium age. Brown and brown. He'd claimed he was a relative of Slezak's from back East and wanted to surprise him. Now, that part Elmer had not related to us, but then, maybe they hadn't told him. The description might have fit a lot of people. It would have fit Rakubian, for instance.

CHAPTER 20

Daunted at the prospect of talking to Kathy about her last night's tête-à-tête with Elmer—always a messy business—and wanting to give Hilda more time before pestering her, I ran errands and then read the last chapter of a novel I'd been trying to finish for a week, this while eating at the counter at Mitchelli Trattoria downstairs from our office.

"Where have you been?" Kathy asked when I got to the office. "It's almost one o'clock." Pressing her fingertips to my chest, she walked me backward into my office, closed the door, and forced me into my chair, then kicked off her shoes and sat on my desk with a foot on either of my chair arms. "I know something."

"That's not a very lawyerly position," I said.

She pressed a stockinged foot gently against my crotch. Her foot was cold. "Is this better?"

"It's better, but it's not very lawyerly either."

"I just asked if it was better. You know, Elmer's been in my office with Ellen all morning."

"Ellen Burgess? The psychologist?"

"Running a battery of tests. I've got the early results. He's recanted."

"What do you mean *recanted*?"

"He admits the alien business was baloney. Said he was seeing her just like the neighbors said he was seeing her. For a period of two weeks."

"How does he explain her death?"

"He doesn't. Nor does he know her real name. But listen to what Ellen says about him." Kathy reached over to a folder she'd carried in with her. "He has a borderline narcissistic personality."

"I could have told you that."

"He's insecure but doesn't want anybody to know he's insecure."

"I could have told you that."

"He spends much of his time maintaining a false front, and he's paranoid. That's why he wears all those guns. His relationships with women are ambivalent. On the other hand he is usually generous and often thinks of others. He has a high-achiever personality, but he's adopted a lifestyle that makes high achievement close to impossible. He's got an addictive personality too. Probably an alcoholic. Certainly a sexaholic."

"I could have told you that."

"Come on. Don't ruin it for me. He doesn't have a whole lot of imagination. He works hard when he works but spends a lot of his life figuring out how not to work. He shies away from romantic entanglements and treats women as trophies. He hates his father to the extent that if he saw him again, he claims he would kill him. He hates his mother, who probably had bipolar disorder—manic depression—and has been missing for nearly twenty years."

"I knew that."

"You did?"

"Snake gets drunk, he tells you all this stuff. Ellen should have got him drunk."

"She had her chance. He asked her out."

"What'd she say?"

"What do you mean, what'd she say? She's married. He's a patient. She told him as much and he said he'd quit as a patient, wouldn't tell her husband."

"None of this explains the alien foolishness. As for the guns, they aren't entirely image. He's been shot four times."

"Then he should be wearing a bulletproof vest, not carrying guns. Oh. Ellen says he has a John Wayne complex."

"I knew that."

"Now you *have* ruined it."

"What time did you get to bed last night, Sister?"

"Three-fifteen."

"Three-fifteen!"

"He needed to talk."

"What did you talk about?"

"The same as last time. His seven girlfriends."

"That's down a little from when I first met him. I think he told me he had nine."

"Including—now, don't you dare say anything to her— Beulah, our receptionist, whom he rattles about once every six months. That's what he calls it, *rattling*."

"Colorful, ain't he?"

"She always calls him, he never calls her, and she brings a pornographic movie over and they watch it together and they drink rum and then . . ."

I put my thumbs in my ears and started babbling, kept it up until Kathy pulled my hands away and whispered, "Okay. Okay. I'll spare your sensitive soul the gruesome details. He wants to be married. That's his problem. He wants a wife and a house and a life. He thinks he's getting old and he wants a wife around when it happens. He's lonely."

"Most guys who live like him are. So what about the psychosis or delusions or whatever? What did Ellen say?"

"Like I said, he's abandoned his alien story. No signs of delusional thinking. No signs of psychosis. Which doesn't mean she can't be fooled. Especially after only one visit. She wants to see him again in a few days."

I told Kathy what I'd learned about our dead nonalien—that her real name was Roberta Capshaw Sams and she had lived by Lake Washington on Ferdinand. I told her about Arnold Haldeman's lies, about Green International, and about Fitt wanting to ride bikes with me.

"What do you know about this Sams?"

"Not a thing. I've got Hilda working on it. I'm going down later to talk to the neighbors."

"I keep thinking about that seventy-five thousand in bail money. Who would put that up? Who could afford to? And this Rakubian person has clearly asked Fitt to scope you out. I think you should go riding with him."

"I will, but I have a feeling he's not going to speak out of turn."

"Do me a favor too, would you?"

"What, my love?"

"Take Elmer away."

"Oh, come on, Kathy."

"He's underfoot here in the office, and if he goes out by himself, I'm afraid he'll get into trouble."

"If he'll get into trouble by himself, he'll get into trouble with me."

"No, he won't. You want him arrested again?"

"Okay. I'll take him. He can give me tips on how to keep nine girlfriends."

"You already have *one* girlfriend, big guy."

"No. I have one wife. The girlfriends are extra. Maybe I'll hold it down to seven. No, wait. I need nine. Otherwise I won't have enough for a softball team."

She smiled and placed her foot against my crotch once more. "Sure you could handle nine more like me?"

"Oh, they wouldn't be anything like you. These would be inferior, more like . . . six-foot Swedish masseuses. You know. That type."

She kissed me in the center of my forehead and stepped into her shoes. "I'll send him in. Be nice. He thinks the two of you are working on the case together."

Hilda called just as Snake came into the office and collapsed into the red chair. "She owned the house on Ferdinand free and clear," said Hilda. "Paying the taxes herself. She'd be twenty-two this week. The birthday on her phony driver's license was accurate. She attended the University of California at Irvine and was in the drama department until she was cast in a small television movie for Miramont. She dropped out of school then and about six months later moved to the Northwest."

"Why would a young actress move to Seattle? Don't they all move to L.A. or New York?"

"Miramont's building a studio in Ballard, I believe. It might have to do with that. She comes from a family with eight children and was on financial grants going to UC, so I don't know how she got the house. If there was a marriage somewhere, I haven't traced it. Her Social Security card, driver's license, and all her credit cards are under the name of Roberta Capshaw Sams."

"You have a next of kin?"

"I'm working on it. The children in her family had several fathers, according to what I'm finding out, all different last names, and the mother died last year. They were raised in Fresno. At least that was the last address before her freshman year."

"Hilda? You happen to know who owns Miramont?"

"A company named BrelCo."

"BrelCo the bicycle-racing team out of Belgium?"

"Now, that I wouldn't know. The last time I was on a bicycle, my butt was sore for a week."

"Do me a favor. Keep after Sams. And I'd like some basic information on BrelCo and Miramont. They're connected to IGP Systems somehow. I want to know how. And who runs them."

"Sure, Thomas. It might be a day or two. I've got some other accounts I'm working on."

"Whenever."

"Thomas me boy," Snake said, when I'd racked the receiver. "Your pretty wife, Katherine, tells me you have some leads."

"She tells me you've taken back your story about the aliens."

Elmer scratched his head, hunched his shoulders, glanced around the room, and shrugged. He looked like James Dean in *Giant*. He put on a look that was almost a smirk and said, "I don't think Ellen's got a single ounce of silicone to her. I believe in my heart she's all woman."

"I bet you do. So tell me how long you knew the dead woman."

"A coupla weeks."

"Why did you say otherwise?"

"Confused? Drunk? I dunno. Thomas. You think Desiree would make a good wife?"

"No. Come on. Let's go."

Bumping into me at the door, Snake said, "Where're we goin'?"

"To do some intergalactic research."

CHAPTER 21

Ferdinand dead-ended two blocks off Lake Washington Boulevard South. From the middle of the street you could catch a narrow glimpse of the choppy lake and beyond that the lumpy green peninsula of Seward Park across the water. On Ferdinand it was a mixed bag of older bungalow-type houses and remodeled jobs.

Sams's place was a single-story stucco structure, the lawn pocked with gray lollipoplike dandelions going to seed, the shades pulled all around in the house. These two blocks on Ferdinand reminded me of a neighborhood in southern California. Maybe it was the stucco or maybe it was the brown lawns.

Parking on the street, we got out and walked to the house. The police were gone. Elmer hadn't said a word on the drive and I hadn't either. We'd passed Beulah, our receptionist, without a look or word exchanged, their affair hidden behind a façade of exaggerated indifference.

"This the joint?" Snake asked, catching me on the walkway. "This belong to Sams?"

"Yes. And you be good."

"She ain't going to be home."

"Dead people usually aren't."

"No, I meant . . . Oh, shit."

We knocked at the front door for decorum's sake, then went around the house to a small fence in the back. As I stepped over it, Snake said, "We gonna break in? I don't have my picks." I ignored him. She was no gardener, though a hummingbird feeder, sadly drained and dry, was hanging near the kitchen window. I stood on tiptoe and peered in. It was a nice little unit, all new appliances, a half-filled wine rack on the counter. I noticed there weren't any doodads stuck to her refrigerator: no notes, wanted posters, or report cards.

"May I help you?" The woman was standing in an adjoining backyard filled with log playground apparatus. Three toddlers bounced around behind her. She wore shorts over a bathing suit and was in her early thirties, a pleasant-looking woman with hazel eyes and sandy hair tied up in a frowzy ponytail.

"Did you see the police here?" I asked.

"They left about half an hour ago."

"They take anything with them?"

One of the children behind the woman fell and began crying. After she comforted the child, I gave her my card. "We're looking into the death of Ms. Sams," I said. "Working for the defense."

The toddler stopped crying and stared at us. Snake inserted his thumbs into his mouth and made faces that seemed to fascinate the youngster; that or she was too terrified to cry. "We got home from the Colorado Rockies two days ago, and it wasn't until late last night I went through all our newspapers. Poor Roberta. Why would anybody do it?"

"Hell only knows," Snake said.

I said, "Mrs. . . . ?"

"Gunderson. Genevieve Gunderson. You're a private investigator?"

"We both are, ma'am," said Snake.

"I see."

"Did you talk to the police?" I asked.

"No."

"You know Ms. Sams very well?"

"Not well. No. Mr. Poulidor owned the house before her. Raymond was such a sweet old guy. He used to sit on the porch in a straw boater. He was getting on in years, and he kept setting fire to his stove. He was deathly afraid of nursing homes and refused to go to one, even for a visit, but he was even more afraid of dying in a fire. In the end he went into the garage one evening and shot himself. My husband found him."

"I'm sorry to hear that. Did Ms. Sams ever talk about her work?"

"She was an actress. She'd been in a couple of movies, but mostly she worked in local theater. I don't know what the last play was, but it was some time ago."

"She have an active social life?"

"Not what I'd call active. She had a sister or two who would visit from California. At least they had California plates. And she used to have a boyfriend. An older man. For a long time we thought he was her father."

"You know his name?"

"She didn't talk about him much. I think his first name was Jud."

"What'd he look like?"

"We only saw him from a distance. Then there was a younger gentleman who drove a limo. I'm not sure what their relationship was. But neither of them have been around for some time."

"How long's she lived here?"

"Two years this summer. She bought the house right after Raymond died. She had it remodeled and moved in."

"You don't happen to have a relative's name, do you? Any kind of contact?"

"I only wish I did."

As we left Sams's yard a black car with four men in it drove by on the street. When Elmer pulled out a gun and pointed it at the vehicle, I grabbed his arm before he let any lead fly. It was the same revolver I'd confiscated last night. "Damn it, Snake. What the hell do you think you're doing?"

"I put some bullets in their britches they'd be shitting sand instead of sashaying around like buzzards after a battle."

"You can't shoot strangers because they're driving by on the street."

"I think those are the people who been tailin' me. Let's follow 'em." The black car was at the corner now, making a slow right turn onto Lake Washington Boulevard.

"Forget it. I'm not chasing a carful of midgets. I don't care who they are."

"Dwarfs. They're dwarfs."

"You still believe you were screwing aliens, don't you?" He gave me a dumb look. "You were trying to look down that woman's cleavage, weren't you?"

"Checking for tattoos."

"You still believe it all. The aliens. The breeding program."

"You had any brains you'd be looking at tits too."

"You lied to Kathy."

"I lied to that damned psychologist. And because they got a house for this one, that don't mean she wasn't an alien. They'll do a paper trail to confuse you."

"You heard that woman back there. Sams has been here two years. How do you explain that?"

"I got no way to explain it. Not yet. And hey. She wasn't bad, was she? The lady with the kids. Genevieve. How'd you like her to wax your bat?"

"Give me a break, Elmer."

"Christ was a corporal. She was packed in there like a sack of wet mice."

CHAPTER 22

Elmer fell asleep on my couch so quickly, I didn't have time to offer him refreshments, accommodations, or a straitjacket. In the kitchen I phoned Fitt at the number he'd supplied. He sounded glad to hear from me, said he could be at my place in twenty-five minutes. He wanted to ride to Mercer Island, which would make the round trip somewhere between thirty and fifty miles, depending. I wasn't a pro on the bike, but I'd done almost five thousand miles since January and doubted his ability to stay with me for forty miles. But then, I wasn't after a ride. It was information that I was seeking.

I called Hilda in Oregon and ate a banana before she took me off hold. "Thomas? I've got nothing on the dead girl except a sister's name. Henrietta Samantha Sams. The only sibling I could dig up."

"Same middle name as the phony driver's license too."

"Right. She lives in Chula Vista. I haven't gotten her occupation, but she drives a Mercedes-Benz. A new one. She owns property in Tahoe with the dead girl. And she's got a small plane. Early twenties, is all I know."

"Did she marry well? Where'd she get all the money?"

"I don't know yet. I called her house on a fake phone survey, but there was no answer. Do the police know about her?"

"Hard to tell. They're not sharing if they do."

"If the police don't know about her, she probably hasn't been told her sister is dead."

"I was thinking that too."

Hilda gave me the number and address for Henrietta Sams. "What about IGP Systems?" I said.

"IGP was established in 1970. The brainchild of a man named Judson Bonneville. Ever hear of him?"

"An hour ago I heard about a man named Jud. It might be the same person."

"He's one of the richest men in the world. Born in Canada, now a U.S. citizen. There are only a few pictures of him. None in public circulation. At least none that my library researcher could dig up. He's a privacy freak and once had a photographer's legs broken when he snapped a picture of his daughters. Or so goes the story. Bonneville owns IGP Systems, which is an umbrella corporation that mainly buys and sells companies. At one time they made airplane parts. Remember Cisco Foods? Bonneville's father owned that. When he was twenty, his parents were killed in a plane crash, and Bonneville inherited the whole schmear. So he's more or less grown up being in charge of about half the world. Wouldn't that be a kick?"

"I'd rather be king of America so that I could take the wheels off every motor home in the country. Give them to the homeless."

"You'd be a dictator?"

"A king."

"My folks have a motor home. The chief executive for Cisco, a man named Mauldin, was given carte blanche by the young Bonneville and built the empire into what it is today. IGP's been in control of a number of smaller companies since it was formed in 1970, many of them in the Northwest."

"You have any names?"

"There's a real tangle here. Even *The Wall Street Journal* doesn't know what all he owns. We know IGP runs the film company, Miramont. The word is Bonneville does a lot of hands-on at Miramont—directing, cutting movies, hiring—but other than that, nobody actually knows where he puts his energies. He is known to be a health fanatic and tends to hire fitness freaks, cyclists, runners, swimmers, former ballet dancers, cross-country skiers—you name it. Cisco's got that new line of low-fat health foods. He says he's going to live to be a hundred and twenty. He once did five thousand push-ups. And he owns that racing team in Europe."

"BrelCo. It's a bicycle team."

"That's it. We found an article in the *Journal* from a few years back that claims he's hired a number of people out of the CIA and the National Security Agency, that he likes to surround himself with spooks."

"Spooks and athletes. I've already met both types. Hilda, there's an arm of IGP called Green International. You know about that?"

"It wasn't on the list I saw."

"The man who runs it was introduced to me as Arthur Rakubian. I'd like whatever you can get on Green International and Rakubian. He has a slightly washed-out British accent. *Shed-jyool* and all that."

"Rakubian. Green International. *Shed-jyool*. Okay."

When I'd dressed, filled my water bottles, and stuffed my jersey pockets with granola bars and bananas, I noticed Elmer had fallen asleep with his dirty boots on my sofa. Meaning to wake him and tell him where I was headed, I picked up one of his feet and tugged the boot off, but his eyes didn't open, nor did his engine slow. When I pulled the other boot off, a derringer fell onto the floor, prompting me to search the first boot, which contained a small knife in a built-in sheath. After having stashed the weapons under the sink, I was writing Elmer a note when Fitt showed up in the alley on a foam-green Bianchi, the same frame the BrelCo team rode.

He wore a BrelCo team jersey with the orange shoulders and blue back, as well as BrelCo shorts. When I carried my bike down the porch, across the yard, and up the concrete steps to the alley, I was surprised to see Elmer's Cadillac parked behind the garage where we couldn't see it from the house. There was a motto on the license holder: HORN BROKE—WATCH FOR FINGER. Quintessential Snake.

As we rode up the small hill to Seventeenth Northeast, it

became apparent Ernest Fitt was as strong as he'd claimed, if not stronger. He looked thinner in his cycling togs, and somehow younger.

We pedaled down through the University of Washington campus, dodging students, waited for the lights at Montlake, crossed the cut on the east sidewalk on the bridge, and took side roads past the Museum of History and Industry. When we stopped for a car before entering the Arboretum, the heat off the road hit us like an oven. Fitt's body took on a sweaty sheen that looked almost like a mirror. Marbles of water dribbled off my chin.

Fitt, who could pull as smoothly as any racer I'd ridden with, talked authoritatively about local cycling events, as well as the Tour de France, which had just started in Europe; about the STP, Seattle to Portland, which he said he did every year.

Fitt and I got on well together, perhaps because we were both bike snobs. Fitt's legs were shaved like a racer's, and he had faded abrasion marks from a recent crash. Though we rode easily most of the way, once, when being caught by a pair of riders who apparently didn't know how to trade off, we hiked our speed up to twenty-three or twenty-four and kept it there until they faded back. We did a couple of easy loops of Mercer Island, then returned to Seattle across the floating bridge, where the breeze off the water was from the north, portending fair weather.

Fitt admired the company he worked for, IGP, said he'd been with them almost thirty years, that they were going to be making movies in Seattle, and that he had written scripts, one of which had a shot at being produced. It was about an Iowa plane crash and a hypnotic dog. "The trick is not to look directly into the dog's eyes," he quoted from the script, smiling wryly.

"IGP's a special place to work," Fitt said. "I'll tell you what I probably shouldn't. Don't piss off Rakubian. He does all the assigning and he could make you rich. You get enough hours in, they set up a pension plan for you, match it dollar for dollar. By next January you could be in Majorca with the rest of us."

"Did I piss him off?"

"You weren't exactly kissing butt."

"Is that what he needs?"

"It's hard to tell. He's got all kinds working there."

"But you work for Diesel Works Matters?"

"Yes. We're a subsidiary of ComCon Consumer Electronics. They own the ComCon Software stores."

"And who owns them?"

"IGP."

"So who runs IGP?"

"It's run by a board. And they're tough, let me tell you. Those guys come down to audit the books or take a tour and our knees are knocking. They're capable of firing a whole department in twenty seconds flat. That's the bad side. The good side is they pretty much leave everybody alone. Plus they generally treat us right. For instance after five years with the company you have a guaranteed pension."

"What about Judson Bonneville?"

Fitt was quiet for a moment or two. "I don't see much of the man."

"Does Rakubian?"

"Bonneville likes that spy stuff. He takes Rakubian and some of the others out on his yacht in the Mediterranean. He likes to get all his ex-spies drunk and listen to state secrets. That's about all I know about him, except he's got some of our actresses in Ballard under personal contract."

"You think he might be employing them for reasons other than their acting ability?"

"I'm not going to repeat rumors."

"Like Howard Hughes, huh? I read a book about Hughes once. He claimed he could buy any man."

Fitt seemed startled at my skepticism. "You don't agree?"

"No, I don't."

"I happen to believe Howard Hughes was right. You *can* buy anybody." He'd said it with such conviction I figured he'd either witnessed the process or been bought.

From the floating bridge we dropped down onto Lake Washington Boulevard and caught a cyclist who asked where we were headed. Fitt surprised me by saying we were going up the hill on Madison, for we had not come that way and neither of us had mentioned returning by that route. It was a long hill and was going to hurt after my hard weekend and the two hours we'd just logged. "Up the hill, huh?" said our companion, who seemed amiable enough. "I guess I'll probably be dropping you then. I drop most of my friends on the hills."

Fitt gave me a dyspeptic look, which I returned. Our companion's pronouncement wouldn't have been quite so irritating if he hadn't chuckled.

We started up the hill fast and found our friend hadn't lied. He *was* strong. At a hundred eighty pounds I was the heaviest of the group and thus would have to work the hardest on the hill. Fitt was steady and a good climber, but he had almost no zip, so I rode second, behind Fitt, letting him build a slow lead over me and our new companion, one length, two lengths, until he was thirty or forty feet out. The pace had been steadily increasing. I could hear our companion breathing heavily, could see his front wheel wobbling when I peered down between my pumping legs. I sprinted up to Fitt's wheel, but so did our friend. We were all gasping now. I let the gap grow again, twice as far this time, watching Fitt pull away a second time. I sprinted again, powered up to Fitt, and took the lead for the next few meters. Then Fitt took it. Then I took it. After we were out of sight, we ducked off onto a side road and headed for the University of Washington Arboretum, laughing so hard we could hardly sit on our bikes.

" 'I guess I'm going to drop you guys on the hills,' " Fitt said.

" 'I usually drop my friends on the hills.' "

"You're going to drop somebody, you don't announce it."

"Not like that, anyway."

At home Snake was still conked out on the sofa. Kathy was preparing supper. "Ride with Mr. Fitt, did you?" she said.

"Yep."

"How'd it go?"

"Bitchin'."

CHAPTER 23

"You learn anything?" Kathy asked.

"I'm not sure." I looked into the living room. "Is Elmer living with us now?" Kathy's smile said it all. He would never be living with us; I needed to be tolerant.

By the time I got out of the shower, Snake was snorkeling in his dinner. I joined them and we ate in silence. For dessert Kathy brought out some Goo-Goo Cluster ice cream, a particular weakness of hers—and mine—and while we scooped it into bowls, I said, "Elmer? You know a man named Ernest Fitt?"

"I don't guess I do."

"Works for IGP? Diesel Works Matters, actually."

"The toy company?" said Kathy. "I didn't know they owned a toy company."

Snake said, "Oh, him. He seemed like a decent enough chap. Why are you interested in IGP?"

"Partly a hunch. You followed Meade Barber for them. Also they seem remarkably intent on getting me to work there. I want to know about Meade Barber. All of it."

"Why?"

"JoAnne Barber swears she saw the dead woman with Meade a couple of years ago. And you've been hanging around with Meade, whom you followed two years ago for Green

International, which is owned by IGP. IGP also owns Miramont, which is building a studio in Seattle, and Roberta Capshaw Sams was an actress who did at least one film for Miramont. And Sams was found dead in your bed. I guess I'm naive, but there's got to be some connection in all of that."

"Sams never made no movie for Miramont."

"Forget that. Tell me about Meade."

"Meade. Oh, man. I don't even like to think about it. After I submitted my first couple of reports, they wanted to know about his sex life. Wanted to know what kind of women he preferred."

"You never told us this," said Kathy.

"I just remembered it. My memory hasn't been so hot lately, what with all that's been happening. I told them he preferred his wife, which he clearly did, but they supplied me with several young women, models I guess—all four of them were in the drama department at the U—and they wanted me to basically dangle these babes in front of Barber to see how he reacted. I was to videotape them interacting with him."

"You mean a setup?" said Kathy. "Like in the old days when private eyes were doing divorce cases?"

"Maybe they set him up later, I ain't sure. We had the first girl fake a car breakdown next to where he'd parked at work. I filmed it from a van. He fixed her car—it was something simple like a disconnected battery cable—and she gave him a big hug and then a kiss. You could tell he liked it. She was maybe nineteen. They were very interested in that film. I didn't do any more work on Barber, and I never figured out what they wanted. Usually I had a hunch why they were gathering information on a pigeon, but Barber worked for *them.*"

"So why were you hanging out with him two years later?" I asked.

"I saw him in the soup line, it got me thinking. So I talked to Fred Rosas, who was also working for Green International. Remember Fred Rosas?"

"Sure. He used to work for the prosecutor's office."

"Then he went out on his own and got a PI license, and then IGP hired him. I used to talk to him."

"I thought IGP went crazy, they caught you talking about their cases."

"Think about it. Fred's in New York going back to school to become a teacher. I'm sleeping on a friend's sofa."

"They found out you were talking?" Kathy asked. "Snake, you think this is all connected to IGP, don't you?"

"Maybe. So Fred and I used to talk about what we were doing, and Fred told me he was setting up cameras in motel rooms. That they would use him to make threatening phone calls to various individuals. All kinds of shit. He was at the other end of the tunnel. I would scout out the victims and he would do the heavy work."

"He know anything about Barber?" I asked.

"He knew something, but he wouldn't tell."

"You find any evidence that Barber was a playboy when you were poking around?"

"None."

"But you tested him with women?"

"All knockouts."

"His wife divorced him after he had an affair. An affair I assume started after you sent in your reports and videotapes and such."

"It was after."

"So IGP set him up?"

"That would be my guess. But that's all it is, a guess. And, Thomas. Meade wasn't involved with Roberta Capshaw Sams."

"His wife says different."

"He wasn't. Unless he was part of the fertility program."

"By the way, Elmer. You've been working for IGP for a couple of years, right? What happened to all the money you made?"

"That prick Fred Rosas got me into futures. I lost about a hundred grand."

I let that sink in for a while and said, "So you think Meade Barber's downfall is related somehow to IGP, or Green International?"

Snake grunted affirmatively. "What you really need to think

about is them tattoos. Always in the same place. A little scrawly butterfly."

"I'll think about them."

"And stop worrying yourself over IGP. Now that I think about it, I realize they're not after me. It's the government."

"Why would the government be after you?"

"My record in the service wasn't so hot. Maybe they're trying to get even."

CHAPTER 24

Rakubian's phone call came after dinner. "You work late," I said.

"I don't get out of here usually until ten, often not until midnight," he said. "Black. I understand you've made plans for this week, but an important situation's come up in the last half hour. You could do us an enormous favor by agreeing to do surveillance on an attorney in Bellingham. Three days. Fifteen thousand."

"Starting when?"

"Tonight."

I looked across the room at Elmer. "I hate to keep turning you down, Mr. Rakubian, but I can't do it tonight."

After a long silence he said, "If that's how you feel," and hung up. Was he teasing with these offers of increased pay and urgency, or was he actually desperate for another operative?

When I'd related the call, Kathy looked at Snake. "Fifteen thousand dollars? Is that business as usual for these people?"

"I've made that," he said.

When we decided to walk to Elmer's apartment, he griped about every aspect of the excursion: that we were suffering the heat on foot and not luxuriating in the air-conditioning in his

Caddy, that we were out in the open and might be targeted by snipers, that the college kids on the street were too damn cheerful, that I'd confiscated his weapons. "Christ on a crutch, I feel naked without them guns."

"What fun for you," said Kathy.

"You won't be makin' jokes when them government dwarfs draw down on us. They're prob'ly the same bunch killed JFK."

At his apartment he topped off a paper sack with fresh clothing and then seemed to be looking for another item, got a shifty look in his eyes, and walked abruptly out the door. On the way home, because Snake claimed he needed beer for his headaches, we detoured to the supermarket at Fiftieth and Brooklyn.

It being summertime, except for the main drags, traffic was sparse in the U District. Sidewalks continued to let off heat from the day, and one corner was saturated with the tantalizing suggestion of spilled ice cream. The Safeway store bristled with summer-school students, hairy-legged men in shorts, and three wisecracking, big-thighed girls selling cookies for their soccer team at the front door.

We'd separated, and I was in the cereal aisle when Kathy careened around the corner in a panic. "Thomas! You have to help. Quick!"

She pulled me to the area behind the checkout stands where the food aisles began, to where a space had cleared around a man and a woman, the man facing us, the woman facing him, expressionless store patrons forming a makeshift ring of the uninvolved. It was clear from the onlookers' reluctance to look away that a hideous spectacle was unfolding.

He was a large man, maybe forty-five, in tight, grease-stained jeans, motorcycle boots, and a sleeveless vest cut from an old army shirt, SANCHEZ written across the name tag. She was in her early twenties, clad in shorts, a halter-top and lace-less deck shoes, no socks. She was so deeply tanned, if she hadn't had long, dishwater blond hair and hazel eyes, you might have thought she hailed from some port in the South Seas. For a moment she turned around and scanned the crowd, looking seemingly neither for help nor for witnesses, simply looking. She was an attractive woman, yet there was a slightly off-kilter manner to the glance she gave us. I'd once seen a dog hit by a car give that same uninformed and out-of-place look of unconcern only a few moments before he died. For a heartbeat or two she caught my eye and held it. I saw a sliver of fear.

He carried himself with an arrogance as bold as the stink of a large carnivore. Fostered by his booming voice, a thatch of greasy black hair, and the heavy stubble on his face, he reminded me of the cartoon character Bluto. His arms were as big as most men's legs. In the background a clerk stumbled toward the store office. Elmer showed up on the other side of the couple and met my eyes, arms laden with a number of six-packs of Budweiser headache medication.

"He hit her twice already," Kathy said.

We were close enough and the store was quiet enough that Sanchez heard Kathy and glanced over the woman's head at her, his angry black eyes garnished with a flat look that might have been madness. I had a feeling he was on drugs. A man that huge on drugs would be able to lift the store at one corner. Nor could I help noticing the karate calluses on his knuckles. Next to a beltful of grenades, it was the last detail I wanted to see.

When he raised his enormous left arm and slapped the woman across the face, everybody in the store heard the blow. He slapped her again. Two women on the far side of the couple quickly abandoned their grocery carts, purses too, and fled the store. Because the crowd around Elmer had melted away, it seemed as if he had crept forward, though he hadn't moved an inch. I hoped he wasn't going to step in. He could have fit into one of Sanchez's pant legs.

A tall male clerk in heavy black-rimmed glasses stepped toward the assailant, mumbling about taking it easy and then saying, "Hey, buddy. Hey, buddy," when he received a hard, open-handed pop to his chest that propelled him ten feet backward. There were at least twenty able-bodied men in the store, and I began to wonder if a cluster of us might not be able to jump Sanchez, or at least to pose enough of a threat to make him stop. Then again, we could turn this into a bad Bruce Lee movie, Sanchez of course playing the part of Lee.

The power in Sanchez's casual push had convinced the clerk to back off. A couple with a baby came in from the parking lot, saw what was happening, and stepped back out again.

The blonde said, "You chipped my tooth! What do you think you're doing, you cretin?"

He hit her again and yet again, her head rolling to either side.

"Thomas. Do something," Kathy whispered.

"The police are on their way," I said loudly.

"That wasn't what I had in mind. He's hurting her."

Stepping forward, I tried to think of words that might convince him to cease and desist without sidetracking all that bulk and dojo training and callused madness toward me. It was hard to think.

Before I could speak, though, he knocked her to the floor on her back. I looked around at the onlookers one more time, but clearly nobody, not even Snake was feebleminded enough to intervene. At the last minute Kathy said, "He's too big."

"No foolin'," I said over my shoulder.

It wasn't until I was beside the blonde and helping her to her feet that he noticed me. What he seemed to notice the most was my hands touching her. Moving far to his right so that she would automatically rotate out of his line of sight, I said, "Hey, pal. You don't have to do this."

As if it were the barrel of a gun, he pointed an index finger with a blackened nail at me and said, "Stay out of my shit."

"I don't think I can do that." The muscles in his arms bunched up, veins bulging as his hands corded into fists.

"You want to die?"

"You can't do this."

"Who's gonna stop me? You?"

"It's not civilized."

"How 'bout if I break all your teeth off? That civilized?" I was starting to feel like a Cub Scout at a gang rape. When he took a step toward me, it was easy to tell he was almost a head taller than my six feet one inch.

"Lane. Leave him alone." Battered as she was, her voice thin and bubbling with blood, the blonde was the only bystander with the pluck to stand up for me.

"Shaddup!"

"There's a domestic-abuse law in this state," I said lamely. "The police will have to make an arrest when they get here."

"The police better bring their own body bags."

"He's an ex-cop," Kathy blurted.

It was obvious to her she'd made a mistake before the words were even out of her mouth, for when he looked at Kathy, his black eyes took on the glow of a neon implosion. His teeth looked like pearl onions, his tongue like shoe leather. "A pig? You kiddin' me? I love it."

Taking two swift steps forward, he thrust his right arm at my chest. I managed to scoot backward, but the box of cereal I'd been holding in front of me exploded with the impact of his blow. His movements had been crude, bordering on awkward, an affectation I thought he might have adopted to throw me off guard. Nuggets of Cap'n Crunch popped under his boots and dropped out of my hair.

He was moving again as I backed into an end display of cans, grasping one in time to hit him over the eye with it while he did a sweep kick that knocked the wind out of me and drove me through the corner of the display and into a heap on the floor. I'd lost track of Kathy, the suntanned blonde, the spectators. I'd lost track of north and south, floor and ceiling, my own hands.

Clearly intending to snap my lower leg with his boot, he pounced into the still-rolling cans, but as he stepped forward, one of the cans rolled under him and he danced on it for a moment. From my prone position I kicked him in the knee as he danced, then like a mechanic on a creeper, propelled myself backward on the rolling cans until I was out of range of his boots.

"Fuck!" he said, favoring his ankle and knee both. A small cut had opened on his brow where I'd struck him with the creamed corn, a very small cut.

Shuffling toward me amid the cans, he punched at my face

with his right arm, then his left. I was standing now and ducked, felt the wind of his fists, found myself flying across the floor, the victim of another sweep kick I hadn't seen him initiate. I flew into a display of toilet paper, but did not go down. It was several moments before I could force any air into my lungs, and when I did, it felt as if my back was broken and I was inhaling bits of broken glass.

"Hey, dick breath!"

Sanchez glanced back over his shoulder at Elmer. I used the breather to look around. The police hadn't arrived, and the onlookers appeared even less inclined to interfere than they had earlier. A pair of young men in shorts and thongs who might have been football players avoided my gaze. The affair reminded me of fistfights after school where three or four self-appointed referees backed up the crowd, saying, "Let 'em fight, let 'em fight," though nobody here was saying anything but, "Stop it. Somebody stop it," this, a mantra from three women on the edge of the group. They'd been at the school fights too.

As hard as I could, I pitched a can of corn at Sanchez's head, watching it bounce off the back of his skull. By the time I wound up to throw a second can, he'd turned around and eluded it with a snap of his head. Snake was behind Sanchez on the floor, on his back, immobile. I couldn't tell if he was dead or alive. I hadn't seen either of them move.

Sanchez's first jump kick caught me square in the chest and blasted me down the aisle as if I'd been dragged off the sidewalk in the door handle of a speeding automobile. Trying to make my lungs work, I got to my knees, then my feet. Near as I could tell, both lungs had collapsed, and if I was breathing, I wasn't aware of it.

Before Sanchez could kick me again, Snake said, "Next time you see your mother, tell her to lower her price. She's not worth the two bucks."

When Sanchez turned back to Snake, who was still on the floor, a small black object skittered along the floor from Snake to me, skating past Sanchez's feet. I stopped it with my shoe.

Sanchez was speaking in his deep, rumbly voice, but none of the words made sense to me. I picked up the object.

I caught him in the left buttock with the prongs of the Powermax Double Shocker. His body convulsed and he dropped to his knees. Snake got up, stomped his feet, cackled like a witch in a bad high school play. A victory dance.

Sanchez had gone down hard, hitting the floor so heavily it shook. He muttered a few syllables that sounded like, "Praise God," though that couldn't have been what he'd said. He huffed and hunched over and rolled onto his side; his face contorted and his eyes went blank. I could see now through the thick black hair of Sanchez's scalp where it was bleeding from the second can I'd thrown.

"Do him again," said Snake. "Do him again!"

In frighteningly short order Sanchez climbed to his hands and knees, blinking the shock out of his eyes. I reached down, pushed the Powermax Double Shocker against his shoulder and triggered it. He spasmed onto his face, moaning, one arm twitching. Again the floor shook.

"Do him!" yelled Snake. "Charge it up and do him." I did.

"For Christ's sake," somebody said. I felt a hand on my shoulder. "Knock it off." Before I knew what was happening, I'd shocked him too, the brave, bespectacled checkout clerk who'd tried to stop the fracas earlier. Lying on the floor, he wasn't nearly so animated as Sanchez had been the first two times I'd dropped him, though the clerk hadn't wet his trousers the way Sanchez had.

"Thomas," said Kathy, stepping out of the crowd. "Are you all right? I thought he was going to kill you."

"Uh, he might have been working up to that. Where's the blonde?"

"She left even before you went into the toilet paper."

A cop and her partner showed up a few moments later. "What's the story?" the first one said, glancing at the two fallen men and the general disarray.

Snake gave an abbreviated version and said, "Sweetheart, you better wrap those bracelets around that sumbitch before he comes to, 'less you want him stomping around here like a rhino in a chicken coop."

They handcuffed Sanchez facedown on the floor, and assisted by several now-eager and suddenly voluble bystanders, we explained fully what had taken place. When he was himself again, the store clerk confirmed our story and mercifully didn't seem to hold a grudge against me for zapping him, though I noticed he was maintaining a cautious distance.

Rivulets of blood dripped down my face into my mouth. It tasted familiar and somehow reassuring. My chest felt as if it'd been collapsed and reinflated with air from a dusty old basement.

"You okay?" Kathy asked, dabbing at my eyebrow with a piece of twin quilted toilet tissue she'd commandeered from the topsy-turvy display.

"Fit as a fiddle. How about you, Elmer?"

"I been throwed by broncs was tougher than this idiot."

"You know, Thomas," Kathy said, "I recognized her from somewhere. I think she works downtown. I *know* I've seen her."

Though he claimed to be unhurt, Elmer was holding a handful of teeth, a curiosity that distressed me until I realized it was a bridge he'd taken out before the brawl began. A woman bystander had handed it back to him wrapped in his own handkerchief. While Kathy and I spoke to the cops, Elmer was trying to get her phone number.

Sanchez didn't say a word, not even when he was finally lifted off the floor by a sextet of officers and fitted horizontally into the back of an SPD car.

Later as we were walking back to our bungalow with the groceries, Elmer said, "None of that shit would have happened if you'd let me keep my ordnance."

"Where did you pick up the shocker?" Kathy asked. "They sell those with the beer? Or over with the flashlights?"

"It was in my closet. You might want to start carrying that little baby around with you, Thomas. You seem to have a knack with it."

"Thomas has always been good with a shocker," Kathy said,

a playful glint in her eye. She seemed glad to see me, as if I'd been away on a trip and we were meeting at the airport.

"You know who that sorry son of a motherless whore was, don't you?" Elmer asked.

"How could we? He wasn't talking and he didn't have ID," I said.

"He was hired by the government. I'll bet every cent I got. I'll bet the stains in my shorts. He's some sort of freelance sonofabitch they hire out for dirty work. I was *supposed* to see him with that woman. It was a setup to get me to fight."

"Then why didn't you jump right in? Why'd you wait until I was committed?"

"I thought we'd team up on him. You know. The old one-two punch. It worked, didn't it?"

"Yes. And thanks. You might have saved my life."

"If I did, that makes twice. Now you owe me big time."

"Of course if you'd stepped in first, I could have come later and saved your life. Then you'd owe me."

"But that's not what happened, is it? And you know what? It was a setup. You can't deny that. It was the government."

"Do-do do-do . . . ," Kathy and I sang in unison.

"Okay. Don't believe me. Sure. Shit. Sooner than you think, you'll be in this web as deep as I am. All wrapped up. You wait. You'll see. This ain't no *Twilight Zone* episode."

When we got home, Elmer parked in front of the television, stacked his boots on our coffee table, and began swilling headache medication.

"Elmer," I said, addressing him as if he were sane, "why would the government send a man to beat up a woman in our local Safeway? I can imagine why they might bug our phones or look into our financial transactions or check out our tax returns. But why this? Where's the gain?"

Without looking away from the television, Elmer slowly shook his head. I'd seen him do this before. We'd mocked his theories and we'd mocked him, and our reward would be a good long dose of the silent treatment.

Later when Kathy was in the shower and I was sitting shirtless in the kitchen trying to figure out if I had any broken bones, Snake emerged from the living room and whispered conspiratorially, "Thomas. You see the blonde's boobies?"

"Uh, gee. I must have missed those. Why? You think she's tattooed?"

"I'm not sure. But I would have liked to have seen her boobies anyway."

Grinning, I glanced at the bathroom door. "Me too."

Elmer guffawed and popped the tab on another beer.

CHAPTER 25

Morning found Elmer asleep on the living-room couch, besieged by a squadron of white beer cans, his open shirt exposing a bruise the shape and color of an eggplant. Aside from my own bumps and a general queasiness from swimming in an ocean of nightmares during the night, I felt nearly human again. Kathy had an early appointment before having to be in court and was already gone before I got up.

After he'd eaten and showered, I drove Elmer to a nearby clinic and waited while they X-rayed him. "How was it?" I asked when he came out

"I told you there wasn't nothin' broke," he said irritably. "I been thrown by bulls, broncs, and bitches enough times, I know when somethin's broke."

We were in my Ford, Snake's eyes bloodshot from beer, pique, lack of sleep, and the beating. "Where to?" I said.

"Where *you* goin'?" he asked suspiciously.

"I've got some calls to make from the office. Then I thought I'd go look up Barber."

"Meade, huh? I've been thinkin' about Meade. He might be the individual people seen sniffing around my apartment that night."

"But that man was bearded."

"So was Meade. Last time I saw him."

"He wasn't when I saw him."

"When was that?"

"A couple of days ago. Why didn't you tell me this when I brought it up earlier?"

"I had other business on my mind."

"What else did you forget to tell us?"

But Elmer was in a world of his own now, staring out the car window.

When we arrived at my office in the Mutual Life Building, he found an empty room and commandeered the sofa. I picked up a slip of paper that had fallen out of his pocket and found a phone number and a name: Muriel, the woman who'd held his false teeth during last night's excitement.

There was a message on my machine to call Ralph Crum at the police department. Ralph had already given me Roberta Capshaw Sams, so I wondered what other goodies he was parceling out. "Thomas? You had a beef with some guy last night at the Safeway on Fiftieth and Brooklyn?"

"What about it?"

"Know who he is?"

"A steroid salesman?"

"Name is Lane Thorne. Owns a gun shop in Santa Clara. The authorities down there tell us ATF has been investigating him for gun running. Rumor has it he's been involved in a local shooting near Santa Clara. No charges. Not yet. The boys at the jail say he had karate calluses on his knuckles the size of golf balls."

"I noticed that myself."

"You're lucky to be alive."

"I noticed that too."

"The police in Santa Clara suspect he's been involved in the disappearance of at least one local businessman. There's also some feeling he might be a part-time hit man. Working another part of the country. Maybe the Southeast."

"What was he doing up here?"

"You tell me. You're the one who put him in jail. He gave his

address as the Four Seasons Hotel. Don't bother to call over
there. He's checked out."

"He's *out*? You let him out?"

"About an hour ago."

"He's out?"

"Don't get all cranked up."

"I'm not all cranked up. Why the hell did you let him out? Do
I sound cranked up?"

"As a matter of fact you do. I called to warn you, was all. His
attorney flew up from California in the middle of the night.
Jesus, Thomas. According to the arrest report, you and him
about tore that store right out of the Yellow Pages."

"Mostly him. The Four Seasons is pretty swanky. He wasn't
dressed swanky. In fact he wasn't dressed like a man who had a
lawyer who would fly fifteen hundred miles to arrange bail."

"I wouldn't know. I only wanted to warn you this wasn't
some college kid on a bender."

"So who was the woman?"

"Hasn't shown up yet."

"He wouldn't say?"

"You hardly expect a critter like him to volunteer the names
of witnesses and victims. His attorney said Thorne was up here
on business, that he'd behaved badly and knew it, and that he'd
show up for trial. They let him out on a five-thousand-dollar
bond. My guess is he's still nearby."

"Probably right outside my office with a meat cleaver.
Thanks, Ralph."

"Watch yourself."

"I'm planning on it."

The thought of Thorne running around loose made me
jumpy, even though, when I intellectualized it, it didn't seem
likely he would bother to look me up. But then, when you intellectualized it, he shouldn't have been slapping a woman around
in Safeway either. For all I knew, he was standing outside my
office with an ice pick, a body bag, and a rose to slip between my
clenched teeth when he was through.

I dialed Hilda's number in Oregon and she answered on the

first ring. "Thomas. I've got more on Henrietta Samantha Sams, the sister. She's working on a degree in dance from UCLA. She owns her house, plus three rentals. And by *owns*, I mean no banks involved whatsoever. She paid off all her credit cards three years ago and doesn't have a cent of debt. And get this. No job. At least no job that's registered with the state or the federal government. She does have a Social Security number, but the last time an employer listed her was three years ago. Inherited money? Gambling wins? I can't tell you. Not yet."

"What about IGP Systems?"

"That's been a little stickier. I have a woman in San Francisco working on it. She should have some information before the day's over."

"And Art Rakubian?"

"There's a man in D.C. who handles spook stuff for me. He's been around D.C. and the agency since it was called the OSS; knows all the skeletons by name. I'm warning you, though. If Rakubian was in MI-six, we'll probably come up empty."

"Thanks, Hilda."

"Talk to you later, hon."

"Thomas. We need guns." Snake stepped inside and closed the door to my office.

"What makes you say that?"

"That asshole from last night is gonna come after us, and I for one don't wanna be shoving dental floss up my ass with a stick trying to clean my teeth."

"Snake," I said. "If he was a wife beater, he might come after us. If he was working for the government like you said, I doubt we'll see him again."

"Just the same, I'd like some guns."

"I don't think so," I said, picking up my keys.

"Who made you boss of the world?"

"Go get your stinking guns, then. I've got more important things to do."

"Where are you going?" Snake trailed me through the office, studiously ignoring Beulah, who, as we passed her island, surreptitiously slid a doughnut behind her computer terminal.

"I'm going to find Meade Barber," I said.

"I think I know where he is. I'll navigate. You drive."

When we got my car out of the lot behind Mitchelli Trattoria, I turned on the air-conditioning and dutifully followed Elmer's instructions, cruising up First Avenue and around the block under the Alaskan Way Viaduct, which we all knew was going to come down when the big quake finally hit. After ten minutes of cruising among the pigeons and the homeless, I said, "Snake. You've been taking me around the block."

"And I'll keep it up until you drive to my office."

It took fifteen minutes, and by the time we were back in the car, he'd strapped on two shoulder holsters, each housing a long-barreled .44 Magnum revolver, had jammed a two-shot derringer under his huge World Championship Bull Riding belt buckle, and dropped a .38 automatic into a rig in his left boot. He'd stuffed enough boxes of extra ammunition into his pockets that his jacket looked like a plastic bag with an anchor in it.

On our second try at locating Barber, we weren't any more in concert than on the first, Snake directing me up First Avenue past the peep shows and the art museum to the vicinity of the Pike Place Market. Noontime traffic was thick and pushy, yet it gave us the excuse to dawdle, to idle at intersections, to scope out pedestrians, and for a while I entertained the notion that Snake and I were searching for the same person. "I thought he got his mail at the Endless Light Mission up the street from the office."

"Shhh. Shhh!"

"Being quiet isn't going to help you check out skirts, Elmer. You haven't looked at a man in ten minutes."

"Shhh! Kathy said she saw that gal from last night somewhere around here."

"We were looking for Barber!"

"*You* were looking for Barber!"

"We're trying to get you out from under a murder rap," I said.

"Trust me."

"Trust you? You think a carful of dwarfs has beamed down from *The Enterprise*. Even *you* wouldn't trust you. And I let you have those guns the way I'd let a baby have a pacifier. First chance I get, I'm going to break off all the firing pins." He gave me a black look and scrunched down in his seat, wedging his back against the door. I noticed the awkward position didn't keep him from peering over the sill at women.

"I don't have to follow your ass all over town, Thomas. I don't have to be here."

"I know," I said in a softer tone. "Why are you?"

"Because they're after you too. And I'm the only one can stop 'em."

"Who's after me?"

"The government. Them aliens. Probably both."

"Okay. Fine. You want to look for the blonde, you do it on foot." I pulled over to the curb. "Going around in circles is making me carsick."

Reluctantly Elmer sat up and directed me to Second Avenue, and then to the Millionair Club at the corner of Second and Lenora. It was a concrete block building with about a dozen men leaning against the wall or standing on the corner waiting for employers in automobiles to come by with work. About the only project my neighbor Horace ever took on that I approved of was driving down here a couple of times a year to pick up men for the heavy work in his yard, men he let drink out of his garden hose.

We parked on Second and walked up the sidewalk under the hopeful eyes of half a dozen of the unemployed.

Barber was inside talking to a scruffy man who had a black eye and wore a Navy pea coat. I heard the name Arliss.

CHAPTER 26

"**S**nake," said Meade Barber, his look of surprise quickly melting into a broad smile. "You got out." He'd been hugging Snake around the shoulders, but he abandoned that to pump my hand. "Brilliant. Absolutely brilliant, Mr. Black. Brilliant."

"He's still charged with murder," I said, finding myself oddly willing to accept raves for an accomplishment I'd had nothing to do with. "Not much has changed."

He looked at Snake again, beaming, throwing his arm around Snake's shoulders. "But still."

We walked back to my car on Second, where Snake leaned against the front fender in the sun and Barber and I stood on the sidewalk and let the heat work on us. "We need to ask you some real serious questions," Elmer said.

"Fire away. You know I'm here for you, man." Barber put down his packsack and smoothed his white hair with one hand.

"We heard," Snake said, "that there was a man outside my apartment building the night of the murder. Heard he looked something like you." We'd actually heard he was a large, hulking man, but that description came from Magdanz, who'd already been wrong about a number of particulars. Meade, however, did roughly fit the man Kathy and I had seen.

"You did?"

"Yes."

"Well, I was there. I guess it was me."

"Why didn't you tell us before?"

Barber turned to me, his clear eyes trustful and a bit vacant. Sleeping under bridges and getting beat up on street corners tended to sap the intelligence from most men. "You never asked."

Snake glanced at me. "What'd you see?"

"I didn't see anything. I needed a touch," he said sheepishly. "A couple bucks to tide me. I waited awhile and then you showed up with a woman. I guess it was that poor Fleegle woman who died. I didn't want to disturb you when you already had company, so I just hung around, but then Mr. Black and some other woman showed up."

"Did you see anyone else enter the apartment during that time?"

"No, but I might have fallen asleep for a while."

"You had a beard that night?" I said.

"I guess. I don't remember when I shaved it off exactly. It's hard to get work, you look scruffy. I got my hair cut at the college too. How is it?"

"Quite dashing," said Snake.

"Elmer," I said. "You mind if I talk to Meade alone?"

Adopting a wounded look, Elmer walked back toward the Millionair Club, shouting over his shoulder, "Honk when you think I'm worth associating with." Seconds later he was conversing with three men on the corner as if he'd known them all his life.

Barber looked at me expectantly. "Did you know Elmer met your wife?" I said.

"Did he? He was probably trying to talk her into taking me back."

"Did he ever discuss her with you?"

"I didn't even know he knew her."

"I understand you had a steady job a few years ago."

"Yeah. Yeah." Barber nodded. The sun reflected off the pale, thin-looking skin of his face and neck. His eyelashes were long and dark, almost as if they belonged on a woman, and he smelled of talcum powder. He was not only clean-shaven and well groomed, he was impeccable. "It's kind of a long story if you want to hear it." I nodded. "My first marriage was to my high school sweetheart, Angie. After a year and a half she ran off with my best friend. Clint. The last I heard, they were in Hawaii. A few years later I met JoAnne at her church. A friend took me there. I was working at Boeings and she was working for her father. I asked her out.

"She was almost twenty years younger than me and seemed troubled. It wasn't until later I found out her family had money. The whole family's always been secretive about the money. Never wanted anyone to know. On top of that she's the only one of her three sisters who *never* got along with their father.

"Anyhow a couple years after we got married, her father offered me a job at IGP at about twice what I had been making at Boeings. JoAnne said she wanted me not to take it, but I could tell she actually had mixed feelings. She claimed it was her father's way of controlling us. She was always a little troubled where he was concerned. It was a very complex relationship."

"So you went to work for him over her objections?"

"At a couple of different enterprises. Life was hunky-dory for a few years. Then the man I was working with in the accounting department told me he had been embezzling money to pay for a woman he'd been running around with. She'd been heavily in debt from a bad marriage and he was helping her pay it off. You want to know the truth, I think she was using him. He begged me not to turn him in. After a while he talked me into helping him cover it up. It was only supposed to be until his father, who had cancer, died, because his father had lots of property and Peter would be able to liquidate that and pay it all back. In theory nobody would know the difference.

"I didn't know what to do. I couldn't let a friend go to prison for a silly mistake, so I overlooked a couple of items and signed a few papers, and before I could blink, the old man was accusing me of embezzlement."

"Who's the old man? JoAnne's father?"

"Right. Judson Bonneville."

"Judson Bonneville? As in *the* Judson Bonneville?"

"Yeah. He was a hell of a nice guy. I never could figure out why he and JoAnne didn't get along. I had the feeling her sisters were the root cause of it. They both live up in Montreal and there's always been bad blood there."

"Your ex-father-in-law's one of the richest men in the country."

"Yeah. Anyway, I could hardly blame him for being ticked off, since I *had* helped Peter. It turned out Peter's dad's cancer went into remission. Peter took off. People tell me Peter left me holding the bag, but that's not the way it happened. How did he know Judson would take it out on me? After all, I was his son-in-law."

"All the same, Peter must have known you were in trouble."

"He couldn't have."

"What happened?"

"JoAnne had a trust her mother left her, but she wasn't allowed to dip into it until she was thirty-five. When she saw I was headed for a courtroom, she talked the trustees into breaking the trust. We took the principal and paid back all the money Peter had taken."

"How much are we talking about?"

"A little over three million. It pretty much emptied her trust."

"How did Peter's girlfriend ever run up debts of three million dollars?"

"I don't know. I never asked."

"Let me get this straight. Your wife's father was going to send you to prison because you helped this fellow named Peter cover up an embezzlement? Did her father know you were not the embezzler?"

"I told him."

"And he let his daughter pay this money out of her trust?"

"Judson was . . . Judson is always very concerned with the bottom line. It didn't matter if it was his daughter or whoever."

It was hard to believe the daughter of one of the wealthiest men in the country was living in a little house in West Seattle, with meager furnishings, a rattletrap station wagon, bikes with flat tires, multiple jobs.

"Was JoAnne upset about losing the trust?"

"Not as much as you would have thought."

"But she was upset?"

"I guess you would have to say that. Yes. I do know having to break her trust like that did serious damage to the relationship with her father. It wasn't long after that she stopped all contact with him."

"So she's not talking to her father?"

"Not for a couple of years."

"But you were still working for him?"

"That went out the window. After JoAnne paid him back, I got a job at Seattle Maintaining for about a quarter of what I'd been making. But we had savings and the place at the lake. Quite a bit in stocks. We were doing all right. It was only her trust was gone."

"What happened to the place at the lake and the savings?"

"We lost it. Piece by piece. I got involved in a couple of bad investments."

"And who were you working for when this embezzlement deal went down?"

"NordCo Brothers Trucking. I don't think there ever were any brothers, but that's what they called it. You see their trucks all over the freeways. For six months or so I worked at a cookie factory down in Kent. Blister Cakes. Know them?"

"There was a time when I lived on Blister Cakes. Bonneville owns all those companies?"

"Yes, sir."

"So what's the situation between JoAnne and her father today?"

"Far as I know, they still don't talk."

"She's living like a redheaded orphan, working seven days a week, taking care of two kids, and her father won't help out?"

"She works seven days a week?"

"Don't tell me you didn't know."

"I didn't. I actually didn't. But I don't feel sorry for her. All she has to do is swallow her pride and go to Judson and apologize. JoAnne's got this mistaken notion her father tries to buy people. That he runs people's lives. But he did so many wonderful things for us when we were married. Sent us to the Virgin Islands. Gave us a houseful of furniture."

"He's such a good person, why are you on the street?" Barber gave me a hurt look. A couple of his cohorts, thinking I was handing out work, had made their way up the sidewalk and were waiting deferentially thirty feet away. "I crossed the line with Judson. I cost him money."

"But it was paid back."

"Well, yes."

"What's going on that JoAnne's sisters don't like the old man?"

"The sisters in Montreal have both reached thirty-five and stepped into their mother's trust. So they don't need him, I suppose."

"So after you were involved in that embezzlement at NordCo, you got a job on your own? At a place the old man wasn't controlling?"

A grimace corkscrewed the lines around his eyes. "Not exactly."

"You said you didn't work for him after the embezzlement."

"You won't tell JoAnne, will you? I couldn't get a job. Then somebody from Judson's office called one day and casually suggested I try Seattle Maintaining. I didn't know much about office-cleaning companies, but I gave it a try. I'd been there about three weeks when I learned Judson owned it. What was I supposed to do? Quit? Tell you what I didn't do. I didn't tell JoAnne. That wasn't so wrong, was it?"

"I don't know."

"I was having a little trouble adjusting to the business, so Judson had a long talk with me one day and decided to give me some on-the-job management training. Brought in a special tutor. A woman named Susan Lee."

"And?"

"It didn't matter. Tutoring or not, whatever I touched turned to shit."

"And then your wife caught you with Lee?"

"How did you know?"

"I'm guessing at some of this."

"She followed us to the motel. I was sick about it. Heck, I was a rotten husband."

"But you didn't get divorced at that time?"

"We patched it up. JoAnne was plenty pissed, but she put all that aside and gave me another chance. I have to hand her that. She's a better woman than I ever deserved. First the embezzlement, then the other woman, and then I got let go from Seattle Maintaining."

"Did it occur to you that Judson was firing you from these jobs?"

"How so?"

"He owned the companies. If you got fired from them, he was ultimately responsible."

"No. I blew it myself. Judson did all he could. He used to call me in and ask me how it was going. Every time he talked to me, he was skipping out on a meeting or an important phone call. I'm not going to blame my problems on anybody else."

"You know how to get in touch with Bonneville?"

"At one time he lived right up the street by the Market. Had the top two floors of a condominium. His security people were living on the floor below. I guess he's still there. I don't know. Mr. Black? I have a question."

"What's that?"

"JoJo say much about me?"

"JoJo?"

"My wife. You did talk to her? She mention me at all? Maybe say she'd like to get back together with me or something?"

"Uh, if she did, I don't recall."

"I see."

"What's this?" I said, picking up his left hand. Using blue ink, he had sketched what appeared to be a lopsided butterfly on the web between his thumb and index finger.

"Oh, that. I was doodling."

"Why that particular doodle?"

"I saw it somewhere."

I brought out the photo of Roberta Capshaw Sams. "You know this woman?"

"I don't believe so. Oh, wait. That might be the woman I saw with Elmer going into his apartment. Is this the woman who died?"

"Your wife says she's the woman you were at the motel with."

"Two years ago? Susan Lee?"

"That's what she says."

"Then you did talk about me."

"A little."

"I don't think she ever saw Susan up close. And anyway that's not Susan."

"You know where Susan Lee is now?"

"Detroit. Or was it Milwaukee? Needless to say we haven't been in touch."

"And she didn't look like this?"

"Her hair maybe. But that was all."

"Did you know the dead woman in Snake's apartment had a tattoo looked a lot like that drawing on your hand?"

"No. How would I know that? I remember where I saw it now. Elmer showed it to me. Said it had something to do with UFOs. Say, are you going to be able to get him off?"

CHAPTER 27

We parked the Ford near the Public Market on First Avenue near Pike. Except for having to feed quarters into a meter, it was not a bad spot for watching rush-hour motorists and pedestrians, bus passengers, reckless bicycling messengers, cabdrivers, the mentally ill, and harried shoppers. I'd asked Elmer some pointed questions about Roberta Capshaw Sams and also about Meade Barber, but what he gave me were evasions, denials, and half-truths.

When he was still married, Meade had had an affair with a woman he called Susan Lee, who JoAnne Barber insisted was Roberta Capshaw Sams, alias Catherine Samantha McFleegle, deceased, whom Elmer had been dating, one or more times—it didn't matter—while under the impression she was a virgin involved in an intergalactic breeding program, one of hundreds of similar virgins. Discount Elmer's theories for a moment, what you had left was Meade Barber claiming Susan Lee didn't look like the photo on the McFleegle driver's license, that Susan Lee and Sams were two different people, his wife claiming otherwise.

The first time I'd spoken to Barber at Elmer's apartment, he'd failed to mention that he was right outside the apartment the night of the murder. It seemed like an extraordinary oversight. Added to that was the fact that he'd been doodling on his hand and come up with the design Elmer claimed had been tattooed on Sams's breast. But then, he had innocuous explanations for both matters.

As we sat in the Ford, windows rolled low, traffic noise and pedestrians whirling about us, I told Elmer what Barber had told me. I explained my doubts too. Elmer said he believed Barber because Barber was too decent a man to lie.

"There are damn few men too good to lie."

"I know that, Thomas. That's what makes Meade so rare, especially for someone in his situation, who has every right to be bitter and cynical."

When I mentioned the lies that must have surrounded his adultery, lies he'd more or less admitted, Elmer said, "Hell, you can't hold that against a guy. How do you think he's going to get action on the side without having to lie to his wife? I swear, Thomas me boy, sometimes I think you just fell off the turnip cart. Technically he lied, but only if you want to be a real stickler about it."

"That's what I said."

Confidence in Barber's nature aside, Elmer came up with another argument for Susan Lee not being the dead woman. Lee, who allegedly had had the affair with Barber over two years ago, had been hired by old man Bonneville to tutor Barber in executive behavior and duties. Sams had died at twenty-two. If she and Lee were the same woman, as JoAnne Barber argued, she would have been barely twenty when tutoring Barber. Could a twenty-year-old successfully mimic an experienced business consultant? Probably not.

"Okay. I got it figured out," Elmer said. "It's been staring me in the face. The *government* conned me into believing I was banging babes from space."

"To what purpose?"

"To drive me crazy. I got reason to believe I was being drugged too."

"And why would they want you any crazier than you already are?"

"To keep people from listening to me."

"Listening about what?"

"*That,* I don't know."

"So where does IGP Systems fit in?"

"I don't know. Maybe they don't."

"Did you ever draw that butterfly tattoo for Barber?"

"I mighta. I wanted people to know what it looked like in case I disappeared."

"*Disappeared?*"

"You know . . . in case they took me with them."

"To the big sperm bank in the sky?"

"Listen, Thomas. If the feds are involved, that tells me Judson Bonneville is working with the government on a secret project. A project I was getting close to."

"And he's also Howard Hughes in disguise, right?"

"In my travels I got too close to it, this secret project. So they began trying to figure out how to shake me loose."

"Are you telling me they murdered an innocent woman in order to frame you?"

"Why not? And what makes you think she was innocent?"

"So you're saying she wasn't from space?"

"Hell, no. She was. She was a clone. I'm thinkin' maybe Bonneville was working with the clones and the government. Doing what, I don't know."

"Snake. Did you ever figure out why IGP Systems wanted this information on Barber?"

"I had me some theories."

"This is probably a pretty good time to enumerate them."

"I figured Barber stumbled onto something while working in Bonneville's business, something he wasn't supposed to know. Another theory was maybe Rakubian or somebody else on the sidelines sabotaged Barber's career. Maybe they were afraid he'd gained too much favor with the old man. The old jealous-of-the-son-in-law syndrome. They ask me to get the particulars on him so they would know what his weaknesses were so they could frame him. Which brings up a bad but highly likely—knowing them—possibility. That they hired some bimbo to screw his brains out so the old lady would catch them together."

On the street a raggedy man on the corner was shouting at a

flower vendor, and for a minute I became nervous thinking it would escalate to fisticuffs. Last night's events in the Safeway had left me jumpy.

"Did you ever see Judson Bonneville, Elmer?"

"Not me. They say he loves the movies. Hires the best writers and directors and then steps in and dabbles, and pretty much scuttles the ship. I've heard that from a lot of sources. They say he's a health freak. Lives at altitude somewhere in Mexico about half the year. I think when he was young, he used to be a runner. He's got about half the ex-marathon champions in the country working for him. A bunch'a swimmers and goddamned cyclists."

"Those goddamned cyclists."

"I always try to run 'em off the road when I see 'em."

"Me too."

A few minutes later I handed Elmer the keys to the car, got out, and leaned against a nearby building, where I made a call on the cell phone. "Kathy?"

"I've been missing you. Where are you? What are you doing?"

"Leaning against a building at First and Pike. Watching women."

"See anybody you're interested in?"

"I haven't seen anyone I'd replace you with, but I'll keep looking."

"Ah, that's sweet. Speaking of sweet, Desiree called. Wanted to know where she could find Elmer. She left a number." I scribbled it down on a small tablet.

"Okay if I drive home with you tonight?"

"Why? Does the old man need your car for a hot date?"

"He needs the car."

"You're such a good son."

"I know. What bothers me is he went up to his office and secured about fifteen pounds of armament."

"Oh dear."

"I know."

When I handed Elmer the scrap of paper with Desiree's phone number on it, he said, "What's this?"

"Desiree called the office looking for you." He pushed the

paper through his whiskers and into his mouth, chewed, and swallowed it. "By the way, Elmer. Why do you ignore Beulah so pointedly?"

"Beulah?"

"Our receptionist. Everybody in the office knows the two of you are having an affair."

"They do?"

"Of course they do."

"Crap."

"What? You thought it was a secret?"

"It shoulda been. Don't you know there's a fat ladies' network?"

"What do you mean?"

"Once they find out you'll talk to 'em, they start coming out of the woodwork from all over. You're smart, you don't ever make eye contact with a fat lady."

"Beulah's beautiful. That's why you were attracted to her in the first place. Stout, but beautiful. Besides, if you're worried about your reputation, you shouldn't be fooling around with Desiree."

"Why? She's not fat."

"No, but she's not doing your rep any good."

After being cooped up in the car, the walk down First Avenue was refreshing despite the noise and traffic. Once at the office, I returned a call Beulah said had come in five minutes earlier. The man on the other end of the line said only, "I know you killed him."

"Who is this?"

"You want to talk about it, you name the time and place."

"Fuck you." I hung up, waited a couple of minutes for him to call back, and when he did not, dialed the phone company. My contact wasn't in, but I was able to squeeze the location of the phone out of another employee by telling her I'd received a call from a retarded cousin who desperately needed his medication, that I had his number but not his location. The number I'd dialed was a booth in the Federal Building only a few blocks away at Second and Marion.

Paranoia setting in like flu symptoms, I called Hilda again. "I don't have what I thought I would, Thomas. It's going to have to be tomorrow."

"That's okay, Hilda. If you can't find it, nobody can. But I have another name for you. Last night a man named Lane Thorne got into some trouble with the police here in Seattle. He supposedly owns a gun shop in Santa Clara. I'd like to know if he's connected to IGP, to Rakubian, or to Green International."

"You're running up a bill on this."

"I know. Lane should be easy to trace, though. You might try one of the local PIs in Santa Clara."

"Will do. Catch you later."

"Let's go, buster," Kathy said, poking her head into my office. "We're late."

CHAPTER 28

We had dinner with friends, friends we hadn't been inclined to discuss recent events with, and we'd driven home in Kathy's cramped Miyata only to be greeted by a flock of phone messages, the one from her mother knocking an hour out of the evening when Kathy returned the call. We went to bed and made love.

Afterward I said, "I'm shocked, Miss Birchfield. You're the first grammar teacher to make me stay after school and do things like that."

"Grammar teacher?" She was quiet for a few moments. "Well, Tommy, you should be proud to learn you're the only boy in the whole class to earn an A-plus." Giggling into her pillow, she added, "So far, that is."

"Careful, Sister."

"Grammar teachers. That's shocking, Thomas."

"You think so? Someday I'll tell you about the last-man-on-earth thing. I guess you can imagine some of the particulars. In that, I'm a pretty busy boy. Populations to reconstitute and all. I'd tell you about the wager in the lingerie shop, too, but it's embarrassing."

"You're not embarrassed by these others?"

"Only by the women's softball team. But let me tell you what happened today."

"You already told me about the softball team. You're the manager and—"

"The water boy. I'll tell you about it later."

"Okay. Sure. Elmer's still got your car. What's going on?"

I explained about Lane Thorne and his release from jail that morning. About my long chat with Meade Barber, about the relationship between Barber and Judson Bonneville, and thus the once-removed connection between Slezak and Bonneville. When I told her about the phone call from the potential blackmailer that afternoon in the office, she grew quiet.

"Let me give you my thoughts in order. First, this Lane person. I know I urged you to step in and help that woman last night, but the minute he turned on you . . . I started planning your funeral."

"Oh, come on. It wasn't *that* bad."

"It was that bad. And when that woman ran away . . . Here you are risking your life, and she takes off."

"Now, don't blame her for that. Anybody would have been scared."

"Do you think it could be possible Elmer's right? That Lane is somehow involved in Elmer's problems?"

"I don't know what I think."

"What are you going to do if he shows up again?"

"Hide under the bed. Blow my Dick Tracy whistle. Sick L.C. on him."

"I see you've made plans."

"Tons."

After a few moments Kathy said, "That phone call you got is really scary. It does something to my stomach to be reminded of Philip's death. Maybe you should have taken your chances with the authorities. By now it would be over."

"I've thought about that. It's a sorry state of affairs when you think you're serving justice by breaking the law."

"Philip's death was an accident. You know that. I know that.

We never could have been sure we could convince a jury of it, though."

We were submerged in the past for a long time before I broke the gloom. "Okay. I'm the water boy. I'm stuck on the left fielder, but she won't give me the time of day."

"I thought she was the center fielder."

"Sometimes the shortstop. It depends on my mood. Once it was the catcher. Never the pitcher. She's always butch."

"So what is it about women softball players? The uniforms? The way they spit?"

"Maybe both. Who knows? The left fielder won't give me the time of day, but all the other players are nuts for me. Really nuts. Hey, stop your laughing. These aren't Barbie-doll players, you know. These are real women. A little chewed up around the edges."

"Okay. Sure."

"So it's a three-day weekend, and we're sharing a beach house—just the team and the water boy—and I make the silly statement that I want the left fielder so bad I'd screw the whole team to get to her. The left fielder says I couldn't possibly get to all of them in three days, but that if by some miracle I could, I was free to take her on. So they all agree, about half thinking I'll never get to them. But I do. I get to them all, and the peer pressure from the ones in the beginning makes the reluctant later players go through with it. The closer to my goal, the more nervous the left fielder becomes. Then finally she has to pay up."

"And of course she loves it."

"Of course."

"That's terrible."

"I know."

"So who am I? Left field?"

"Tryouts are tomorrow. Oil up your mitt and be ready."

"Somebody already oiled my mitt."

"Maybe you had a tryout and didn't know it."

"Come on. I know I'm left field. Right?"

"No, you're always third base." I had to roll over onto her to stop her giggling.

It was hours later when the phone woke us. "Thomas? It's me, Snake. I found her. She's across the street in a diner. I got her, Thomas."

"Who is it?" Kathy asked.

"Elmer."

"Does he have another dead woman?"

"This one's alive. I think."

"Of course she's alive," Elmer said. "Get down here before she skedaddles."

"Who are we talking about, Elmer?"

"The blonde who ran away last night. She came through the intersection in a white BMW about half an hour ago. Parked in a private lot under the building."

The address he gave me was in the heart of downtown Seattle. "Snake. Promise you won't make a move until I get there."

"She's having coffee. Reading a newspaper. She gets up to leave, I'm going to nab her."

"Don't do anything."

Kathy didn't get dressed before I did, but she was quick enough that I couldn't get out the door alone. We took my old pickup truck and were downtown in under twelve minutes. Snake was sitting in my car outside a small eatery called George's, which was on the first floor of a combination office building and condo tower near the Greyhound bus terminal. The upper floors of the tower were dark. Except for some all-night neon lighting, the rest of the block was dark too. It was almost two o'clock.

I parked the truck and walked to my car, where Elmer was slumped below the window. It occurred to me that I could get two parking tickets at once. Kathy approached the other side of the car. Elmer glanced past me and into the diner. "She's got a friend now. See 'em?"

There were three people in the tiny eatery, a counterman, the blonde huddled over a table facing us, and a raven-haired woman with her back to us. When Elmer saw me squinting, he handed me the field glasses from my glove box.

She was an attractive woman with a somewhat mannish

face, stolid and serious; high, wide cheekbones that were almost too big; a wide brow and a full mouth with even, newscaster teeth and glossy lips. She spoke animatedly, almost angrily to the other woman, whose face I could not see. Her blond, shoulder-length hair was a trifle disheveled and hung freely. From where I stood with the binoculars, it looked as if one side of her face might still be swollen from last night.

CHAPTER 29

Heading across the street alone, I heard the Ford's door open and close behind me, Elmer's hard-heeled cowboy boots rapping the pavement as he trailed me across the empty street. To the west a stoplight winked red. Next door two homeless men in dirty sleeping bags lay curled up in the doorway like caterpillars in a boy's shoe box.

I reached the diner alone, opened the front door, and strode across the floor toward the women. Spotting me, the blonde grabbed her purse, spun out of her chair, and exited through a rear door. When I went after her, the dark-haired woman tipped her chair onto its side in the aisleway in front of me. I leaped it, but caught the toe of my shoe and almost went down, my agility hostage to the pain in my ribs and side from last night. It was a dirty trick and could have hurt me badly.

Catching the rear door as it closed, I followed the blonde into the lobby of the building next door. She'd already thumbed the up button on the elevator when I walked across the polished floor and turned her around.

Behind us in the diner a commotion had ensued, Snake yelling, "Hey, hey, hey," as if he were trying to keep somebody at bay, possibly the counterman, whom I'd only glimpsed. My impression had been of an extremely tall, youngish man with stooped shoulders and a bad complexion. For the moment the blonde and I were alone in the lobby.

Outside the building two running figures passed the glass doors. Neither of the men in sleeping bags in the doorway stirred. Taking advantage of the distraction, the blonde shook herself loose and ran for the stairwell at the end of the lobby. I caught her, cornered her. She was tall for a woman, a husky, well-put-together female who might have put up a battle if she'd been inclined.

"I'm not here to hurt you," I said. "I want to talk."

"Leave me alone." Up close it was clear she was wearing heavy makeup over last night's bruises.

"Tell me about Thorne."

"I don't know what you're talking about."

"At the Safeway store on Brooklyn. He was knocking you around."

"You're crazy."

"He landed in jail."

"You trying to say I'm safe now?"

"Not exactly. They released him this morning."

It was hard to tell which frightened her more, my presence or the mention of Thorne. Whichever it was, she was clearly terrified, had been from the moment I'd entered the building. She breathed through her mouth so forcefully I could smell coffee and cream on her breath, as well as a whiff of lipstick, as if she'd just kissed me.

"I don't have any friend named Thorne, and I don't know you. Leave me alone."

"The more you protest, the more you make me think last night was a setup." Her knees buckled and she sank a few inches, managing in the end to remain on her feet. "All I want is for you to tell me about Thorne."

"I'll call the police."

I dug into my jeans pocket and offered her a quarter, stepped aside so that she could reach a bank of pay telephones racked against the far wall. When she balked, I said, "Tell you what. I'll call the police."

"Shit." She went around me to the elevators. "We'll talk upstairs."

While we waited for the elevator, she eyed the empty street through the thick glass doors at the end of the lobby, not that she could see much against the reflection of the lobby lights. For some reason Kathy and Snake had not followed us through the diner.

We rode the elevator in silence while she looked me over. She wore a long, white garment that might have been a coat if it hadn't been lace, black leggings, high heels, and a sleeveless silk blouse. Her arms were thick and somewhat muscular, had felt solid and icy when I'd touched her. She had run heavily and powerfully.

We got off on the fourteenth floor, where she went to the end of a well-lit, white-carpeted corridor and stuck a key into an off-white door with a little gold nameplate that read, T. WOODS.

Somewhat late it occurred to me that Thorne might be inside. Or that she might pull a gun on me. She could tell the police I'd accosted her and forced my way into her condo. At this juncture she could have claimed a lot of things. I didn't even know her name.

"Wait a minute," I said, watching her hands shake as she tried to fit the key into the lock. "You *were* at the Safeway last night?" She nodded. "And you *do* remember me?" She nodded again.

It was a plush apartment with carpeting so thick that walking on it shined your shoes. Somehow it suited her and at the same time didn't suit her. The unit was dark and still, and though I couldn't be certain, I believed it gave off the aura that nobody else was in it. It was oddly quiet, as if the rooms were soundproofed.

She turned on a couple of lights, dropped her purse on a table, and faced me, tongue dabbing at the edge of her dry mouth. "I don't know what you're selling, but I don't need any."

"Let's begin with your name."

"Jill Jones."

"Try T. Woods. What's the *T* stand for?"

She looked down. "Tammy. Tamantha."

"Tell me what happened last night, Tammy."

"You were there. You know what happened."

"Who is he to you?"

"Oh, for God's sake. I've only known him a few days. He called himself Street or Alley or some damn name."

"Lane?"

"If you knew, why'd you ask?"

"Where'd you meet him?"

"How did you find me?" I didn't reply. She sighed deeply. "At the pier at a concert. I don't know why this is so damned important to you. I knew him a couple of days. And then last night he went bad on me." She started weeping, though she made no show of it, the tears rolling quickly down her cheeks. After a few moments she glanced at a clock on a table against a wall. Next to the clock was a glass art piece that looked almost as costly as my Eddy Merckx. "Look, mister, whoever you are . . ."

"Black. Thomas Black. I'm a private investigator."

"I can't really talk now. I have an appointment I have to be ready for. How about tomorrow?"

"You have an appointment at two in the morning?"

"I've been in a play all evening, and now I have a date. Okay? You got my name. You know where I live, and now I want you to leave. I was there last night. My understudy took the play. So what? Goodbye."

"Did Thorne tell you why he was up here?"

"Up here?"

"He's from California."

"I met him at a concert, okay? I'm sorry if you got banged around, but you might have noticed I got banged around too."

The doorbell rang. "Oh, shit," she said, hurtling past me and stopping at the closed door. "He's going to be pissed. Can you do me a favor and hide?" Cowering in the back of a closet while Lane Thorne or another man spent the remainder of the evening with Ms. Woods would have been worse than getting slammed around. "Hide? Please?"

Giving me a disgusted look, she opened the door. "You were supposed to be downstairs five minutes ago," said a man in a suit, all business and familiar contempt. Approximately thirty, he had jowls and a look of total control. The look dropped from his face when he saw me. Even Woods appeared surprised when he turned and fled.

Slamming the door, she stood against it with her arms crossed over her breasts, glowering at me. "Thanks a heap."

It occurred to me that she wasn't peeved so much as she was barricading my path, that she had slammed the door not out of anger but as a roadblock.

She tried to throw the lock as I made my way past her to the door. I ran down the carpeted corridor just as the elevator doors closed with the soft sound of rubber kissing rubber. If the lobby had been closer than fourteen floors, I might have used the stairs, but I thumbed the down button and waited for a second car. Woods, who had been watching from her doorway, sealed herself back inside when I glanced her way.

On the trip to the lobby I thought about what she'd said. Had she been in a play tonight or had all that makeup been only to cover bruises? If she was an actress, she had that career in common with Roberta Capshaw Sams. And of course that was the question I hadn't asked. Had she known Sams? And why was she having a date at two in the morning? Had Thorne been a customer?

The lobby was well-lit but empty, the same two homeless men outside the glass doors in their sleeping bags. Kathy and Snake were nowhere to be seen. Stepping back into the elevator car, I pushed the button for the parking garage.

The garage was under the building, supported by concrete pillars, slots for forty or fifty vehicles, six or seven of which were occupied.

When I stepped out of the elevator, a snootful of fresh car exhaust and the sound of the closing metal exit gate were all that greeted me.

I rode the elevator back up to floor fourteen, but Ms. Woods refused to answer the door. It was hard to blame her.

CHAPTER 30

During my second descent to the lobby in five minutes, I tried hard to dissect my motivations. Elmer was unshakable in his belief that Ms. Woods was related to his case, but I labored under no such illusion. Still, like a sociopathic debt collector, I had harassed and pursued and interrogated her, had made her weep, had ruined her evening and chased her "date" out of the building.

Was it possible I was upset at not being given the hero treatment? Woods was an abused woman, a beaten woman, a woman in hiding, yet I'd burst through the deli door like a stampeding moose. Expecting what?

When I stepped out of the elevator, Elmer Slezak was in the lobby, along with Kathy, an agitated Tammy Woods, and, surprise of surprises, an even more agitated Desiree Nash.

Woods, chasing her boyfriend, must have ridden the elevator down while I'd been traveling back up. Desiree's arrival was an event I couldn't account for, unless she'd been following Snake, or he'd regurgitated her phone number and called her. The counterman loitered in the doorway between the deli and the lobby with his mouth open and his back hunched like some sort of carrion-eating bird on a fence. Another young man stood back by the glass doors with a stuporous, drugged look on his face. It took me a second or two to recognize him as Dale, the neighbor I'd seen at Desiree's house. He looked as if he'd been sniffing gasoline again. Desiree had brass balls to drag one lover around while chasing another so that she could accuse him of philandering.

As I took the scene in, Desiree, clad in a pink waitress outfit that suppressed only some of her buxomness, was shoving the smaller Woods with the palms of her hands against her chest and shoulders, moving Woods back a step at a time, hollering unintelligibly into her face.

"Hey, girlie," Desiree said when she'd calmed down enough to be understood. "You're going to find a man, why don't you find one ain't already taken?"

Incensed both at the charges and at Desiree's roughness, her second physical altercation in two nights, Tammy Woods said, "I don't even know the little runt."

"I ain't no runt," said Snake, pulling one of his four guns out of its holster, a .44 Magnum. For a split second I thought he was going to shoot Woods, or Desiree, or both of them, or all of us, but then I realized he thought the menace alone would bring peace to the lobby. It didn't.

"For God's sake." I grabbed Snake by the shoulder. "Put that back."

Like a pro lineman working over a rookie on the second team, Desiree continued to shove Woods across the polished lobby floor. Elmer holstered his revolver and scratched the stubble under his chin, clearly pleased to be the cause of conflict between two women.

While we were pondering how to break it up, Woods surprised us all by sideslipping Desiree, gripping her wrist, and flinging her into a wall, using the larger woman's own weight and momentum to do the work. Obviously she was the product of some martial arts training.

"You want to get rough?" Desiree said, peeling herself off the wall. "Come to mama, you little peroxide prick-tease."

When Woods didn't move, Desiree rushed forward clumsily, and Woods threw her against the opposite wall. The counterman whistled in appreciation. Dale watched in a fog. Kathy turned to me.

"Why do I always have to be the one?" I said.

When we heard the sharp sound of high voltage, I turned to Snake, who was holding the Powermax Double Shocker above his head, grinning like a mischievous ninth-grader who'd successfully phoned his first dirty nine-hundred number. He offered it to me as Desiree came sailing toward us; she stumbled, fell, and skidded across the polished lobby floor on her stomach. Without climbing to her feet, she tackled Woods around her ankles, and together they crashed to the floor, Woods making a guttural sound as the wind was knocked out of her. Before I could pull them apart, they rolled across the lobby in a snarl of arms and legs and wild hair.

From her knees Desiree doubled up her fist and hit Woods in the head, knocked her three feet backward. Before she could slug the smaller woman again, I stepped in with the Powermax Double Shocker and touched it to her back.

She flopped onto the floor on her side, eyes wide, arms akimbo, shuddering like a fish in the bottom of a boat.

"Geez, I love these things," I said.

Wheezing, Tammy Woods rose to her knees, then her feet, hands on her kneecaps. "Who the hell is that?"

I said, "I wish I could say it was the Avon lady trying a hard sell, but it's Elmer's girlfriend."

"Who the hell is Elmer?"

"*One* of my girlfriends," Elmer corrected, moving closer to Woods. Without provocation Elmer leaped at Woods, prying her arms away from her torn blouse. Looping an arm around Elmer's waist from behind, I picked him up and carried him across the lobby. When I set him down, I let some random voltage shoot out from the Shocker as a warning.

Kathy stepped up to Woods and said, "I like the tattoo. Where did you have it done?"

"I don't have to talk to you people."

Elmer sneaked past Kathy again and grabbed Woods a second time, pushed her up against the wall, holding her there with his hips, pulling her arms down and away from her neck. "That's it. See? There's the goddamned tattoo right there."

Grabbing him from behind a second time, I tossed him across the room, where he landed on his feet. "I'm getting sick of this, Elmer."

"Look at her goddamned titty!" We all looked, the counterman goggle-eyed and bewildered, Dale moving closer—alert for the first time. Desiree stirred, rolled over, and moaned, a discarded gum wrapper stuck to her cheek. "Sonofabitch," she said, eyeing me. "Who the fuck hit me?"

"I told you I wasn't nuts," Snake said. Then, turning to Woods, he added, "Go ahead, baby. Tell my friends what planet you're from."

"You people are all crazy," said the counterman.

When I flicked the switch on the Powermax, he jumped. Woods began crying. "God," she said, huddling against the wall. "I can't stand it. They're going to kill me."

"Did you know Roberta Capshaw Sams?" I asked. She turned away from us and pressed her face and hands into the wall. It was hard to know if it was a performance. "What does that tattoo mean?"

"Would any of you all like a cappuccino before I close?" asked the counterman, making an attempt at normalcy and profit.

Woods continued to cry. Desiree, still on the floor, moaned and began to put her torn uniform back together. Dale tried to look inconspicuous. Elmer chewed the inside of his cheek and stared at Woods. Kathy looked at me pleadingly, then at the blonde. "We want to help," Kathy said. "Tell us what you're afraid of."

"You can't even help yourselves," Woods said. Myopic with tears, she shuffled to the elevators, stepped into an open car, and closed the door. The elevator went up, and we let it.

"I don't feel so hot," said Desiree, getting shakily to her feet.

"You ever follow me again," said Snake, "I'll tie you up and sell you to the Arabs. Fifty cents on the pound."

"I didn't hear that," said the counterman. "I didn't see this. I don't know any of you people." He locked the glass door behind himself.

"Where'd she go?" Kathy asked.

"Upstairs. The fourteenth floor."

"Are we going to follow her?"

"She won't talk to us. She's frightened."

"Damn right, she's frightened," said Desiree. "Now I know where to lay my hands on her, she'll be more scared than ever." She brought out a switchblade from somewhere in her clothing and flicked the blade open.

Snake took the Powermax out of my hands, zapped Desiree, and watched her drop to the floor. When the knife clattered to the tile beside her, Elmer stooped, picked it up, stabbed the blade into the crack of a door, and broke it off. I took the Powermax away from him. "This isn't a toy, Elmer."

"It was that or shoot her stupid ass."

Kathy removed the Powermax from my hand and said, "Look who's talking."

"I'll come back and talk to the woman upstairs after she has a chance to calm down a little," I said. "I want you to stay away, Elmer."

"Hey, man. I *found* her."

"She's got nothing to do with your case."

"Oh, no?"

"No."

"Then how come she was talking to one of my clones?"

"What?" I looked at Kathy.

"Don't ask me. I only caught a glimpse of her," Kathy said.

"I chased her out in the street and she took a coupla potshots at me," said Snake. "Damn. I was like to shoot her down 'cept I don't want the whole hive on me."

Kathy said, "I didn't follow them outside, but I did hear shots."

"You lost her?" I said.

"I felt one of them bullets come right past my ear. Yeah, I lost her. Don't bother about asking him," Snake said, nodding toward the deli. "Neither one of them paid and he don't know who they are."

When we left, Dale was standing by the door trying to be invisible, waiting for Desiree to fully regain her senses and get up off the floor.

On the trip across the street I got the Shocker back from Kathy and snapped some voltage into the night air. She gave me a severe look. "I wonder if they'd put my picture on the box. You know. Satisfied customer Thomas Black zaps two assailants in two nights."

"Thomas?"

"Yes, my dear."

"I'm not sure I like you with that in your hand."

"I'm not sure I like myself with this in my hand. But it sure is a gas."

CHAPTER 31

Fretting over the complications from last night, combating the loss of sleep she'd been suffering all week, worrying about the lawsuits I might bring down on us with the Powermax Double Shocker, Kathy had left the house for work like a puppy dragging a laundry line.

As I was fixing breakfast, Ernest Fitt phoned and asked if I wanted to ride. The sky was beginning to cloud over, so when he suggested an eleven o'clock start time, I readily agreed. It would give me a chance to make some phone calls, and if we were lucky, we'd beat the rain.

Elmer hadn't made himself visible, but I could hear him sleeping in the spare bedroom, sounding off like a refrigerator going bad.

Hilda gave me a phone number in Washington, D.C., and told me to call back after I'd spoken to her expert. "Ask for Kermit," she said. "Kermit Jackson."

Jackson let it ring twenty times before picking it up and barking, "Yeah?"

"My name is Thomas Black. Hilda Nardo asked me to call."

The line was quiet for a few moments. Jackson sounded old, phlegmatic, and curmudgeonly when he finally spoke. His lungs were worn out and his wheezing sounded like a paper sack with a duck in it. "You tangled up with somebody named Art Rakubian?"

"I've been offered some work by him."

Another long pause. "Rakubian worked for MI-six. Came here eighteen years ago and worked contracts for a company named Inteller Search Universal. It's gone now, but it was an outfit did a lot of favors for the CIA and the NSA. You get ahold of anybody worked there, they'll swear it was a mail-sorting operation. Rakubian worked there until about five years ago, when he apparently received a better offer. He's called himself Greene, Smith, Smythe, Barney, and Middlestone, but Rakubian is his given name. There are rumors he actively participated in torture sessions in South America, that he volunteered to go down special for the CIA. Later he got involved with electronic eavesdropping."

"He seems the perfect gentleman."

"I'm sure he does. As a little bit of a trade-off, what's he doing now?"

I told Kermit Jackson about Rakubian and Green International. He warned me that the female receptionist at Green probably served double-duty as a bodyguard and undoubtedly had experience in wet work. I found it hard to believe Cynthia Webber had committed any crime worse than leaving a rest room without washing her hands. "Did you happen to find information on a man named Lane Thorne?"

"Hilda mentioned him. He was CIA."

"You think Thorne and Rakubian knew each other?"

"They mighta. On the other hand, it's possible for two people to work for the company right up to their pensions and never run across each other. Hard to tell at this point."

"What's the word on Thorne?"

"He was a field operative for a CIA cover company, or rather a series of companies. Africa. Central America. Mostly airlines. Chopper pilot in Vietnam. After the company he was a mercenary for about five years and then a private investigator. Now he runs a gun shop in Santa Clara. I don't know if this is true, but somebody told me he killed his wife in 1980. Did a few years for it in San Quentin. And there's an off-the-wall rumor he occasionally works as a hit man in the southeastern United States. I can't verify that."

"How'd he kill his wife?"

"You've run into him, haven't you?"

"Just the once. How'd he kill her?"

"Threw her out the window of their apartment. Eight floors. Then sat down, had dinner."

Hilda gave me a long rundown on IGP Systems and the intertwining business commitments between IGP and two dozen smaller companies. The only interesting fact to come out of it was that Judson Bonneville's personal discretionary income, his pocket change, amounted to close to a million dollars a month, or thirty-three thousand dollars a day.

She had almost no new information on either of the Sams sisters, but was able to report Lane Thorne had returned, at least temporarily, to Santa Clara. I hadn't been aware of my own nervousness over Thorne, yet news of his departure to southern California worked on me like a soporific.

After a few more calls I got outfitted and went riding with Ernest Fitt. We were more competitive than on our first ride together, so that by the time we got down alongside the shore of Lake Washington, we were trading off in one-minute stretches, hard, each trying to burn the other off his wheel. The plan had been to ride thirty miles and get Fitt back to the office before lunch break was over, but by the time we reached Renton, dark clouds had marched in and rain began stinging our arms and legs. Weeks of sunny weather ensured that Seattle's streets were quickly laminated with an oily sheen. On top of that, Fitt and I were both riding treadless clincher tires. For safety's sake we slowed the pace.

When I told him about the job offer from Rakubian two nights before, he said, "Don't take any bullshit from Art. He'll run you over, you let him, and most do. Be firm."

"Seems like a strange bird," I said. We were riding side by side now, the spray from our rear tires making concealment in the other rider's windbreak impractical. Previously I'd guessed he was in his early fifties, and he looked every inch of that today, though he was probably the fittest man for his age I'd ever known. I wondered how many others like him were working for IGP.

"I never have gotten a good handle on Art. I go up once a month, sometimes twice a month to sit in on an interview and then give my two cents' worth. Some of them he hires. Some he doesn't. Whether you know it or not, you have a reputation in this town, Black. Trade on it. Art's not going to be around forever. In a few years, with stock options, matching Keogh contributions, bonuses, paid vacations to Majorca, and whatnot, you could be rolling in dough. It would get you out of that neighborhood you live in."

"Where I live? I *like* where I live. It's not the Street of Dreams, but it suits Kathy and me." The U District had diversity and a feeling of life being lived. We liked walking to bookstores and theaters, liked the campus being close. I even liked complaining about our grumpy neighbor, Horace. If we moved, I'd have to take him with us.

"I don't think you're taking in the full import of what I'm trying to tell you. Rakubian pulls down probably, with options and so forth, three-quarters of a million. Some years more. He's got a villa in Italy he's restoring. Six hundred acres in Montana where he's planning to build a ranch and retire. He has an enormous amount of power."

"I haven't even been hired yet, and you're telling me I'll be running the show?" I laughed. "You sound like a huckster conning a high school kid into magazine subscription sales." I'd offended him. I could see it on his face. "If I like the work, I'll do it. Otherwise I've got everything I need." When Fitt gave me a scornful look, I added, "How many good meals can you eat in a day? How many shirts can you wear at a time? I do work I like. I ride my bike. I water my roses. My wife keeps me warm at night. Life is grand."

Fitt gazed across at me and smiled enigmatically. We were returning, riding north on Rainier Avenue now, a small plane taking off at the Renton airport to the east, a mist spinning up off our rear wheels and skunk-striping our backs. "I have a feeling the old man's going to like you. I have the feeling he's going to like you a lot."

"Who's the old man?"

"Don't you know by now?"

"Judson Bonneville?"

"You called it."

"Is it true he's never seen in public?"

"I heard he said once all these millionaires in the news are like nervous virgins at a church picnic, bragging about it as much as they can before they lose it. New money. Tacky lifestyles. In his world people don't brag about their money or their power. They wield it."

Fitt glanced across at me again. We were balancing side by side at a stoplight now, the rain having ceased, though the streets remained wet. "You'll meet him. Don't worry. You'll meet him. Most likely it'll be in the middle of the night. He keeps strange hours."

"Did you know his son-in-law?"

"Which son-in-law would that be?"

"Meade Barber."

Fitt smiled as if he'd thought of a joke he didn't want to explain. "Meade used to drive us crazy. For a while I was the coordinator trying to get him shipshape, but I wormed out of that. It was a lose-lose proposition. Whatever they gave him to do, he bungled." Fitt laughed a mean laugh, the first I'd heard from him, and it surprised me. "As a manager he was a one-man disaster. He couldn't fire anybody, even somebody who came to work drunk and fell asleep in a tub of batter, but he would hire people he met on the street—bums. Then he embezzled. I don't recall the exact amount or any of the details, but it was a lot."

"Somebody told me it was all paid back." It occurred to me that I was giving away more than I was getting here, by admitting that I had information on Barber, that I even knew about him.

"I don't know where you heard that. I do know it was the end of him and the old man. Bonneville doesn't tolerate thievery."

"I guess it was the end of him and the old man's daughter too?"

Fitt looked across at me. "I wouldn't know. I didn't know any of the family except Meade."

"Was there some friction between the old man and his daughter?"

Fitt gave me a funny look and braked to a stop. I let a car go by and circled back. We'd ridden through a dry patch, but now the streets on Seward Park Avenue were wet again from a shower we'd just missed. "Where'd you hear about the old man and his daughter?"

"Gossip."

"From somebody in the company?"

"I don't know anybody in the company except you."

Fitt reached back to his rear wheel and pressed his thumb against his tire, found it going flat. "You go ahead. No sense both of us getting cold."

"I'll come back," I said.

"Sure. And Black?"

"Yeah?"

"Don't gossip about the old man. It's a lesson I learned a long time ago. It'll get you in a heapa shit."

"Thanks for the tip."

Pedaling alone, I found myself thinking about Meade Barber and JoAnne, about her two jobs, about the boys waiting around the house trying to best the odds of unsupervised children getting into trouble, Meade meandering around town with a bedroll and a headful of smashed dreams. He'd seemed particularly vulnerable in the street environment, happier in former times, but a man as proud and as filled with his own personal integrity and demons as ever. Despite a history of embezzlement and adultery, Barber exuded a feeling of promise and, believe it or not, reliability. But then, there were certain people who simply looked and sounded reliable, even when they were screwing up. I had a feeling Barber might be one of them. I believed what he'd told me about the lost money, that he'd been taken in by a friend. It was harder to believe the adultery was somebody else's fault.

Three minutes up the road I turned around and headed back. It took someone on clinchers five to ten minutes to change a flat, but Fitt was already pedaling toward me. When I slowed to turn around again and join him, a large black car passed between us, and I was stunned to realize the driver was the man from Tammy Woods's apartment last night. The lost date.

Alongside Ernest Fitt once again, I waited until we had a rhythm going. "You know that man?"

He gave me a quick look. "What man?"

"In the limo."

"Do you?"

"Saw him last night."

"He's one of our drivers. Just happened to be delivering papers down here and had some of the team wheels in the trunk. Leftover from a group ride we did a couple of weeks ago. He was the sag wagon."

"That's some classy sag wagon."

"You'll get used to it, you work for us."

"What's his name?"

"The driver? Betcher, I think. Or Bretcher. Dick Bretcher. Dickie, I think they call him. He's probably the one who'll pick you up from the airport—you have a job out of state."

"He ever drive the old man?"

"Bonneville? I wouldn't know. I wouldn't think so. Bonneville's got bodyguards. People you don't ever want to mess with."

"I'm not in the habit of messing with anybody," I said. "Leastways not on purpose."

It had occurred to me to ask Fitt about my nemesis from Safeway, Lane Thorne, but I found myself holding back. Fitt was a stalwart company man, and any subversion from my mouth was bound to be repeated. I'd said too much already. During the remainder of the ride Fitt talked about training theory and a hill climb he was entering that fall.

An hour later as I was stepping out of the shower, the phone rang. "Black here."

"Mr. Black?" It was the voice from the Federal Building phone booth, the man who claimed to know about an unsolved murder I had been involved in.

"Who is this?"

"Everybody knows the cops cleared you of one killing, but what they don't know is you killed two men. The cops never pinned the other stiff on anybody, did they? What does your wife think about being married to a stone-cold killer?"

"Who are you and what are you after?"

"I want a talk, a long talk. I want to save your life. Just bring your checkbook."

"Screw you." I hung up and a moment later dialed the phone-company combination that provided the last number that had called in. It was the same pay phone in the Federal Building downtown.

CHAPTER 32

After we'd cleared the dinner dishes, I headed for the living-room couch to let the meal settle while wading through a tome called *Gunfighter Nation* by Richard Slotkin. Kathy and Elmer sat at the kitchen table, Elmer regaling Kathy with facts and speculations apropos of his ongoing romance with Desiree Nash, as well as other indiscretions, Kathy patiently offering advice.

For my part I was trying to figure out when we were going to have our privacy restored, as Elmer had shown no inclination to return to his own digs. What kept us from booting him out was an unstated fear that living alone might make him even crazier than he was.

When the phone rang, Elmer picked it up, as was his habit recently, and said, "Yep?" He brought it into the living room with his palm clamped over the mouthpiece. "Thomas. It's Genevieve, the neighbor woman with the kids."

"Who?" He handed it to me. "Black here."

"My name is Genevieve Gunderson. We met the other day when you and your partner were at Roberta's house. You gave me your card, remember? I thought you might want to know the lights are on over there."

"In Sams's house?"

"Yes. I didn't know whether to call the police or to go blind."

"Have you gone over and spoken to whoever's there?"

"Heavens, no. Bruce is out of town and I have three kids here."

I told her I was on my way and gave her my cell-phone number in case she had more news.

Elmer was already on the floor like an eager boy at the first sight of snow, tugging his silver-toed cowboy boots on over his floppy red wool socks. He didn't bother to pull the socks tight to keep them from bunching up around his toes. He stuffed the .38 into his left boot, then grabbed his coat and two shoulder holsters sagging with pistols.

"When do you think you'll be back?" Kathy asked.

"Not to worry," said Elmer, hobbling down the porch steps.

"Maybe an hour," I said to Kathy.

Once in the car, Elmer said, "They've landed, haven't they? Them aliens."

"You calm down."

"Okay, okay, but I got a feeling we're going to see a whole mother ship full of tattooed—"

"I know. I know. You don't have to say it every time."

After passing the University Hospital I followed my biking route over the Montlake Bridge, through the Arboretum and down along Lake Washington Boulevard. That noon we'd cycled along the lake to within a block of the dead woman's house. The roadway was dry, but the weeds in the yard on Ferdinand had a crust of glittering droplets. In front of the house sat a new Mercedes the color of deep cherry wine and flaunting California plates.

We went up the walkway to the stucco house, Elmer falling into his short-man's walk, bouncing on the balls of his feet, explosions of momentary height coming with each step. He was so charged up, if he'd been a teapot, he would have been whistling. Using one of his rodeo rings, the one that served as a makeshift brass knuckles, he rapped on the front door, and then, even as I was reminding him to be a good little scout, the door opened and closed partially. It might have closed farther except for Elmer's boot.

After a few moments of pressing the door against Elmer's boot, the woman slowly opened the door.

She was small, well groomed, exotic, dark-eyed, dark-skinned, and dark-haired, identical to the woman we'd found in Elmer's bed. Except this one was breathing. For a split second I thought all the stories Snake had told us about the breeders and clones were true.

She wore jeans with tears in the knees and a cropped green T-shirt, her tight midriff exposed.

Remembering his depredations on Tammy Woods the previous night, I kept close enough to shoulder Elmer away if he made a move for her bra. "See what I been tryin' to tell ya, Thomas me boy?"

For almost a minute the three of us stood in the small living room studying each other.

"Who are you?" I said finally.

"Who do you think she is?" Elmer said, dancing around the carpet like a drunk who had to pee. "She's one of them clones. What's your number, baby? You kinda resemble one-nineteen." He stopped dancing and we looked at each other a while longer. It wasn't until Elmer said, "Where's your spaceship?" that she laughed bitterly.

"You son of a bitch," she said, glaring at Elmer. "You killed my sister."

"I did not."

"The police arrested you. The papers said she was found in your apartment."

"I didn't do it, sweetheart."

When he made a move to reach out to her, I barred his way with an outstretched arm, feeling one of his huge guns under his coat as it bumped my wrist bone. "You're Henrietta Sams," I said. "Roberta's twin."

She turned to me. "You work for Rakubian?"

"Not so's you'd notice."

"Who?"

"I'm employed by Mr. Slezak's attorney."

"I was charged with it, but I never did it," said Snake.

She looked at him coldly. "I drove back up to take care of Roberta's stuff." With that, Sams collapsed into an armchair, her face in her hands.

"You were with Tammy Woods last night," I said.

"Yes." Her voice had become mouselike, shrunken in the presence of the man she thought was her sister's murderer.

"Wait a minute," said Elmer. "She's lying. Tell him you're a clone, baby."

"Not a clone, a twin," I said.

They stared at each other for a moment, and she said, "Roberta was my sister."

"Liar."

"I was working with her until last week. The night before you killed her, I left for California."

"You're all dangerous," said Snake. "The one last night fired shots at me! And you *are* a goddamned clone. Don't try to tell my friend here you're not. I oughta know. I rattled dozens of you."

"You saw two of them, Elmer. Two."

"I knew conning you like that was going to lead to something bad. I just never could have guessed you would kill one of us," she said.

"How many times do I have to tell you? I never killed her. Why do you think we're here? We're trying to break the case. Somebody else came in and killed her. I'm trying to prove that." She thought about what he'd said, wiping tears from her eyes with the backs of her slender wrists. "Don't give me no shit, baby. There were dozens of you."

"*He's* right," she said. "There were *two* of us. It was our last gig. Tell me the truth. You really didn't kill her?"

"His door was unlocked that night," I said. "We're working on the theory that somebody came from outside and killed her."

She seemed incredibly young, though I knew her to be twenty-two. It was easy enough to see how she and her sister could make some gullible fool believe they were virgins from another planet. She had an ethereal, otherworldly quality.

"Damn it, you're a clone," Elmer said, rushing through the

house. He came back a few moments later. "Where are the others?"

"It was a job," Sams said, ignoring Snake, her dark eyes boring into mine. "It was one last job before we both moved back to California. He wanted us to come on to Snake, sleep with him, and be mysterious. Snake never saw us together. We were supposed to pretend to be one woman at first, but make him suspicious. We would mispronounce common American words. One of us would come to his apartment two nights in a row and on the second night walk into the closet pretending we thought it was the bathroom. We would seem to have forgotten everything he'd told us the night before. Our perfume would be slightly different, our style of dress different."

"No!" said Snake. "They were different goddamn women! Not two of 'em! Dozens. I screwed dozens. Are you trying to tell me I have to take some two dozen women off my lifetime count?"

Sams and I looked at each other and rolled our eyes. "After a few days of this, when he realized something was fishy, one of us was to let him think he was dragging our story out of us," she said. "We were to tell him that we were clones involved in an intergalactic breeding program, about the hive, and how he'd been chosen to help us save our race. I didn't believe anyone would really fall for a story like that, but he seemed almost anxious to believe it, said he'd fertilize the whole planet if we wanted him to. First my sister would be with him, then I would, and each time we'd pretend we'd never seen him before. His mind seemed to snap, like they told us it would."

"That's a damn lie," said Snake. "My mind never snapped. And I ain't changing my count. I still can't believe you're not clones."

"Your apartment. The Thunderbird Motel. The backseat of your car. You particularly like it up on the sink in the bathroom—not the most romantic place for an intergalactic virgin."

"Your clone sisters told you about them things. That don't prove nothin'."

"Who put you up to it, and why?" I asked. "Rakubian?"

"Rakubian?" Snake screamed. "What the fuck is going on? Thomas, screw your head on straight. You're being taken in. She's got a butterfly on her booby and a Slezak in her belly."

Before he could move forward or I could stop him again, Sams unbuttoned her blouse and bared the top of her right breast, revealing the same small tattoo Tammy Woods'd had, the same design Elmer had sketched for us that first night. It was a simple blue outline of a butterfly, one side larger than the other.

"Rakubian hired us," Henrietta Sams said. "And it's not a butterfly. If you'd ever looked at it, you'd see it's handwriting."

"Initials," I said. "J.B."

"Listen. I gotta take care of some details here and get out. I'm sure they know I'm in town. I just needed to get some of my sister's belongings."

"No, no, no, no," Snake said. "Back up a minute here, baby, number one-nineteen, or whoever the hell you are. Rakubian hired you to rattle me? Why the hell would he do that?"

"We were to convince you we were from space. That we were clones. Sex was the lure. He said you couldn't resist, and he was right. We did it because we were paid very well for it. Why he wanted it done, I have no idea."

I turned to Elmer. "Snake. Assume for a minute this is all true. Why would Rakubian do something like this?"

"Everything he does is on orders from Bonneville. The question is, why would Bonneville want this done. I don't know. It's the way Rakubian does his shit, though. He likes to try to make people crazy. He discredits them. Ruins them, but makes them think it was all their fault, like they brought it on their own selves. But why me?" He turned back to Sams. "You enjoyed it, right? The bed part?"

"After a couple of years of hanging around waiting for Judson to put us in a movie, it became clear that money was all we were going to get out of him."

"But you enjoyed it, right?"

"She's trying to tell you she was paid," I said.

"Wait a goddamned minute," said Snake. "J.B.? Judson

Bonneville? Those initials on your tit stand for Judson Bonneville? You're one of his women?"

"We *were.*"

"What? He puts a stamp on his women?" Elmer said. "You really weren't born on Trianbria?"

"We were born in San Jose."

"Where's San Jose?" Snake asked.

"Just south of San Francisco," I said. Elmer gave me a sour look.

"We were in college when Judson saw us in a student play. He started courting us. Fancy restaurants. Expensive clothes. Jewelry. Cars."

"And he put you each in a house?" I said. "What else?"

"The tattoo," said Elmer.

"It was proof of loyalty. He put a million dollars in a trust for us after we were tattooed. Of course he controlled the trust, which meant he controlled us. We found out later all of his girlfriends had tattoos."

"A million dollars?" Snake said. "Hell, for a million bucks that fucker could tattoo the U.S. Constitution on my butt. What were you two? Operatives?"

"Girlfriends. We were J.B.'s girlfriends."

"Both of you?" Snake said. "At the same time?"

Sensing Sams's embarrassment, I said, "What are you talking about, Elmer? You thought you had a *hundred* girlfriends at the same time." I turned back to her. "A man doesn't generally send his girlfriends out to sleep with other men."

"You go through a cycle with J.B. We were at the end of it. He was through with us and we knew it."

"I need to know more about this tattoo," Elmer said. "Your sister had hers removed. I know, because when I tried to show it to people, they thought I was nuts."

"She was leaving. She didn't want to be branded when she moved back to California."

"So what's this Bonneville like?"

"In the beginning we saw him once a month, sometimes not even that. There were rules of course, and Rakubian was responsible for enforcing the rules. We couldn't see other men, and we were expected to be there when he called, usually late at night. No traveling unless we were with J.B. In turn we were under contract at Miramont and received cars and a monthly allowance, and of course the million-dollar trust. He was nice to us. He gave us everything we wanted."

"You're actresses?" Elmer asked.

"We were supposed to be. Roberta got a part in some little potboiler. Looking back on it, you can see a regular progression. He flatters you and takes you places. Buys you jewelry and puts you up somewhere. Gets you to quit your job. Quit school. Move away from your family. Pretty soon you don't have any friends because your whole world depends on him. Eventually he drops you, but before he does, you have to do some dirty job for him in order to get your trust money. Tammy knows three other girls from Miramont and they all went through the same progression."

"She must be on the way out too," I said. "She was in a public skit the other night that got her hurt."

"I wouldn't know about that. All I know is Judson likes proving he can get you to demean yourself."

"You mean he was *trying* to humiliate you?" I asked.

"We thought so."

"Christ," said Snake.

She looked at him, not unkindly. "Maybe I shouldn't say this, but we were given pills to put in your drinks."

"What kinda pills?" Elmer asked.

"We were told they were antipsychotic medication."

"Antipsychotic? Goddamn. It was LSD. At least once it was. And sleeping pills. I know it was. That explains a few things. Like the rattlers in my bed that weren't there after I shot 'em. It explains why I sometimes slept for two days after seeing one of you."

"I'm sorry. I thought that was why you killed my sister. I thought you found out."

"I mighta killed her, I found out. Damn, that makes me mad!"

"I'm sorry."

"Aside from what we've discussed here," I said, "is there any reason somebody might kill your sister?"

"She was writing a book. The writing was her therapy. I don't know that she was even thinking about publishing it, but they knew about it and they even broke in here looking for it."

"Do you have a copy?"

"I've been looking, but I can't find it. They probably stole it."

"You think the book caused her death?"

"I don't know. I thought Snake killed her."

"What do you know about Rakubian?"

"Only that he makes bad stuff happen. We were at a Huskies basketball game once and Judson got jostled in the crowd. It was nobody's fault really, but he got all teed off and tried to get into a fight with some kid. A kid! He made a phone call on his cell phone. I know it was to Rakubian. Two days later Roberta sees this newspaper article. The boy from the game is in the hospital. Hurt bad."

Elmer was slump-shouldered and slack-jawed, as depressed as I'd ever seen him. "Did they bug my place?"

"They had some little electronic gizmos we were supposed to put into light-bulb sockets."

"*You* bugged my place?"

Ignoring his question, she looked at me. "Do you think Rakubian had my sister killed?"

"When did you meet Rakubian?" I asked.

"Three years ago. He bought this house for Roberta. Bought my condo in Redmond. He had drivers pick us up when we were to meet Judson. All the money came through Rakubian."

"What about Tammy Woods and the Safeway?" I asked. "Was it connected to this?"

"All I know is when I called her yesterday to talk about Roberta, she was scared. Real scared."

"What *did* she tell you?"

"Nothing. You came in before we could talk much."

"Why did you run?"

"I was afraid. I didn't know who you all were."

"Except for me," said Snake. "You recognized me."

"I did. I thought you came to have sex with me. I ran."

"Because I wasn't paying you. Women'll do anything for money," he growled to no one in particular. Sams straightened her blouse. "Goddamned women are all for sale. It ain't got nothing to do with love. It never did. It's all who can pony up the nickels. A million dollars for a tattoo. Keeeriste!"

"Love? Look who's talking," said Sams. "You were willing to go to bed with aliens. For nothing."

"I was doing a species-to-species favor. Replenishing the race. I thought I was going to get a medal for it."

Before the name-calling could escalate, a Jeep Cherokee pulled up in front of the house, not quite blocking my Ford.

Looking wan and small and red-nosed, Arthur Rakubian got out, straightened his jacket and bow tie, stooped to look at his hair in the side mirror of the Jeep, then walked to the front door. I saw him first, then Elmer, then Henrietta Sams, who had gotten out of her chair.

When I opened the door, Rakubian said, "Well, isn't this a surprise? Two of my favorite ops." He stepped in, looking hard at Sams. "Henrietta. How've you been?"

"Not so good."

"Yes. Well. What are we all doing here? Chitchat?"

"That's right," Elmer said.

Rakubian was smaller than I remembered, more frail, more British in his tweeds, vest, and cockeyed bow tie, his gray eyes livelier and deader at the same time. They were flicking over us and the room behind us, but aside from their movement there didn't seem to be much behind them. "I was saddened to hear about your sister," Rakubian said.

"Thank you." Sams moved to the window, where she nervously looked out at the dark street, presumably for more of the enemy.

"You men been here long?" Rakubian asked.

"Ages," said Elmer.

"Is that right?" Rakubian looked at me.

"We've been here a spell," I said.

"Say, listen," said Sams, whisking up her purse and running for the door. "I have to be going. I just remembered something."

"Don't be in a hurry." Rakubian gestured with his hands as if gentling a skittish horse, but she was already out the front door and onto the stoop.

Mumbling words none of us could quite distinguish, Sams pedaled down the steps and jogged along the pathway to her Mercedes. Rakubian started to follow, but I blocked the center of the doorway. "Hey, you know I've been meaning to phone you. We ran into some idiot the other day in the Safeway. Thought you might know him."

"I rather doubt it," Rakubian said, trying to squeeze past.

"Art, baby," Elmer said, pulling on Rakubian's arm. From the look Rakubian gave him, being touched was not an offense he took lightly. "You got any work for me? I been incurring legal fees. Costing a goddamned fortune."

When Rakubian spoke, we could smell alcohol and hot mustard on his breath. He'd probably been called away from dinner and drinks. I wondered who'd called him. "You gentlemen planning to hold me here until she leaves?"

"I was," Elmer said, grinning. "I'm not sure about my *compadre*."

"I think I was too."

"I'm sorry," Rakubian said. "What was it you were asking? Perhaps we can get together and talk the situation over. I have an opening tomorrow at eleven."

"See you then," I said.

"Looking forward to it," Elmer added, glibly, as Rakubian made his way down the walkway. Sams was already out of sight. Rakubian did not turn around.

Left to our own devices, we searched Roberta Capshaw Sams's house, looking for, among other items, evidence of a book, a diary, notes. I cast about for a photograph of Judson Bonneville but uncovered none. We found CDs, fashion magazines, a stack of romance novels, a small library of mainstream videos, and two spare bedrooms filled with new clothing, some with the tags still on, none of it worth selling your soul for.

"Hell," muttered Snake. "For a million dollars he could staple his family tree to my lip. He could scribble the Old Testament on my skull. For a million bucks I'd let him stitch the Koran on my testicles with a sewing machine."

"You'd probably even sleep with a woman for a million bucks. Right?"

"Any man would. So what's that got to do with the price of tea in China?"

"Not a thing."

CHAPTER 33

On the drive to Elmer's office in the International District, Elmer was decidedly glum. He said, "I was sorta thinking I might round up five or six of them little honeys, find myself a sailboat, and start down Mexico way. Me and a buncha breeders. I was even thinkin' of invitin' you."

"If you haven't noticed, I've got my own breeder."

"Damn, it woulda been something, though, wouldn't it? To sail around with all that quack-quack."

"It would have."

On the way out of his office, arms filled with electronic para- phernalia, he stopped and dropped boxes of bullets into his jacket pocket until I heard the stitching on the pocket squeak.

As expected, we found bugs in his apartment. Two were in light sockets, one in the phone. We worked silently, but the more we found, the angrier Elmer became. He went into the bathroom and threw his toothpaste and all his medications into the trash, then rummaged through the kitchen shelves and refrigerator, discarding all perishables and any open containers. "Damn these bastards," said Snake. "It's one thing to pull these stunts on the great unwashed public. But I'm one of their own. How could they?"

Peeping through a chink in her curtain, Mrs. Magdanz

watched us leave. Perhaps Snake's pounding his fist on the outside walls had alerted her. He saw her and said, "She's got Marilyn Monroe's bra."

"Pardon me?"

"Showed it to me once. Wears it around the house stuffed with Kleenex."

"Hmmm."

When we reached our house, Kathy was reading in the living room. Elmer, who was carrying an armload of transmitter detectors and other electronic surveillance paraphernalia, managed to put a finger to his lips signaling silence, and then wordlessly we ran our tests.

Afterward the three of us went outside, squeezed into my truck, and began driving. Elmer turned the radio on loud. "What is it?" whispered Kathy, sitting between us. "You think our house is bugged?"

"Six ways from Sunday," I said.

We drove up Ravenna, went around the grassy traffic island by Green Lake Elementary School and onto the freeway toward downtown. We rolled the windows low and let the summer air whip through the passenger space, splashing Kathy's hair across her face, occasionally across mine. I explained about Henrietta Sams, about Rakubian and the plot against Elmer Slezak. About the con job.

"This is very hard to believe," Kathy said.

"Yeah?" said Snake. "Believe it."

"Why would Rakubian go to such lengths to make it appear as if you were crazy?"

"That's how he works. If you hadn't heard what we just said and taking into consideration my last couple of weeks on this planet, what would you have thought if I'd committed suicide? Or had a fatal car accident?" Kathy was silent. "That's right. You wouldn'a thought much of it. Rakubian gets you into this sort of box, you might as well nail your nuts to a stump and fall over backwards."

"But why you?" Kathy asked.

"I must have stumbled onto something. I don't know what,

but I must have stumbled onto something. I guess in one of the jobs I did for them."

"What do you want to do about the bugs?" I said to Elmer.

"Wiretapping's a federal offense," Kathy offered.

"I know," I said. "But proving who did it could take years."

"Nobody in that organization's going to squeal," said Elmer. "You'd never pin it on them."

"Oh, I almost forgot to tell you," said Kathy. "Hilda called. Said to tell you Lane Thorne flew back up to Seattle this evening."

"Oh, shit," I said.

"I thought that's what you'd say. What did you find out about the dead twin?"

"She was writing a book about Judson Bonneville—an unauthorized biography, you might say."

"I see."

"I'm convinced now Elmer was framed for the murder. Somebody sneaked in and killed her while he was sleeping. They had the place bugged. They knew when he was asleep and they knew when he was in the bathroom. They knew Elmer had been on hallucinogenic drugs and was entertaining a noggin full of theories certain to discredit him with the police and with his own attorney."

"In other words they had a sitting duck," said Snake. "You were probably the only two people on earth wouldn'a thought I was stark staring bonkers."

"Hell, we thought you were crazier'n a bagful of cats," I said.

"We did think you were crazy," Kathy added softly.

He looked across at me. "Shit. And I was going to take you sailing."

"Sailing?" Kathy said.

"The way I figure it," I said, "we only have one arrow in our quiver and it's an arrow we don't want to deliver."

"What's that?" said Elmer. "My ordnance? Go in there and blast the bejesus out of them?"

"Out of who?" I said. "The only person you know about is Rakubian."

"We know who's in it. Thorne. That blond babe. What was her name? Woods? We know."

"No, we don't. Woods may have been playing a part the way the twins were playing a part. She may not know anything. And who killed Sams in your apartment?"

He thought about it for a moment. "Who?"

"You tell me. This is our arrow. The fact that we know about the bugs, but they don't know we know."

"We really should take this to the feds," Kathy said.

"And how long do you think it would take the feds to unravel it?" Elmer asked. "Ask the feds where Jimmy Hoffa is. In six months I'll be in prison for a crime I didn't commit. Besides, they're never going to get Sams to repeat what she told us. Her life wouldn't be worth two cents. She knows that."

"So how is knowing we're being bugged going to help?" Kathy asked.

"I can think of several scenarios. For instance we could go back home and discuss how somebody in the company's asked us to pull a fast one on Rakubian. Hint that he's about to be terminated and we know who's going to do the job."

"Why would we do that?" Kathy asked.

"To shake him up," said Elmer. "Get him moving. Pull the same shit on him he's been pulling on me. Us." Clearly Elmer had taken to the idea.

"Maybe we could convince him this whole murder rap on Elmer is a trap set for him, that people working on it are going to testify against him."

"Rakubian's paranoid," Elmer said. "He was a spook, and they're all paranoid. He works a paranoid job in a paranoid business in a paranoid world. He's done so much wickedness to other people he's always looking over his shoulders to see what somebody else might be doing to him. Hell, at one point the CIA was trying to poison Fidel Castro's toothpaste. Spooks dream paranoid. It wouldn't take much."

"So what do you think he'd do if he thought there was a conspiracy against him?" Kathy asked.

"Hard to say. He's cold-blooded enough," Elmer said, "he might start killing off the participants."

"We can't be a party to that," she said.

"You're right. It's a lousy idea," I said. "Thorne, Tammy Woods, Elmer, us. And who knows who else. We could get innocent people hurt. The other hazard is it might not be Rakubian who's bugged our place. If it's the feds and we put on some act that sounds like a conspiracy, we're in trouble."

"It's not the feds." Elmer hung his head out the open window and sniffed the breeze like a dog. "It's not the goddamn feds. That alien impersonator said her and her sister bugged my place under Rakubian's orders."

Kathy said, "Maybe we can find some of the operatives who worked on this. *Somebody* bugged our house too, and it wasn't fake aliens. He might turn state's evidence—"

"And Julia Roberts is going to take off her clothes in Times Square." Elmer pulled his head back inside. "Rakubian never worked it so's anybody knew what anybody else was doing. Trust me, somebody put bugs in your house, he's from outa state. Somebody's listening to tapes at your place, they don't know who you are or what they're listening to. Rakubian is the hub of the wheel, but none of the spokes even know it *is* a wheel."

"So you think Judson Bonneville is behind this?" Kathy asked. "Or is this something Rakubian might be doing on his own hook?"

"Elmer thought it had to do with Bonneville's family life," I said. "Bonneville's had trouble with his daughter. Trouble with his ex-son-in-law, Meade Barber. Elmer investigated Barber two years ago. Then he saw him on the streets a few weeks ago and got curious."

"You know, I *did* ask Rakubian a couple of pointed questions about Barber," Elmer said. "At the time, he just gave me a queer look, but I guess it was around the same time I stopped getting work from them."

"Probably wasn't too much later the twins showed up."

"No, it wasn't."

On the drive home, Kathy said, "They were listening to us. They even had our backyard bugged. We talked about the wife beater the night before we saw Thorne in the Safeway. We talked about it in the backyard, and the next night we ran into it. It *was* a setup. Or am I getting paranoid now?"

"Rakubian's good," Elmer said. "Makes you think bizarre coincidences are ruining your life. Destroys your peace of mind, wrecks your sanity, knocks you off balance, and then he springs the coop de grass. With me it was the space girls, the drugs, the murder."

"If he wanted to get rid of you and he's that ruthless, why not simply have you killed?" Kathy asked.

"You ever see a matador walk into a bull ring with a gun? Rakubian's victims have to self-destruct. He has to work the magic with the cape and sword."

"And he went after us because we're defending you," Kathy said. "They were trying to buy Thomas off with those jobs."

"He would have been working eighty hours a week, bringing down so much money he wouldn't have been able to quit. That didn't work, they'd harass him till he went nuts."

"There must be something they want to protect pretty badly," I said. "I wonder what it is."

CHAPTER 34

We walked into the house agreeing that for the time being we'd pretend we didn't know the bugs had been installed. What that might gain us other than time, we had no way of knowing, but we figured if we brainstormed long enough, we'd find some profit. Contacting the authorities, we had decided, could wait, at least until we'd checked our offices for bugs.

"So," said Elmer when Kathy had shut the front door behind us. "They're going to hit him tonight?"

"What?" Kathy said.

"Don't do this, Snake," I said.

"No, no, no. You can't talk me out of it. I've made up my mind. That fucker's made my life miserable. I'm going to jail because of him, and if the callus king from California doesn't do him tonight, I'll do him in the morning. I'm crazy. I been drugged. It's the perfect crime. I might spend three years in the jug. So what? I need a rest and I need the money."

"Elmer," said Kathy, drawing the word out. "No!"

"You can't talk me out of it. I've accepted the deal. Thorne tonight or early tomorrow morning and if not, then me."

"Don't be saying this," said Kathy.

"Snake, this wasn't the plan," I said.

"It's *my* plan." Snake walked toward the back door and got

213

his car keys off the hook on the wall. "He needs it and I'm going to give it to him."

"This is an act, Elmer," I said. "We know it's an act."

"We know you're joking, Snake," Kathy said.

"No act, folks. I'm going over to his place this very minute."

"We talked about this earlier," I said. "About making him think we were involved in a plot against him. Because we know the house is bugged."

"We all know the house is bugged," Kathy said. "You can cut it out any time."

"Sorry, folks." Elmer opened the back door and walked out. A minute later we could hear his Cadillac firing up in the alley.

"Where's he going?" Kathy said.

"Probably where he said. To stake out Rakubian. Hoping he'll panic."

"Where does Rakubian live?"

"Upstairs in the Meany, according to Elmer."

"This is crazy." Kathy paced in the kitchen. "We don't want to do this. Snake's made it all up. He's made it up!" She spoke the last to the walls. "Nobody's hired anyone."

In astonishingly short order the phone rang, Rakubian on the other end, though he didn't identify himself. It was pretty hard to mistake his arch English accent. "You *are* bugging our house," I said. "You sonofabitch."

"Let's postpone the castigations and get down to brass tacks. What do you know about your friend's plans?"

"What? Are you listening to our conversations yourself?"

"Use your own dime to entertain your paranoid delusions about people spying on you, Mr. Black. Right now you're on my dime. Tell me what you know."

"I'm not telling stink."

He was quiet for a few moments. "There are going to be consequences. Dire consequences. Do you wish them on your conscience?"

"What would you know about conscience, you jackass?"

"People are going to get hurt, Black."

"What I know is we used debugging equipment on Elmer's apartment a couple of hours ago. We found bugs and we know you put them in. We came here and found more bugs. Elmer decided to play a practical joke. That's all."

"You expect me to believe such a fairy tale?"

"Yes."

"How did Elmer know Thorne was back in town?"

"We told him. Didn't you hear it? Kathy got the call this evening. You're slipping. You did hire Thorne, didn't you?"

"So you and Slezak haven't been in touch with anyone else?"

"What do you mean?"

"From the company?"

"Are you talking about Green International or IGP Systems, or what?"

"You know what I'm talking about. Quit hedging."

"As far as I know, Elmer hasn't been in touch with anybody in the company since he last worked for you."

"But you did talk to Henrietta Sams."

"She didn't tell us anything. She still thought Elmer killed her sister."

"And you went riding with Fitt."

"Fitt was the paragon of corporate virtue and loyalty."

"He didn't speak to you about Green International?"

"Not a peep."

"I'm not sure I believe you. How did Slezak know where to find Woods the other night?"

"That was an accident. My wife thought she recognized Woods from somewhere around the Market. Elmer staked out First and Pike for about ten hours and she drove by. Bald-faced luck."

"You think I'll accept that, Black?"

"Accept what you want. It's true."

It was more than eerie hanging up the phone and realizing Arthur Rakubian was still listening. I explained what had taken place, self-conscious of my word choices and tone, angrier now that we knew for certain he'd set the bugs in our home. He'd been listening for over a week. He and assorted technicians had listened to us making love. Kathy said, "Did he believe you?"

"I don't think so."

"What's he going to do? He won't come here, will he?"

"I don't see why. He's got loose cannons all over town. Or he thinks he does."

"Isn't there any way to convince him Elmer was putting him on? If he talks to Thorne?"

"You saw Thorne. Would you ask him if he's been hired to kill you?"

"I suppose not."

We sat at the kitchen table for a long while, neither of us able to summon the energy or desire for bed, neither capable of sleep. From time to time I worked the Powermax Double Shocker.

Finally Kathy said, "Wouldn't it be awful if somebody did kill Rakubian?"

"What do you mean?"

"It's probably on tape that Elmer said he was going to do it. If somebody else killed him, Elmer would take the rap, just like he's taking the rap for the Sams woman."

It was nearly one o'clock before we decided to sleep, and even then we were distracted by the phone. Before answering, I turned on the electronic noise generator we'd picked up at Snake's office. "You got it on?" Snake asked.

"Where are you?"

"And you're using a plug-in phone? I'm at the Meany. He just shot out of here like a spitball out of a substitute teacher's class. I saw him checking the clip in a Glock. He's armed and dangerous. Driving a black Volvo Eight-fifty. Headed west on Forty-fifth. So am I." I told Snake about Rakubian's phone call. "Good. I bet he's scared shitless, he thinks Thorne is after him. Trust me. No matter what you tell him, no matter what anybody tells him, he'll think his boss is out to nail his ass to a tree. That he's hired two of us to do the job. Believe me. I know about paranoia."

"I know you do. Where do you think he's headed?"

"Either the big man or Thorne. He'll hit them before they hit him. That's what I'd do."

"You've got to warn them. Elmer?"

"Are you shittin' me? You saw Thorne. Warn him? And the big man's got bodyguards coming out his ears."

"Elmer. You—" But he broke the connection.

Eight minutes later the phone rang once more. "It's me again. Guess where?"

"Don't play games, Snake."

"Tammy Woods's condo. He went straight up. Didn't lock his car or nothin'. Double-parked and ran inside. He's in a hurry and the only luggage he's carrying is that Glock. Guess what else? He's wearing a bow tie. Must've put it on during the drive. You think it's a clip-on?"

"How would I know?"

"And I just now pulled a caseful of floppy disks out of his backseat. Betcha these are his records. Pretty nifty, huh?"

"Don't follow him inside, Snake."

"The records'll be locked in my trunk."

"Snake. He thinks you're going to kill him. He'll shoot on sight."

"That makes two of us. Listen to me, Thomas. I started this fandango, and I need to make sure the girl upstairs is all right." The line went dead.

"Come on. We're leaving," I said.

"I'm not dressed," said Kathy, scrambling around the dark bedroom for clothes. I was already in jeans. Shoes with no socks. A pullover shirt. By the time we reached the truck, Kathy had it figured out. "You think he's coming here, don't you? Rakubian's coming here."

"Not this minute. Maybe later."

"Don't drive so fast. What if we have an accident?"

"We won't."

"We'd better not. I'm not wearing any underwear."

CHAPTER 35

Snake's Cadillac was parked eighty feet away from the doorway of Tammy Woods's condominium, but I didn't see a black Volvo 850 anywhere.

I left the keys with Kathy and told her to lay low, to keep the doors locked, and to burn rubber if anybody approached. Anybody. This business had made us all paranoid.

As they had been Tuesday night, two men in dirty sleeping bags lay curled in the doorway. In the lobby I found a security guard in uniform. "Can I help you?" he said. I shook my head. His hair was grizzled at the temples, and he was short and squat. He was not wearing a gun. I spotted a cooking pot incongruously sitting on the floor as I waited for the elevator. A rivet was missing from the handle—had been replaced with a nut and a bolt.

When the elevator doors opened, I found Elmer slumped on the floor in the corner of the car, a knot the size of a hamster rising into an ugly point over an eye, which was already swollen shut. With his remaining eye he squinted up at me over the sight of a .44 Magnum revolver.

"Elmer. What the hell happened?"

The security guard and I helped him out of the elevator, helped him holster the gun, and walked him to a low padded bench against the wall in the lobby.

"What's going on?" asked the guard, thinking he had to take command of the situation but not quite knowing how.

"I dunno," Elmer said. "The door opened and somebody slammed me. Never saw who."

"Come on, Elmer. You can do better than that."

"I swear I never saw him, Thomas. But it had to be Rakubian. I followed him in here. I was right on his tail."

"That your name? Thomas?" asked the guard. "That's my name."

"Nice," I said. "What'd they hit you with? A brick?"

"I don't have any idea. I just now woke up."

"What time did you come in?"

"I don't know. It must have been right after I called you."

"They hit you upstairs or down here?"

"I don't recall."

"Sure you do."

"Damn. I don't even know what day it is. I think I got it upstairs."

"Were you here all the time, Thomas?" I said.

The guard said, "I got rounds to do. I move around."

"Was it this?" I asked, walking across the lobby to point out the pot that I noticed had a caved-in brass bottom. "Somebody bean you with this?"

"Couldn't have been anything that flimsy."

"Did you see Rakubian once you were inside the building?" I asked.

"I saw him come in. After that all I saw was the ceiling in the elevator. Oh, yeah. And I saw a bear in pink shorts. But I think I was dreaming."

I walked over to the open elevator car and inspected the interior. When I stooped, a smear that might have been a footprint became visible, appeared to be blood. Elmer hadn't bled, and it wasn't his boot print nor my footprint. The guard hadn't entered the elevator.

"I'm going upstairs," I said to Elmer. "Kathy's across the street. Go over and make sure she's all right."

"I'm with you," he said, but when I turned him around by the shoulders, he hobbled toward the street like a dizzy old man with a tack through his shoe.

Taking a clean elevator, the guard and I rode to floor twelve, then took the stairs to fourteen. The guard's nostrils flared and whistled with the effort as we climbed. I said, "Did you see the other man come in?"

"I didn't see anybody come in but you."

"Nobody in the last half hour?"

"Who's askin'?"

I did not reply as the stairs dumped us out onto the fourteenth floor. The foyer was empty. Dark red fingerprints defaced the closed door of Woods's apartment. I pressed the bell. No answer. I pressed it again, thought I heard a sound inside, and tried the knob. Locked.

Stepping back, I kicked it without result.

"What are you doin'?" asked the guard.

"Call the police."

"What are you doin'?"

"We have one known assault in this building in the last ten minutes and blood all over hell up here. Call the police." I kicked the door again.

"I'm keepin' an eye on you." He took out his nightstick.

I kicked the door again. "You're not going to hit me, are you?"

"I might."

"Do me a favor. Tell me before you swing that. I had a head injury last year. Another one might kill me."

"I might knock you."

"I really wish you wouldn't."

The door popped open on my third try. Blood had mottled the inside of the doorframe, and a trail of droplets led to the interior of the unit. You could smell it. Metallic.

"Hello. Hello?" I stepped into the foyer.

"I gave at the office," came a weak voice, a man's.

For a moment I thought it was a trap, but then I saw Ernest Fitt on the floor beside a davenport, and realized it was a bad joke. He wore only a disheveled robe and was bleeding profusely from his midsection, his hands clutching the wound.

"What happened?" I asked.

"She's okay, isn't she?" he said.

"Who?"

His eyes were dull, and from the look of the carpet around him, he'd lost a fair amount of blood, yet he had the strength to hold his head horizontal to the floor as if it were being supported by a nonexistent pillow. I pulled him away from the sofa so that he could rest on his back, elevated his legs with cushions from the davenport, and put another cushion under his head.

"What the fuck is goin' on?" asked the security guard.

"Call 911," I said. "And don't use this phone." He left the apartment at a trot. "Who did this, Ernest?"

"You know what? I shouldn't have laughed. I opened the door and it was so unexpected, I laughed. Some people . . . you just don't think have the guts. Now, tell me she's okay."

"Woods? Is Tammy here?"

"Not Tammy."

I stood and made a quick survey of the room. Drinks for two on the coffee table. An opened bottle of Scotch on the liquor cabinet. Soft music piped in from a hidden stereo system. There was no telling where Rakubian was. I hadn't seen his car in front where Snake had said it was during our phone conversation, but that didn't mean he wasn't lurking somewhere. Snake was clearly messed up and might have been messed up when he phoned me. And Rakubian's car might have been stolen. Snake said it had been open.

The blood in the room was fresh. I moved from room to room, the Shocker in my hand. It felt like a harmless toy.

She'd concealed herself in the bathroom.

When I pulled the shower door open, a small, broken shard from one of the bullet holes in the glass fell to the floor with a sound like a dropped coin. Woods, who wore a gold robe matching the one Fitt wore, was huddled in the corner with her back to the wall. Of the four bullets, one had gone into the tiles beside her ear, another into the flesh of her thigh, another had nicked her shoulder and pierced the tub enclosure behind her. The fourth had punched a small hole in her head just over the hairline. A trickle of red that looked like a small lightning bolt had wended down her deeply tanned brow and stopped in the corner of one staring hazel eye.

As I walked into the other room and knelt beside Fitt, the theories began to coalesce and solidify in my mind almost more quickly than the blood was coagulating and drying on the carpet. My first thought was that Rakubian had shot Fitt because Rakubian believed Fitt had been feeding me information I wasn't supposed to have. But I had an epiphany when the wounded man looked at me and said, "She won't have to worry now. She'll get a good chunk of change if I die."

I was not inclined to tell him *she* wouldn't be around to receive his gift, that *she* was dead already, but when I thought about it, I wasn't so sure he was referring to Woods. "Who shot you?"

He smiled, and it was tentative and grim and smudged with blood where he'd fingered his face. I thought about trying to staunch the bleeding, but it was mostly internal, his abdomen swollen and hard as a melon. "Who?"

"You're the hotshot detective. You should be able to guess. You don't—ask Dick. You'll find him around somewhere."

"Dick?"

"Dickie Bretcher."

"You're Bonneville," I said. "Aren't you? Judson Bonneville."

"You figured that out, eh? When?"

"Not until a minute ago."

"I've got a doctor in New York I want called. He should be out here by morning. And I want private nurses. Green International will hire them. I told Art you were smart."

"Not smart enough to stop this."

"Art said not to mess around with you. I always played around too much with people's lives. Sometimes I think about the pranks I've pulled and begin to feel a little regret, sometimes, late at night. Not much, but a little."

"Maybe you should have felt more."

"You might be right." He sighed, and I was glad not to hear any wheezing or blood in his lungs. "You can't know how surprised I was when I opened the door."

"Who did it?"

Clearly in pain, he smiled. I couldn't tell whether the smile was to mask the pain or to hide from my question.

From the window in the kitchen I could see my truck and

Elmer's Cadillac in the street in front of the building. The fire department medics hadn't arrived yet. Neither had the police.

"Maybe you'd better make some sort of statement in case you lose consciousness," I said, walking back to Bonneville. But he'd already passed out.

After the police took command of the scene, Elmer, the security guard, Kathy, and I were segregated in the lobby of the building. The man from the deli next door watched through the glass doors with a look approaching satisfaction. The police should have separated us, but hadn't. A few minutes later Bonneville was brought down on a gurney and trundled away, still breathing but even paler than he had been upstairs. Kathy, who had her arm wrapped around my waist, said, "That's Judson Bonneville? You positive?"

"Yes. When we were riding yesterday in the rain, he got a flat and a trail car changed the wheel for him. He must have had bodyguards following everywhere we rode. They probably stayed back when he was with me so that I wouldn't notice."

"Rakubian's a murderer," Elmer said, speaking to no one in particular. "He bashed me with a brick. I followed the fucker to this building, watched him come inside. He had a Glock. He shot 'em with it and then pistol-whipped me."

"As far as I know, Glocks are all pretty large caliber," I said. "Nine millimeter. Forty caliber. The bullet holes I saw looked more like a twenty-two."

"He's not dumb enough to walk around with only one weapon. Probably had a silenced twenty-two automatic. It's a favorite for hit men and with the CIA. He'll cut it up with a torch or have it crushed. It's probably gone already."

"You think he's got Swiss bank accounts and a waiting jet and all that?" said Kathy.

"All of it," Elmer said. "Two people shot because I had to play games with a psycho. I feel like shit."

A uniformed sergeant approached us and said, "Who found the bodies?"

"We did," I said. "Mr. Snyder and myself." I nodded at the security guard, who had been hired as a temporary measure after complaints over our fracas Tuesday night.

I told the sergeant what we'd seen. Snyder gave a slightly more detailed version, which included his frantic search for a telephone. When we'd finished, the sergeant said, "Either of you know anything about the dead man in the parking garage?" I looked at Snake. "Male. Around thirty. Wearing a suit. Seems to be connected to a limo down there. Had the keys on him."

"Rakubian?" said Elmer. "Bonneville musta got a coupla shots in."

"Rakubian's not thirty. More likely it's Bonneville's driver," I said. "Dick Bretcher. How did he die?"

"I don't think I'll get into that," the sergeant said. He turned to Elmer Slezak. "What's your story, and who is Rakubian?"

Elmer explained how he'd followed Arthur Rakubian from the Meany Tower Hotel, how he'd come into the building behind him and entered the elevator, told how he'd been coldcocked.

When Arnold Haldeman sauntered through the door wearing a suit with a nicely knotted tie, a big gob of what appeared to be cat hair clinging to his backside, he conferred with the sergeant near the doors, his eyes on us.

"Well, well, well, Mr. Slezak," he said, walking toward us. "Here you are at the scene of yet another murder. Fancy that. Nice eye. Somebody open a door into it? That's what you get for living on your knees in front of keyholes. In fact all three of you were at my last murder. What'd you do, Elmer? Kill these people and call your lawyer again?"

"I think with this kind of luck I'm going to stop buying Lotto tickets," said Snake.

"It's gonna get worse." He turned to me. "What's your story?"

I reiterated what I'd said to the sergeant. Haldeman looked at me dubiously, a look he undoubtedly practiced in front of a mirror, because he was very good at it. "They tell me the lone survivor from this fiasco is hanging on by a thread."

"Let's hope he makes it," I said.

"I just bet that's what you hope." Haldeman looked at Kathy. "And where were you during all this, honey?"

"She didn't come inside the building," I said. "She hasn't been upstairs."

"I see. Well, you'd better bring your blanky, Mr. Thomas

Black, because it's late already and I believe we're going to have some questions." He turned to Elmer. "You're under arrest. Hal? Cuff him!"

"On what grounds?" Outrage ripped at Elmer's voice like a blade. I got ready to push the Powermax against his shoulder if he tried to resist.

"You, my good friend," said Haldeman, savoring the moment as he eyed Snake, "are a material witness. We'll figure out something more substantial later."

While they were frisking and cuffing Elmer, Haldeman turned to me and said, "Didn't you say you thought the wounded man was Judson Bonneville?"

"I did."

"*The* Judson Bonneville?"

"I couldn't swear to it. Haldeman?" He had begun to move away. "There's a cooking pot over there by the wall. It's evidence."

"Tag it," he snapped to an evidence technician passing through the lobby.

Haldeman stopped a second time and looked back at me. "You *knew* Judson Bonneville?"

"We went bike riding this afternoon."

Elmer, who was being frisked against a wall, a stack of weapons and their accoutrements at his feet, said, "If you weren't so fat and ugly, they might have invited you."

Kathy groaned.

I glanced at my watch. One forty-five A.M.

I didn't get loose of the cops until almost five. They let Kathy drive my truck home, but Elmer didn't get loose at all.

CHAPTER 36

"You look like hell," said Kathy. I rolled over in bed and switched on the noise generator, the gizmo that supposedly made the electronic eavesdropping devices in our house ineffective.

I'd grabbed two hours of sleep to Kathy's four. Once again, she'd refused to let them question Snake without her presence, was headed downtown this morning to confer with him. Tugging on a pair of sweatpants, I followed Kathy into the kitchen. "What a mess," she said. I hoped she was referring to recent events, not the kitchen, since it had been my turn to clean.

"Two dead and one critical at Harborview. Three dead, counting Roberta Capshaw Sams."

I made some toast while she telephoned the hospital for an update on Bonneville, only to be informed that he'd died an hour earlier. "Four dead," she said glumly, tears making her eyes sparkle in the morning light. "I feel so awful."

I went over to her and put my arms around her.

"Unless something breaks, we're going to have a hell of a time defending Elmer. It was a nightmare last night. We've got one thing, though. The policeman who arrested Elmer said none of the weapons they found on him appeared to have been fired recently. If he did shoot those people, I'll feel worse than ever. I was beginning to like the old goat."

"Now, don't break down and go against your principles."

"He's still a misogynist, a misanthrope, and a general all-around scumbag, but I am beginning to like him."

"Grows on you, don't he?"

We were eating in a moody silence when the phone rang.

"Black? This is Ralph Crum. Did you hear about last night?"

"Depends on which part of last night you're talking about."

"Your old buddy, Lane Thorne. Somebody went up to his room in the Westin and blew his brains out."

"Shit. Any suspects?"

"Not a one, unless you want to count your friend Elmer Slezak."

"Let me guess. Twenty-two caliber?"

"That's what I heard. Two slugs in the head. A third in the heart. Almost like pros did it."

"And no witnesses?"

"*Nada.*"

"What time did it happen?"

"The neighbor thought he heard shots around one-thirty. Called security. Otherwise they wouldn't have found him until housecleaning went in this morning. Neighbor was an ex-colonel spent some time in the Pentagon."

"Any connection to Thorne?"

"Not that I heard."

"You might tell somebody to check it out. Thorne used to work for the CIA. Thanks for the information, Ralph."

"Any time."

Kathy said, "Somebody killed Rakubian?"

"No. Lane Thorne. At the Westin. Twenty-two caliber."

"Rakubian? What if Snake were lying? Maybe he didn't follow Rakubian to that condo at all. Maybe he only said so on the phone to put the blame on somebody else. Nobody saw Rakubian. Nobody except Snake. Rakubian's car wasn't there when we showed up, and we got there in minutes."

"What about the computer disks he claims to have swiped from Rakubian's car? Did you find them?"

"They were in Snake's trunk like he said. I stashed them in the office safe. But he could have gotten those disks anywhere. Anytime."

"He could have."

"It seems so odd that Bonneville would ride bikes with you while a multimillion-dollar corporation ran itself."

"And riding in Seattle's traffic when he could ride anywhere in the world. From what Hilda's expert told her, all he did was throw sand in the gears when he got involved with business anyway. He knew that. What he wanted was to ramrod a couple of pro sports teams and become a Hollywood player. He had a pair of hard-headed business-school types operating the corporation while he diddled actresses and wrote bad screenplays."

"And he bought a collection of tattoos. Why didn't he give some of this money to his daughter, who's working two jobs?"

"I may ask her that when I go over this morning."

"You're going to see her?"

"Last night Bonneville kept asking if 'she' was all right. I assumed he was talking about Tammy Woods. Then he said 'she' was going to get a good chunk of change. At the time I still believed he was talking about Woods. But he had women stashed all over town. And they were all living off his largess. Not only that, but would he have cast Woods as the beating victim in the Safeway scenario if he cared about her? When he asked if 'she' was all right, he was talking about his daughter, JoAnne. I'm sure of it. And he refused to tell me who'd shot him. It was almost as if he were covering up for his attacker."

"For his daughter? You think his daughter might have shot him?"

"She's got as good a motive as anybody. Bonneville wouldn't have any reason to cover up for Snake if Snake was the one who shot him, and why would he cover up for Rakubian?"

"But if Bonneville didn't want the police to know whodunit so that he could deal with his attacker in his own way after he recovered, it could have been Rakubian or Snake or just about anybody."

"You're right."

"It's creepy."

"About as creepy as bugging our house and bollixing up our lives. About as creepy as trying to make people think Snake was nuts, as having twins con Elmer into thinking they were clones."

"These are the people who were calling you with threats, aren't they?" Kathy said.

"They had to be. Just throwing more loose nuts and bolts into the motor. So. You're going to go through the computer files Elmer took from Rakubian's Volvo?"

"Allegedly took. Yes. In a few hours. I'd give them to the police if I knew they were stolen, but all I know is they came out of the trunk of Elmer's Cadillac. I find anything pertinent, the police will want to review it."

"You find anything pertinent, call me on the cell phone."

It was almost nine when I got to the house on Twenty-first Avenue in West Seattle. The ramshackle station wagon was still in the carport, and the bicycles I'd doctored looked as if they'd been unused since my last visit. I looked along the side of the station wagon and saw the crease Felix Trosper had told me about.

Clothed for work in a blue dress that accentuated her gray eyes, JoAnne Barber answered the door as if she were expecting visitors. Her eyes were wide and unblinking. Shoeless and unhassled, she did not look as if she'd been crying, nor did she look as if she were headed to work in the next few minutes. She did, however, appear to be mildly disturbed.

"You heard?" I said.

"I'm not sure what—"

"Your father passed away."

"Yes. Somebody from his office called a few minutes ago."

"I'm sorry."

"Don't be sorry. I'm not."

"I was there last night after he was shot. In fact I was probably the last person to speak to him."

She swung the door wide and led me into the kitchen.

CHAPTER 37

The boys, Cormick and Powell, were playing Tetris on their Nintendo machine, the dog between them pretending he knew what was going on. "Level twelve," I said. "You're good."

"Powell can do level eighteen," Cormick said.

"You must have been a hit the other night," JoAnne Barber said, offering me coffee and a seat at the kitchen table. "They don't usually open up with strangers." I took the seat, declined the coffee, and tried to assess her mood as she sat across the table from me, clasping her plump hands together on a paper place mat that had weathered more than one meal. Her nails were polished, but bitten down to stubs. Mickey and Minnie Mouse salt and pepper shakers stood between us like paint-chipped porcelain chaperones. "They said he was murdered."

"Your father, a woman friend of his, and a bodyguard were all shot."

"You mean his mistress."

"Whatever. They're not sure who did it, although there's some evidence it was a man who worked for him."

"Rakubian?"

"Do you know him?"

"Judson doted on him."

"To get past the bodyguard, it would almost have to be

230

somebody who worked for him, or knew him, and Rakubian was reported to have been in the building around the time of the shootings. He's currently missing. What are your thoughts on it?"

"Why do you ask me?"

"I thought you might have some insight."

"Don't put anything past Arthur Rakubian. He's a freak."

"If it's any comfort, your father mentioned you at the end. Asked if you were all right."

"Did he now?" she said bitterly. "Why would he do that? Ask about me?"

"He loved you?"

"He might have loved me the way he loved one of his cars or planes, or one of his companies, but he never loved me the way a father loves a daughter. Judson was into ownership, not love."

"If it makes your life any easier, he said you'd have a good chunk of change coming."

"Even when he was dying, he was trying to buy me. He bought everything. Wives, mistresses, his kids. You know anybody else has three kids who haven't spoken to him in years? It wasn't until I had my own children that I realized the extent of his failure as a parent. Now tell me why you really came here."

"Elmer Slezak, the dead woman from his apartment, your father, and your husband are interrelated in some way I don't understand. I was hoping you could help me."

"I don't see how."

"Our client, Elmer Slezak, is being charged with the murder of the woman whose picture was on your refrigerator the last time I was here." I'd noticed it had been removed. "Elmer was at one time working for Green International, a company owned by your father. One of the assignments Rakubian gave Slezak when he was working for Green International was to investigate Meade. Did you know that?"

"I might have guessed, but I didn't know it. Why didn't Slezak tell me this?"

"I'm assuming he was ashamed of the role he'd played."

"What role?"

"His role in the conspiracy."

"I *knew* it. Judson engineered our divorce, didn't he?"

"I think he did."

"And I let him. I told Meade. I warned him from the start Judson was a manipulator. But Meade couldn't see it. He actually liked Judson. It was the quality I'd admired in Meade when we met—he liked everybody—but it was that quality, in the end, that drove a wedge between us."

"Why didn't your father like Meade?"

"Maybe because Meade was older than he was by a year. Maybe because he thought Meade was a simpleton. Or because he wasn't a physical specimen like my father. I don't know. Meade was over here yesterday trying to get back together. I don't know what he thought was going to happen. I can hardly feed three mouths, much less four.

"My father ruined Meade. Oh, he'd smile and joke and slap Meade's back, but all the time he was looking for weaknesses. When I became pregnant with Cormick, Judson was furious. He'd hoped we'd divorce before we had children. That was when he began giving Meade work. Every job seemed to fall through, and every time it did, it was Meade's fault. But big-hearted old Dad would spot him a new one. And *that* would fall through. He masterminded every downward step, didn't he?"

"I'm sure you know more about it than I do."

She took a slow, deep breath and then looked as implacable, as unmovable, and as resigned as a melting snowman. "Judson was never happy with my choice of a husband, but he decided there was nothing he could do about it. At least at first. I believe he gave Meade that first job with the intention of making it work, but then Meade got a little too familiar with him— something Judson hates. Meade thought they were close enough buddies that he could joke around with him. That was when my father pulled a few strings and made things go wrong with Meade's work. I went to Judson and blamed him. He denied it and then, just to prove he'd been right about Meade, he somehow tricked Meade into an affair with that woman. Later he tricked him into stealing money, which I *always* thought was a setup. I didn't know it at the time, but it was the end of our marriage and the end of me and my father too. After Meade moved out, Judson sent flowers and offered me a job, but I got my own job. I didn't want anything to do with him."

"This is a sad story. A meddler with too much money and power."

"Not to mention ego. I keep thinking if I hadn't accused my father in the first place, if I'd kept my mouth shut, he might have left Meade alone. I think in the beginning he only wanted to show that Meade was a fool. A simple demonstration. Judson was always big on demonstrations. He once paid a boy who was dating my sister a thousand dollars to walk out of the house and never speak to her again."

"Did he do it?"

"You bet he did. The funny thing was, every boy in town wanted to take her out after that."

"Elmer called this house, you know. Many times."

"I don't think so."

"And you spied on him, didn't you?"

JoAnne Barber looked out the sliding glass window that comprised one end of the kitchen, stared at the hummingbird feeder, a duplicate of the one behind Roberta Sams's house. A rufous hummingbird hovered beside it, dipping its beak into the reservoir of red liquid. "I got suspicious about why he was asking all those questions. I had his card and stopped by his apartment after work one evening. He wasn't there, so I waited in my car across the street. When he showed up, he had that woman with him. The woman Meade cheated on me with. I drove home but almost had an accident on the way. I couldn't figure out what they might be doing together. A couple of days later he came by again and asked more questions. I asked him then if he knew Susan Lee, but he denied it. I went back a couple of times and sat outside his apartment. I'm still not sure what was going on."

"You didn't happen to be there on Monday night a week ago?"

"The night she was killed? I was there three times, but that wasn't one of them."

"Where were you that night?"

"Monday night? Here. Sleeping."

"You said you knew Rakubian. How well?"

She shook her head. "Rakubian was . . . he was not in his right mind. I don't think. But let me ask you something. It sounds like you've been poking around in this. The woman Mr. Slezak was with? She *was* the woman who stole my husband, wasn't she?"

"She was one of your father's ex-mistresses. She and her twin sister."

"She had a twin sister?" JoAnne was as shocked as if I'd spit on the table.

"What did Meade tell you about Susan Lee?"

"Nothing. He never admitted any of it. He made me so angry. If he'd just admitted what we both knew, maybe I could have forgiven him. Then came the embezzlement, which I know was a setup also. That was when Judson said if I would divorce Meade, there would be no charges and nobody would have to pay it back."

"But you paid it out of your trust?"

"You bet I paid it out of my trust. Otherwise Judson would have held it over me until the day he died. I went to work in a savings and loan in Stanwood, but he bought the institution, or one of his corporations did, so I quit. Anybody can be bought. That was his motto. It worked on everyone he came into contact with, but he could never figure out why it didn't work on his children."

"Why didn't it work on his children?"

"Because we wanted something else."

"And what was that?"

"I've thought about that a lot, what we wanted. It wasn't until I had kids of my own that I realized what it was. It's what all children want and need. Unconditional love."

"When Meade was here yesterday, did you discuss your father's manipulations?"

"No. He wouldn't have believed any of it. He never has. He liked Judson. I think he needs to believe people are as nice and as uncomplicated as he is. It's part of his nature. He *has* to think that."

"What did you two talk about?"

"I told you he wanted to get back together. One last college try."

"What did you say?"

"I told him he'd been a lousy husband and a worse ex. I told him to get out of my life."

"And how did he take it?"

"Hard to tell."

"JoAnne, you were married to him for years. Surely you know how he took it."

"I don't."

"And what about the boys? What was the arrangement there?"

"We didn't discuss the boys. I was too busy worrying about where our next meal was coming from."

CHAPTER 38

The first day after the killings I squandered seven hours trying to locate Meade Barber. I expected to find him in an ill-fitting suit, panhandling under the viaduct, with pigeons, tourists, and little green trolleys flitting about in all directions. From what I knew of him, Meade would have been a world-class moocher: sincere, hygienic, intelligent-looking, and almost stately with his bloodless complexion and white hair. It would be a bit like having a senator ask you for a buck.

On day two, four hours of scouring the alleys and missions produced no signs of Barber until I spoke to a volunteer working at the Endless Light Mission down the street from our office on First Avenue. She was a gray-haired woman with a soft-looking face and hard gray eyes besieged by folds of tanned and crinkled skin.

"I'm not sure what his name was, but there was a man staying here—gets his mail here too—hung himself off a fence down by the south entrance to the Kingdome last night. It could be him."

I described Meade Barber.

"Sounds like the one," said the volunteer. "Several of our customers watched the police cut the body down. There was a lot of talk about it. Sounds like him."

"What sort of talk?"

"Oh, you know. Miserable talk. People down here don't usually talk of how bad they have it, unless something like that happens."

It took three hours to confirm Barber's death and get the details.

Meade Barber had left a handwritten note for his ex-wife, then had climbed a cyclone fence near the south rim of the Kingdome and hanged himself at the end of a short, knotted piece of rope at the top of the fence. He was dangling fourteen feet in the air when the fire department arrived. After a brief investigation the medical examiner's station wagon had carried him off to the morgue in the basement of Harborview Hospital.

Snake was finally released and came to our house begging and whimpering. Gone were the allegations of dwarfs shadowing him, of clones conspiring against him. Now we were feted with treatises on the horrors of prison life. "You can't let me go in there, Thomas. You've got to get me out of this."

"I'm working on it."

"Working on it? Goddamn. You haven't done anything but ride your damn bike and sit around watching old Marilyn Monroe flicks."

"Have you seen *Niagara*?"

"I'm headed for the big house. Don't you understand? I'm headed for the concrete mama where gorillas are going to be chasing me through the laundry room with Vaseline on their hands, and you're doing nothing."

"That's not true, Snake."

"What? Tell me one thing you're doing?"

"Thinking. I'm thinking."

"Yeah? Well, I know this clown thinks he can make himself float in the air by thinking. But he can't do it and neither can you."

"I never said I was going to float."

Friday night I phoned JoAnne Barber and arranged a meeting with her for late the next morning at the office. Saturday morning she was five minutes early, had both bright-eyed boys with her, Cormick and Powell.

She wore a red sweatshirt and seemed shorter and smaller standing in our office foyer, sturdier and somehow—happier. Two important men from her past had died in the last week, but she looked happier. It was a sunny Saturday in the middle of the summer, and except for us the office was empty. "We're going to the Seattle Center," said Cormick. "What d'ya think?"

"I think you're going to have a great time."

"Can we go downstairs and look at the totem pole?" Powell asked.

"Why don't we all go down and look at the pole and then go to Ivar's?" I said. "If it's not too early, I'll treat. Fish and chips?"

"I'm afraid we skipped breakfast," JoAnne Barber said. "An early lunch would be nice."

So we went across the street and surveyed and touched and speculated about the totem pole in the park and then walked the three blocks to Ivar's on the waterfront next to the fire station, the boys galloping ahead. We hauled warm sacks of fish and chips past the Coleman Ferry dock, past an ornamental fountain where a man in tattered britches was washing his long hair, to the Washington Street Public Boat Landing. The small park adjacent to the boat landing was full of ne'er-do-wells, but we found an empty bench and sat facing the water. Cormick and Powell were too energized to sit, so they gobbled their meal at the railing over the bay, gulls swooping down at the prospect of sloppy boys with food.

"First I'd like to say I'm sorry about all you've gone through in the past week. I know it's been hard," I said.

"I didn't think it would be. I didn't think I loved my father or Meade, but it has been difficult—sorting through all the feelings. I never thought Meade would do that. I never did. I was so abusive the last time we spoke. I keep trying to tell myself it wasn't my fault."

"People commit suicide by themselves. It's the last mistake of the despondent or the desperate."

"And which was Meade?"

"I was hoping you could tell me."

Gulls squawked overhead, landing in troops on the water. Tourists wandered the sidewalk behind us on Alaskan Way, herding kids and wielding cameras. We watched a ferry steadily grow larger out on the Sound. The speeding-tire noises from the traffic on Alaskan Way and the viaduct above were so loud we could barely hear each other. The sky was clearing up, mostly blue now with a few puffy white clouds over Alki Point across the bay. The sunshine felt so good on my jeans and on my bare arms that I wanted to lie down and bask in it like an old dog.

JoAnne Barber looked out past her boys and the gulls at a deadhead floating in the water, watched the incoming ferry on the mirrorlike surface. "I brought the letter. You said you wanted to see it."

"Thank you." She handed me some wrinkled sheets of notebook paper from her purse.

"The boys haven't read it yet. I don't know if they're old enough to see a suicide note from their father."

"I don't know either. The police are sure he wrote this himself?"

"It's his handwriting." The summer sunlight on the off-white paper made me squint as I read:

JoJo,

It wasn't until the other night I finally realized we were finished once and for all. What a terrible realization it was for me, for, you see, for all these hard months on the street, I've clung to the tenuous belief that we would eventually be reunited. At times it was the only hope I had to keep me going. I always loved you, and I love you now. I think about you and the boys, and miss you all, virtually every hour of the day. I know you think I haven't been a good father, that I haven't visited . . .

I know you're working hard for the boys. I'm proud of you and I wish I could get myself together and help, but I can't. All I can think about is how I've failed, and every time I try something new, that knowledge keeps me hostage. I'm a lost cause, and finally even I realize it.

Let me apologize now to the boys for what I've done and am doing. The only thought that might have kept me around was knowing they needed me, but you made it abundantly clear they didn't, that I've been an inconvenience for all concerned. Let Powell and Cormick grow up strong and smart, relaxed and free, the way I never could. And you, my love, lead a happy life.

Meade

P.S. Let's hope Slezak and company can prove he did not kill Fleegle, as I am confident he did not. Thank him for his kindness toward me, and ask the boys to remember me.

CHAPTER 39

JoAnne was crying when I looked up from the wrinkled note. "I lied to you the other day. I did talk with Meade about Judson the last time we saw each other. I told him everything I'd ever suspected about my father's manipulations, and for the first time he acted as if he believed me."

"Why did you lie to me about it?"

"I was afraid he'd killed my father."

"So what you told him caused the type of reaction you felt might lead to him killing your father?"

"*Reaction* isn't even the word for it. Meade was in shock when he left here. I've never seen him so angry or fierce. He didn't deserve any of what had happened to him. Whatever he had been, he'd never been mean. Never. You could lead him around by the nose. That was all. Maybe that was my attraction to him in the first place. Maybe after being pushed around by my father for so many years, I was looking for somebody I could influence."

"Near as I can tell, your father had been driving him toward suicide from the minute they met."

"Yes, but I didn't have to say what I did to Meade. I was hateful. I told him he was worthless. I told him horrible things."

"And the next night your father was killed."

"That's why I didn't want to say anything to you about telling Meade, or about how angry he'd been. I don't think I can remember Meade being angry before. Ever. It wasn't in his nature."

"So you think he killed your father?"

She shrugged and licked a tear as it ran off her cheek and onto her upper lip. "I never saw Meade after that night. Do you think he killed them?"

"He did or you did."

"What are you saying?"

"Both your lives were ruined by your father's manipulations. You had as much motive as he did."

"But I'm not . . ."

"Capable of killing? No, I don't suspect you are. But then, I didn't think Meade was either."

"The papers are saying Arthur Rakubian is wanted for the shootings."

"They're looking for him. I don't know what kind of case they have."

"For what it's worth, Meade shot them. You go around and ask his friends, I bet you find out he had a gun that night."

"Is that what you want me to do? Go around and ask his friends?"

JoAnne stopped crying and looked into my eyes. "I want you to bring Meade back, is what I want. And clean him up. Get him a decent job. Give him his self-respect back. Have him visit his sons. Can you do that?"

"I wish."

"Other than that, I don't want anything." At the railing the boys were feeding the remains of their lunch to the broken flock of gulls. "Why did my father have to prove all the time that he could ruin people? He didn't have any right."

"No, he didn't. All he had was the power."

"He could have given Meade some little job, and Meade could have worked at it and come home and made me and the kids happy, but no, he had to tear us apart."

"Did Meade say anything that night about visiting your father?"

"He said he was going to kill him. He kept thinking of things Judson had said or done that were part of it. Part of the conspiracy. It was like an avalanche, all the little things he finally put together."

Her father, wounded and dying, had been covering up for the killer, and at the time I'd found it hard to believe he would have held back telling me Rakubian was the shooter, or Meade either, even if he had wanted to go after them personally. But he might have kept his mouth shut if his daughter had done it. A daughter would have been worth keeping his mouth shut for.

"Why didn't you tell anybody he said he was going to kill your father? Why didn't you warn Judson's people?"

"You really do think I had something to do with it, don't you?"

I was quiet.

"At first I was afraid my father would hurt him. And then, after I heard about the shootings, I wasn't sure how I felt about it. On the one hand, I found it hard to believe, but on the other it seemed . . . I can't explain it."

"As if justice had been served?"

"Something like that."

I explained to her how I'd met Judson Bonneville under the nom de plume Ernest Fitt, about our rides, our talks. "Why would he ride bikes with me and pretend to be somebody else?"

"You didn't know him. He was always pretending to be somebody else. It was part of his act. He thought he was a junior-league spy, or something. And he was *the* most competitive man in the universe. You said you could climb a mountain, he'd challenge you. You said you could ride a bike, he wanted to race. That was part of why he didn't like Meade. Meade was neither athletic nor competitive."

"He had to have known I was working with Slezak's attorney," I said, thinking aloud. "He and Rakubian had worked long and hard to undermine Slezak. They didn't want me messing in it."

"What did they do to Mr. Slezak?"

I explained.

"I thought he worked for them."

"He did. He found out what had happened to your husband,

the manipulations, the destruction of the man, and he felt guilty for his part in it. Your father was afraid Elmer would tell you about it and confirm your worst fears. On top of that, one of his mistresses was writing a book. He thought he was protecting his privacy and his past by destroying Elmer's credibility. The mistress writing the book was the one who died."

"They killed that woman in Mr. Slezak's apartment. To frame him and get rid of her."

"I'm not quite sure yet," I said.

She gave me a startled look. "You don't really believe I might have done it?" She stared at me for thirty seconds. "I didn't do it. I never had any proof, but I'm sure my father ordered at least one murder in his lifetime. *He*'s your killer. Not me. He and Rakubian."

"Did Meade own a gun?"

"Not after the divorce. We sold everything."

"Did he ever speak to you about Slezak's girlfriends? About the fact that—"

"He'd slept with one of them himself two years ago?"

"Did he ever talk about it?"

"Never. And I never brought it up. Until you explained what Slezak was doing with her, I was totally confused on that issue. I couldn't figure out what they might be doing together."

"Slezak didn't know she'd been involved with your husband."

"I thought he did."

"Is that why you were stalking Slezak?"

"I didn't stalk anybody."

"You went to his apartment and waited in your car. More than once. The police call that stalking. What did you see? Besides Slezak and the woman? Did you see your husband there?"

"Ex-husband. And no. I never saw him there."

"Do you know any of your ex-husband's street friends?"

"He never brought anybody around. Tell me the truth. You don't think Meade also killed the woman in Mr. Slezak's apartment, do you? Black? I swear it wasn't me."

"Then he did."

Four hours later I found the man named Arliss outside the

Millionair Club. There were four men standing on the corner, but when I pointed at him, he dutifully climbed into my truck. I drove to Mercer Street and caught Highway 99 northbound. The black eye he'd had when I'd seen him with Meade Barber had faded to a half-moon of charcoal. He wore the same Navy pea coat, and as I drove, the truck began filling up with a peculiar aroma best described as essence of mankind. It wasn't foul really, but neither was it pleasant. It was just acrid and earthy. He had watery blue eyes, deeply lined cheeks, and a scruffy, reddish beard. "What kind of work?" he said. "I ain't got all evening. I gotta get back by six for supper."

"No work," I said, handing him a twenty-dollar bill.

"You just keep your money. I ain't no rump ranger."

"Talk is what I want. You were friends with Meade Barber."

"Barber?"

"White hair. Distinguished-looking. You were friends?"

"Yeah. So?"

"Tell me about him."

"For the longest time I thought he was the worst liar on earth. Told me his ex-father-in-law was so rich, he had bodyguards or some dadblamed thing. I didn't even listen, I thought he was a godawful liar. And then it turned out to be true."

"How'd you find out it was true?"

"I read it in the paper after he died. Them people was all shot up and he was nervous. That's all I know. He was nervous, and the next night he hung himself. I didn't see it, but one of the boys at the Light said his tongue was all black and swollen and stuck out like a dead cat."

"Where'd he get the gun?"

"How'd you know about the gun?"

"He had to get it somewhere."

"What makes you think it was mine?"

"I didn't say it was yours."

"Hey, listen. Why don't you let me out here? I'll hop a bus back." We were beyond the zoo, abreast of Green Lake, the jogging path pulsing with runners and in-line skaters. "Listen. You want the truth? I thought he was going to rob a grocery store. That's what I thought. So I loaned him my piece. Told him I wanted half of the proceeds; you know, like an investment. He said that was okay. Next day he gives me the piece back and tells me I better dump it. That's when I knew something happened. He was all shaky. His teeth were chattering. I thought he had a fever, but he was scared. I never seen anybody quite that chicken."

"He say anything else?"

"He said they laughed. He said they laughed at him, so he killed them. I never asked who. But it was in the papers that night. He didn't lie, did he?"

"No. Bonneville used to be his father-in-law."

"I guess they didn't get along too hot."

"Something like that. Where's the gun?"

"You know where the aquarium is?"

"On the waterfront."

"We threw it in the bay there. The light's right, you can look right in and see it."

"And you were never going to tell anybody?"

"If anybody asked. Way I figured it, somebody'd be around to ask. Sooner or later. And here you are. By the way. Why'd you look me up? You knew Meade killed them folks?"

"I had a pretty good idea he did."

"Yeah. I was just waiting for somebody to ask."

That evening at dinner I told Kathy what I'd learned. She promised to call Arnold Haldeman Monday morning and arrange a meeting.

CHAPTER 40

Haldeman knocked softly and entered my office like a ferret who knew there was a serpent in the room. Other than the fact that he was sweating, he was as dapper as ever, a red tie and a navy sport jacket over gray slacks. He looked smaller, as if he'd lost some weight, and his smile was as tight as stolen shoes. "Mr. Black. Your wife says you have something to discuss with me."

"Have a seat." He took the red chair and crossed his legs. They were short and so fat that crossing them so that the top one didn't slide off was an art. "I have something to propose to you. A deal, of sorts."

"I don't make deals, Black," said Haldeman, making as if to get up and leave. "You should know that."

"Hear me out and then decide."

"Is this about your friend, Slezak?"

"It's about three dead people and no weapon. No suspects. No nothing."

"On that deal downtown last week? We have a warrant out. It's just a matter of time. We'll find Rakubian."

"Maybe you will. Maybe you won't. If you do, you'll need motive and a weapon, and I know where you can find both."

"You telling me you have the murder weapon?"

"I'm telling you I want a deal."

"Listen here, Black. You have the gun, you hand it over. You don't, you're up to your chin whiskers in chicken shit."

"I want you to look into Slezak's case again."

"Slezak's case is gone. We've handed everything we got over to the prosecutors. You listen to me. You got a murder weapon, you turn it over. You don't, I'll jail your ass like I jailed your friend's ass."

"I believe you've got some tape recordings you confiscated from Rakubian's office?"

"We might have some tapes."

"Here's what I want. Sort through them until you find some from Elmer's apartment. I believe you have a tape of the murder night."

"Wait a minute. Wait a doggoned minute. You're telling me Arthur Rakubian was bugging Slezak's apartment and it was bugged the night of the murder?"

"Yep."

"Why would he do that?"

"You'll have to ask him when you catch him."

"I've seen the tapes. They're in stacks three feet high. Rakubian bugged a lot of places. A lot of people. So what is it you think I'm going to hear?"

"If we're lucky, you'll hear Slezak with the woman. You'll hear them go to sleep. Later you'll hear somebody enter the apartment. You'll hear one party get out of bed to use the bathroom. And then, if you're lucky, you'll hear the murder committed. I'm hoping you'll hear the murderer leave the unit before the first party comes out of the bathroom."

"And who would this be tiptoeing into Mr. Slezak's apartment in the dark of the night just in the nick of time to throttle his girlfriend?"

"A man named Meade Barber."

"And where do we find this Meade Barber?"

"He hanged himself on a fence last week."

"Convenient."

"Not for him, it wasn't."

"This wasn't down by the Kingdome? The bum?"

"He wasn't what I would call a bum, but it was down by the Kingdome."

"So let's assume for a minute I look through these tapes and come up with something. What do I get in return?"

"You put a diver in the water near the aquarium and you should get plenty."

"A murder weapon?"

"That's what I was told."

"From the triple homicide?"

"That's right."

"Where'd you get this information?"

"From a man you can find at the Millionair Club. Name is Arliss."

"What makes you think what we find in the water will have anything to do with that triple?"

"If it doesn't, don't bother listening to the tapes."

"Oh, I'll listen to the tapes. No matter which way this goes, I'll listen to the tapes. There's too much of a chance they'll prove Sleazy murdered that girl not to listen to those tapes. Who threw the gun in the water?"

"Meade Barber."

"You're telling me Barber killed Roberta Capshaw Sams and then went downtown a week later, talked his way into a security condominium, and murdered three more people, one of whom was about the richest man you or I will ever run across?"

"Barber was the ex-son-in-law of Judson Bonneville. He had an old grudge to settle. The grudge involved the dead woman, Sams."

"And you figured this all out by your lonesome?"

"It took a while."

"Assuming you're correct, it must have been some grudge."

"It was."

"Okay. There's his motive for the triple. What was the motive for Sams?"

"Sams had had an affair with Barber years earlier. Along with some other things, it broke up his marriage. She'd been paid to do it. Barber found out."

"Paid? By the old man?" I nodded. "So you figure that's why he did old man Bonneville?"

"There were other reasons, but basically that was it. That pot we found in the lobby. I bet his prints are on it."

"The gun we're going to find in the water didn't belong to Arthur Rakubian?"

"The man at the Millionair Club, Arliss. He'll tell you Barber borrowed it from him the night of the murders, that he was upset when he gave the gun back. That he said he'd done the worst thing you could do. Together they walked down to the water and tossed it."

"I'm not promising anything, but if we find that gun, I'll take another look-see at those tapes. You're all right, Black. You know that? You're all right." He got up and walked to the door. "So, Black. You've known about these tapes for some time, haven't you?"

"Not long."

"A week, I'd say. Maybe longer. Why didn't you clue me in to the tapes before?"

"We thought you would listen to them as a matter of course."

"Oh, sure. Ten thousand hours of tapes. Like we've got nothing else to do." Haldeman eyed me and laughed. It was a sniggering, piggy kind of laugh. "You thought he did it all along, didn't you? You thought your friend murdered the girl. You were afraid the tapes would incriminate your friend. And it wouldn't do for the defendant's investigator to be pointing out evidence that would trap his client, would it?"

"It never even occurred to me."

"I'll believe that when . . . Sure. We'll listen to the tapes. You know why? Because you're wrong. Slezak did do it. And the tapes may prove it. We'll listen to your damn tapes. And we'll put a diver in the water."

"Good. As a taxpayer I appreciate your diligence."

"Fuck you," he said amiably.

"We clear this up, there might be a medal in it for you, officer." I winked.

"Why do you jerks always have to be such clowns?"

"Maybe because you make it so easy for us."

CHAPTER 41

The evening Elmer came in with his final check for Kathy's services, drawn out of the seventy-five thousand dollars bail money nobody had claimed, the four of us had dinner at a sidewalk table at Mitchelli's: Kathy, myself, Elmer, and Desiree— Desiree an unbidden guest, showing up at the last minute on a Harley Sportster whose unmuffled cacophony put an end to all conversation as well as any coherent thought on the street. Elmer and Desiree were flying to Hawaii in the morning for a seven-day vacation.

Desiree parked across from the restaurant on Yesler while about fifty people from one of the underground tours came out a doorway in Post Alley and watched her strip off most of her leathers. After she slammed her Nazi helmet down on our table, I noticed her earrings were colorful images of bloodied, headless children. When she saw Kathy eyeing them, Desiree bragged she'd made them herself, had the heads at home in another set.

"Charming," said Kathy.

Traffic was light, and it was the first Thursday of the month, gallery night, so the restaurants and sidewalks were anthills of movement, men with sunburned faces and Chablis in their bellies strutting the streets alongside women in summer dresses, their tanned legs flashing as they walked. Laden with the odor of vanilla from the city's cleaning and flushing project, a hot wind blew up the alleys, pushing hoarse laughter at us from across the street where a group of winos gathered in front of the Pioneer Square Hotel.

"There's a few aspects to what happened I'd like to get straight, Thomas, you don't mind," Elmer said as Desiree reached under the table and began fondling his leg. At least I hoped it was his leg. "How did you know it was Meade? I pegged Rakubian for killing Bonneville and his friends, and the cops had *me* pegged for Roberta Sams. What made you think different?"

"For a while I did think it was you killed Sams. Let's face it. The cops had a terrific case. You wake up with a dead woman next to you in bed and then make yourself the only suspect by claiming your apartment was locked and nobody else had a key. The autopsy revealed she had been drugged. They found evidence of sleeping tablets in a drink in your kitchen."

"Sure she was drugged. I was starting to get suspicious after seeing lobsters climbing up the walls of my apartment, so that night I switched drinks on her. She drugged her ownself."

"The kicker was Meade kept calling the dead woman *Fleegle*, the same as Kathy had that first night. There was a key lying across her driver's license, and it covered up the *Mc* in her name, so if you saw the license, it was an easy mistake to make. Meade called her *Fleegle* when I spoke to him at the Millionair Club and once again in his suicide note. It was a mistake most likely made the way Kathy had made it, seeing the license on the nightstand with the key across it."

"He said he knew her, but she told him it was baloney. Now that I think about it, he did seem a bit riled over it."

"Because he knew Sams was the woman he'd had the affair with. So he had a motive, maybe not to kill her but certainly to be awfully suspicious, certainly enough motive to sneak into your apartment. I think he went in, not intending to kill anybody but to investigate. He also had opportunity. He was there at the apartment that night. And whether you want to believe it or not, the door *was* open when we got there. The pathetic thing was the woman he killed wasn't the one who'd played the part of Susan Lee. That had been her sister, who'd already left for California that morning."

"What about Bonneville and the others?"

"Several things pointed to Barber. Or his wife. The pot. The fact that Bonneville had laughed at his attacker. You go to the door and somebody's standing there in a threatening manner, possibly with a gun, which we have to assume was the case, you don't laugh at them. Not unless you know them well enough that something strikes you funny about the situation. Nothing would ever strike you funny about that situation with strangers. And I couldn't see him laughing at Rakubian. He said he never figured his assailant had the guts. He knew Rakubian had the guts. It had to be somebody else. Somebody with a powerful motive.

"The way I figured it, he went to the building and got intercepted by the bodyguard, Dickie Bretcher, who took him to the basement to talk. Meade shot him and took the elevator up to the fourteenth floor. He shot Bonneville in the doorway, and then he must have seen Woods. Maybe she screamed. He chased her and shot her in the bathroom.

"Rakubian went up to confront Bonneville, saw the carnage, and scrammed. Then you went up. Barber saw the elevator coming, probably with a passenger. Arliss, the man who'd loaned him the gun, said he'd only given him a handful of bullets. He'd run out of ammunition. So when the elevator doors opened, he smacked you with a pot he took off his packsack."

"Nobody hit me with any damn pot! You couldn't knock me out with a pot unless you shot it out of a cannon. It was a goddamned brick. A crowbar."

"Oh, darlin'," Desiree said, "I've knocked you out with a sixpack of Red Hook and a little kiss."

"Let me guess. The elevator doors opened, your head was down, and the brim of your cowboy hat was blocking your vision."

"Oh, honey," said Desiree. "If he'd had any bullets left, you and I wouldn't be flying to Hawaii."

"That's why I always carry plenty," Elmer said, patting his

jacket pocket. "Running out of ammunition is why it took so long to win the West."

"Are you joking?" said Kathy.

"Hell no. They ran out of bullets fighting Indians."

"Ninety-five percent of the Indians in this country died from the diseases we gave them," said Kathy. "The settlers shot more of their own wives than they did Indians."

"Another good reason not to run out of ammo," said Snake.

"Barber had motive, opportunity, and that pot, which didn't belong in the building. It had a bolt where the rivet should have been holding the handle on. Most people would have thrown it out."

"You know, it was for that very reason I purposely didn't let on to Barber what all I thought happened to him," said Snake. "It was an awful accusation—that his former father-in-law had destroyed him. I thought it might make him deranged, he found out."

"It must have. Meade killed Sams. He tried the door, found it unlocked, went in, and waited in the living room. Trying to work up his courage. Then you woke up and went to the john. He probably had a penlight or a cigarette lighter. He went in there and was poking through her purse. That was how the license got on the table. If we want to keep speculating, I'd say she woke up and tried to scream. He wasn't there to kill her. But he didn't want to get discovered either. He covered her mouth with his hand. She fought. He was trying to keep her quiet. After all, he knew you were behind a door twelve feet away. He knew you had guns."

"He must have been incredibly upset over the fact that she didn't recognize him," Kathy said. "But Elmer? You say you didn't hear anything."

"I had the fan on."

"Not loud enough they didn't hear the struggle on the tapes," said Kathy.

"And I came out and thought we'd have another go-around . . ." He glanced at Desiree. "But she was dead."

"When we got there, Meade was still outside," said Kathy,

turning to me. "Why did he hang around? What on earth did he think he would accomplish?"

"I bet he was going to turn himself in and lost his nerve," I said. "I was suspicious of JoAnne Barber for a while. I thought she'd lied to me about not having received phone calls from you, Elmer. What had happened was she'd received calls from Meade on your cellular phone."

"I loaned him the phone a few times."

The .22 the police fished out of the bay hadn't been in long enough that the ballistics tests didn't prove a match to bullets found in Bretcher, Bonneville, Woods, and the shower stall wall. Arnold Haldeman, who was busy taking full credit in local news reports for having solved a triple homicide single-handedly, believed Barber had killed Roberta Capshaw Sams, too, else the charges against Slezak would not have been dropped. The police had found a recording of Sams's murder on the tapes confiscated by court order from Green International a week earlier.

Our working hypothesis was that Rakubian, who'd gone to Tammy Woods's apartment only to find Woods already dead and Judson Bonneville fatally wounded, had subsequently proceeded to the Westin Hotel, where he shot and killed Lane Thorne, thinking Lane had been hired by Bonneville to kill him. It was anybody's guess what Rakubian had made of a wounded Bonneville and dead or dying Tammy Woods. Whether or not he'd intended to kill Bonneville, too, wasn't a question anyone had asked and now didn't seem relevant.

The floppy disks Snake swiped from the backseat of Rakubian's car and the bugging tapes the SPD confiscated from his office had supplied ample proof that Green International's hired agents had wiretapped and electronically eavesdropped on Elmer's office, his apartment, and our home, as well as dozens of other businesses and individuals. While scanning the computer files, Kathy had found an intimate account of the destruction of Meade Barber's life, a campaign that had been run like a major election launch. Authorship was in doubt, although Elmer had read it and said it looked like Rakubian's handiwork.

Snake scratched his beard and said, "It's hard to know what

a fella would do, he found out his life had been stolen. I got him odd jobs, but it was hopeless. Barber sometimes went two, three days without food. A woman beat him up one night and stole his shoes. He's laying there, some kids come along and just for the heck of it swipe his socks. Bonneville not only put him on the street, he broke him to the point he couldn't defend himself."

Desiree said, "I still don't understand the old man's game."

"JoAnne told me Judson spent his life trying to control others," I said. "The sick part of it was he usually didn't have any trouble. Nobody called them bribes. They were gifts, favors, friendly gestures. The few times he found moral pillars of resistance, he sicked Green International onto them. Ruin a marriage. A series of home break-ins. Ruined people are easier to manipulate."

"Now I know why L.C. was acting so cowardly," Kathy said. "When they broke into our place to put those bugs in, they must have frightened him."

"And you were blaming me," I said.

"Now, don't pout."

Snake said, "I can't believe after all I did for that peckerhead Barber, he was going to let me swing."

"He thought you were part of the conspiracy," I said. "After all, you were running around with the woman who'd initiated the destruction of his marriage."

"Hell, I didn't know she was part of that. I thought she was from space."

"Now don't you feel like a dope?" said Desiree. Without waiting for an answer, she turned to me. "And why all the space stuff? How'd they get Elmer to believe that horseshit?"

"They researched him," I said, "in the same way they researched Meade and others. Found out he was a sucker for alien stories."

"So what was he doing with alien women?" Desiree asked. "I don't get that part."

"Never you mind, honey. Let's just say it was a mission of mercy," Elmer said, patting her knee. He turned to me. "What about the men in black? Them midgets in the Buick?"

"Never saw them," I said.

Kathy said, "There wasn't any mention of them in the records."

"The police never found them either," I added.

The three of us looked at Elmer, who looked as if his eyes were going to squib up.

Later that night, very late, when Kathy and I were in bed and the house was dark and L.C. was on the back porch barking at some poor cat, I said, "You realize, tonight's your night to spill the beans on a fantasy."

"A what?"

"Now, don't stiff me, not after I handed over the whole softball team."

"If you're good, I might tell you one."

"Wasn't I good tonight?"

She thought about it a few moments. "Well, yes, I suppose you were. Okay. But don't laugh. There's this wedding. It's in a different culture. The bride and groom have never met before. An arranged marriage. When it begins, the bride is completely covered by a veil and a long gown . . ."

"Go on."

It was about the wildest fantasy I'd ever heard, uncivilized elements mixed with current Western marital rituals. She realized I was being very quiet and said, "Is this sick? Of course neither the groom nor the bride is experienced or even knowledgeable, so there are . . . helpers. This is sick, isn't it? I shouldn't have told you."

"This is why your hands get sweaty at weddings?"

"Don't tease. I never teased you about the softball team."

"Not much. Besides, the ball team doesn't embarrass me."

"Why not?"

"Because I made it up."

She sat upright in bed, the dim light from the window reflecting off the curved ridge of muscle running along her spine, highlighting the roundness where her hip flared. "I made up the wedding too."

"You'd like me to think so, wouldn't you? Not only do you perspire at weddings, but your eyes glaze over during the vows."

She laughed. "Did you really make it up? The softball team?"

"Maybe. Did you make up the wedding?"

"Yes," she lied. "And my eyes don't glaze over."

"Sure they do, Sister. And what's more, I always get lucky afterwards."

"You *always* get lucky anyway, and you know it."

"I guess I'm just a lucky guy."

About the Author

Earl Emerson is a lieutenant in the Seattle Fire Department. He is the Shamus Award–winning author of the Thomas Black detective series, which includes *The Rainy City*, *Poverty Bay*, *Nervous Laughter*, *Fat Tuesday*, *Deviant Behavior*, *Yellow Dog Party*, *The Portland Laugher*, and *The Vanishing Smile*.

Earl Emerson lives in North Bend, Washington.